THE KERRIGANS
A TEXAS DYNASTY
JOURNEY INTO VIOLENCE

THE KERRIGANS
A TEXAS DYNASTY
JOURNEY INTO VIOLENCE

WILLIAM W. JOHNSTONE
with J. A. Johnstone

PINNACLE BOOKS
Kensington Publishing Corp.
www.kensingtonbooks.com

PINNACLE BOOKS are published by

Kensington Publishing Corp.
119 West 40th Street
New York, NY 10018

PUBLISHER'S NOTE
Following the death of William W. Johnstone, the Johnstone family is working with a carefully selected writer to organize and complete Mr. Johnstone's outlines and many unfinished manuscripts to create additional novels in all of his series like The Last Gunfighter, Mountain Man, and Eagles, among others. This novel was inspired by Mr. Johnstone's superb storytelling.

All Kensington titles, imprints, and distributed lines are available at special quantity discounts for bulk purchases for sales promotions, premiums, fund-raising, educational, or institutional use. Special book excerpts or customized printings can also be created to fit specific needs. For details, write or phone the office of the Kensington sales manager: Kensington Publishing Corp., 119 West 40th Street, New York, NY 10018, attn: Sales Department; phone 1-800-221-2647.

PINNACLE BOOKS, the Pinnacle logo, and the WWJ steer head logo are Reg. U.S. Pat. & TM Off.

ISBN-13: 978-0-7860-3583-0
ISBN-10: 0-7860-3583-8

First printing: August 2016

10 9 8 7 6 5 4 3 2 1

Printed in the United States of America

First electronic edition: August 2016

ISBN-13: 978-0-7860-3584-7
ISBN-10: 0-7860-3584-6

BOOK ONE
Death in Dodge

CHAPTER ONE

"She ran me off her property, darned redheaded Irish witch." Ezra Raven stared hard at his *segundo*, a tall lean man with ice in his eyes named Poke Hylle. "I want that Kerrigan land, Poke. I want every last blade of grass. You understand?"

"I know what you want, boss," Hylle said. He studied the amber whiskey in his glass as though it had become the most interesting thing in the room. "But wantin' and gettin' are two different things."

"You scared of Frank Cobb, that hardcase *segundo* of hers? I've heard a lot of men are."

"Should I be scared of him?" Hylle asked.

"He's a gun from way back. Mighty sudden on the draw and shoot."

Hylle's grin was slow and easy, a man relaxed. "Yeah, he scares me. But that don't mean I'm afraid to brace him."

"You can shade him. You're good with a gun your own self, Poke, maybe the best I've ever known," Raven said. "Hell, you gunned Bingley Abbott that time. He was the Wichita draw fighter all the folks were talking about."

"Bing was fast, but he wasn't a patch on Frank Cobb," Hylle said. "Now that's a natural fact."

"All right, then, forget Cobb for now. There's got to be a better way than an all-out range war." Raven stepped to the ranch house window and stared out at the cloud of drifting dust where the hands were branding calves. "I offered Kate Kerrigan twice what her ranch is worth, but she turned me down flat. How do you deal with a woman like that?"

"Carefully." Hylle smiled. "I'm told she bites."

"Like a cougar. Shoved a scattergun into my face and told me to git. Me, Ezra Raven, who could buy and sell her and all she owns." The big man slammed a fist into his open palm. "Damn, I need that land. I want to be big, Poke, the biggest man around. That's just how I am, how I've always been, and I ain't about to change."

The door opened and a tall, slender Pima woman stepped noiselessly across the floor and placed a white pill and a glass of water on Raven's desk.

"Damn, is it that time again?"

"Take," the woman said. "It is time." She wore a plain, slim-fitting calico dress that revealed the swell of her breast and hips. A bright blue ribbon tied back her glossy black hair, and on her left wrist she wore a wide bracelet of hammered silver. She was thirty-five years old. Raven had rescued her from a brothel in Dallas, and he didn't know her Indian name, if she had one. He called her Dora only because it pleased him to do so.

Raven picked up the pill and glared at it. "The

useless quack says this will help my heart. I think the damned thing is sugar rolled into a ball."

Hylle waved an idle hand. "Man's got to follow the doctor's orders, boss."

Raven shrugged, swallowed the medication with a gulp of water, and handed the glass back to the Pima woman. "Beat it, Dora. White men are talking here."

The woman bowed her head and left.

"Poke, like I said, I don't want to take on a range war. It's a messy business. Nine times out of ten the law gets involved and next thing you know, you're knee-deep in Texas Rangers."

Hylle nodded. "Here's a story you'll find interesting, boss. I recollect one time in Galveston I heard a mariner talk about how he was first mate on a freighter sailing between Shanghai and Singapore in the South China Sea. Well, sir, during a watch he saw two ironclads get into a shooting scrape. He said both ships were big as islands and they had massive cannons in dozens of gun turrets. Both ships pounded at each other for the best part of three hours. In the end neither ironclad got sunk, but both were torn apart by shells and finally they listed away from each other, each of them trailing smoke. Nobody won that fight, but both ships paid a steep price." He swallowed the last of his whiskey. "A range war is like that, boss. Ranchers trade gunfire, hired guns and punchers die, but in the end, nobody wins."

"And then the law comes in and cleans up what's left," Raven said.

"That's about the size of it," Hylle said.

"I don't want that kind of fight. Them ironclads could have avoided a battle and sailed away with their colors flying. Firing on each other was a grandstand play and stupid."

Hylle rose from his chair, stepped to the decanters, and poured himself another drink. He took his seat again and said, "Boss, maybe there is another way."

"Let's hear it," Raven said. "But no more about heathen seas and ironclads. Damn it, man, you're making me seasick."

Hylle smiled. "From what I've seen of the Kerrigan place it's a hardscrabble outfit and Kate has to count every dime to keep it going. Am I right about that?"

"You're right. The KK Ranch is held together with baling wire and Irish pride. She's building a house that isn't much bigger than her cabin. She's using scrap lumber and the first good wind that comes along will blow it all over creation." Raven lifted his chin and scratched his stubbly throat. "Yeah, I'd say Kate Kerrigan's broke or damned near it."

"So answer me this, boss. What happens if her herd doesn't go up the trail next month?"

A light glittered in Raven's black eyes. "She'd be ruined."

"And eager to sell for any price," Hylle said.

Raven thought that through for a few moments then said, "How do we play it, Poke? Remember them damned ironclads of yours that tore one another apart."

"No range war. Boss, we do it with masked men— night riders. We scatter the Kerrigan herd, gun a few waddies if we must, but leave no evidence that can be tied to you and the Rafter-R. Stop her roundup and the woman is out of business." Hylle smiled. "Pity though. She's real pretty."

"So are dollars and cents, Poke. The Kerrigan range represents money in my pocket." Raven was a big, rawboned man, and his rugged face was bisected by a great cavalry mustache and chin beard. He lit a cigar and said behind a blue cloud of smoke, "We wait until the branding is done and then we strike at the Kerrigan herds, scatter them to hell and gone before Kate can start the gather. Can we depend on the punchers?"

Hylle nodded. "They ride for the brand, boss."

"Good. A two-hundred-dollar bonus to every man once the job is done and I own the Kerrigan range." Raven slapped his hands together. "Do you think it can work?"

"No question about that. No cattle drive to Dodge, no money for the KK."

"Hell, now I feel better about things, Poke. It's like you're a preacher and I just seen the light. How about another drink?"

Hylle grinned. "Don't mind if I do, boss. We'll drink to the ruin of the KK and the end of pretty Mrs. Kerrigan's stay in West Texas."

CHAPTER TWO

Kate Kerrigan stood on her hearthstone and watched the rider. He was still a distance off and held his horse to a walk. The weight of the Remington .41 revolver in the pocket of her dress gave her a measure of reassurance. The little rimfire was a belly gun to be sure, but effective if she could get close enough.

That Kate could stand on her hearthstone and see the man at a distance was not surprising since her new home was still only a frame and a somewhat rickety one at that. She'd scolded the construction foreman, but Black Barrie Delaney, captain of the brig *Octopus*, had assured her that he had inspected the work and the basic structure was sound. As she often did, Kate recalled their last conversation with distaste.

"I did not bring, all the way from Connemara, mind you, a slab of green marble for your hearthstone, Kate, only to have your new house fall about your ears." Delaney wore a blue coat with brass buttons. Thrust into the red sash

around his waist were two revolvers of the largest kind and a murderous bowie knife.

"Barrie Delaney, I'll never know why I let a pirate rogue like you talk me into building my house," Kate said. "Why, 'tis well-known that you should have been hanged at Execution Dock in London town years ago."

"Ah, Her Majesty Queen Victoria's mercy knows no bounds and she saw fit to spare a poor Irish sailorman like me."

"More fool her," Kate said. "You've sent many a lively lad to Davy Jones's locker and a goodly woman or two if the truth be known. Well, here's a word to the wise, Barrie Delaney, fix this house to my liking or I'll hang you myself or my name is not Kate Kerrigan."

Delaney, a stocky man with a brown beard and quick black eyes full of deviltry that reflected the countless mortal sins he'd committed in his fifty-eight years of life, gave a little bow. "Kate, I swear on my sainted mother's grave that I will build you a fine house, a dwelling fit for an Irish princess."

"Fit for me and my family will be quite good enough," Kate said.

Kate shook her head at the memory. As she watched the rider draw closer, she pushed on the support stud next to her. It seemed that the whole structure swayed and she made a mental note to hang Black Barrie Delaney at the first convenient opportunity.

Kate's daughters Ivy and Shannon, growing like weeds, stepped out of the cabin, butterfly nets in hand, and she ordered them back inside.

Ivy, twelve years old and sassy, frowned. "Why?"

Her mother said, "Because I said so. Now, inside with you. There's a stranger coming."

"Ma, is it an Indian?" Shannon asked.

"No, probably just a passing rider, but I want to talk with him alone."

The girls reluctantly stepped back into the cabin and Kate once more directed her attention to the stranger. He was close enough that she saw he was dressed in the garb of a frontier gambler and he rode a big American stud, a tall sorrel that must have cost him a thousand dollars and probably more.

The rider drew rein ten yards from where Kate stood and she saw that his black frockcoat, once of the finest quality, was frayed and worn, and a rent on the right sleeve above the elbow had been neatly sewn. His boots and saddle had been bought years before in a big city with fancy prices and the ivory-handled Colt and carved gun belt around his waist would cost the average cowpuncher a year's wages. He seemed like a man who'd known a life and times far removed from poverty-stricken West Texas. His practiced ease around women was evident in the way he swept off his hat and made a little bow from the saddle.

"Ma'am." The man said only that. His voice was a rich baritone voice and his smile revealed good teeth.

"My name is Kate Kerrigan. I own this land. What can I do for you?"

"Just passing through, ma'am." He'd opened his frilled white shirt at the neck and beads of sweat showed on his forehead. "I'd like to water my horse if I may. We've come a fair piece in recent days, he and I."

Kate saw no threat in the man's blue eyes, but there was much life and the living of it behind them. His experiences, whatever they were, had left shadows.

"Then you're both welcome to water," Kate said.

"The well is over there in front of the cabin and there's a dipper."

The man touched his hat. "Obliged, ma'am." He kneed his horse forward. His roweled spurs were silver, filigreed with gold scrolls and arabesques.

Kate fancied they were such as knights in shining armor wore in the children's picture books.

The rider swung out of the saddle, loosened the girth, and filled a bucket for his horse. Only when the sorrel had drank its fill did he drink himself, his restless, searching eyes never still above the tin rim of the dipper. Finally he removed his coat, splashed water onto his face, and then ran a comb through his thick auburn hair. He donned his hat and coat again, tightened the saddle girth, and smiled at Kate. "Thank you kindly, ma'am. I'm much obliged."

To the Irish, hospitality comes as naturally as breathing and Kate Kerrigan couldn't let the man go without making a small effort. "I have coffee in the pot if you'd like some."

To her surprise, the man didn't answer right away. Usually men jumped at the chance to drink coffee with her and she felt a little tweak of chagrin. The man was tall and wide-shouldered. As he studied his back trail, there was a tenseness about him, not fear but rather an air of careful calculation, like a man on the scout figuring his odds. Finally he appeared to relax. "Coffee sounds real good to me, ma'am."

"Would you like to come into the house?" Kate said. "Unlike this one, it has a roof and four walls."

The man shook his head. "No, ma'am. Seems like you've got a real nice sitting place under the oak tree. I'll take a chair and you can tell your girls they can come out now."

"You saw . . . I mean all that way?" Kate said.

"I'm a far-seeing man, ma'am. I don't miss much."

Kate smiled. "Yes. Something tells me you don't."

After studying the cabin, the smokehouse, the barn and other outbuildings, the man said, "I reckon your menfolk are out on the range, this time of year. Branding to be done and the like." He saw the question on Kate's face and waved a hand in the direction of the cabin. "The roof's been repaired and done well, all the buildings are built solid and maintained. That means strong men with calloused hands. Your ranch isn't a two by twice outfit, Mrs. Kerrigan. It's a place that's put down deep roots and speaks of men with sand who will stick."

"And a woman who will stick," Kate said.

"I have no doubt about that, ma'am. Your husband must be real proud of you."

"My husband is dead. He died in the war." Kate smiled. "Now let me get the coffee."

As Kate walked away, the man said after her, "Name's Hank Lowery, ma'am. I think you should know that."

She turned. "Did you think your name would make me change my mind about the coffee?"

"Hank Lowery is a handle some people have a problem with, Mrs. Kerrigan. They rassle with it for a spell and either run me out of town or want to take my picture with the mayor. Either way, they fear me."

Kate said, "Now I remember. I once heard my *segundo* mention you to my sons. A lot of unarmed men were killed in some kind of fierce battle, wasn't it?"

"The newspapers called it the Longdale Massacre, but it was a gunfight, not a massacre. The men were armed."

"We will not talk of it," Kate said. "You will drink

your coffee, Mr. Lowery, and we will not talk a word of it. Does that set well with you?"

Lowery nodded. "Just thought you should know, ma'am."

"Well, now you've told me. Do you take milk and sugar in your coffee? No matter, I'll bring them anyway."

"Is the sponge cake to your liking, Mr. Lowery?" Kate asked.

The man nudged a crumb into his mouth with a little finger. "It's very good. I've never had sponge cake before, and seldom any other kind of cake, come to that."

"I'm told that sponge cake is Queen Victoria's favorite, one with a cream and strawberry jam filling just like mine."

Lowery smiled. "You're a good cook, Mrs. Kerrigan."

"No I'm not. I'm a terrible cook. I can't even boil an egg. The only thing I can make without ruining it is sponge cake."

"Then I'm honored," Lowery said. "This cake is indeed your masterpiece."

"Thank you, Mr. Lowery. You are most gracious. Ah, here are the girls at last, and Jazmin Salas is with them. She's the one who cooks for the Kerrigan ranch and her husband Marco is my blacksmith."

Kate made the introductions.

Aware of her twelve-year-old blooming girlhood, Ivy played the sophisticated lady and shook Lowery's hand, but seven-year-old Shannon was predictably shy and buried her face in her mother's skirt.

"Beautiful children, Mrs. Kerrigan," Lowery said. "They do you proud."

Jazmin's gaze lingered on the man's holstered Colt, fine clothes, and the silver ring on the little finger of his left hand. She guessed that Mr. Lowery had never done a day's hard work in his life. Although she had heard of such men, they were as alien to her as the strange little Chinamen who toiled on the railroads.

"Is the gentleman staying for supper, Mrs. Kerrigan? If he is I'll set an extra place at table."

Kate hesitated.

Lowery read the signs. "There's no need. I should be riding on."

"Of course you'll stay for supper, Mr. Lowery," Kate said, recovering from her indecision. "I will not allow a man to leave my home hungry." To lift the mood, she added, "We're having chicken and dumplings. Is that to your taste?"

"If it's as good as the sponge cake then it most certainly is."

"Better," Kate said. "Jazmin is a wonderful cook."

"Will we eat in the dining room . . . again?" Jazmin said.

"Of course. Where else would we eat?"

Jazmin's eyes lifted to the table and chairs set up within the wobbly frame of the new house. "Yes, ma'am. Let's hope the weather holds and there is no wind."

If Hank Lowery was amused, he had the good manners not to let it show.

CHAPTER THREE

Kate Kerrigan's menfolk rode in just as day shaded into night and Jazmin lit the candles on the dining room table. The men waved to Kate as they rode to the bunkhouse to wash off the trail dust. By the time Frank Cobb, her sons Trace and Quinn, Moses Rice, and eight punchers she'd hired for the gather and drive up the Chisholm had finished with the roller towel it was black. Moses changed it in a hurry, fearing Kate's wrath because he hadn't done it earlier.

The hired hands ate in the bunkhouse, but Kate and her children considered Moses Rice family, even though he was a black man. He sat at the dining room table, as did Frank Cobb. The tension between Frank and Hank Lowery was immediate and obvious. As a guest, Lowery sat on Kate's right side and Frank opposite him. In the flickering candlelight, the two men's eyes clashed, challenged, and held. Trace Kerrigan, seventeen years old that spring and used to being around rough men, dropped his hand to the Winchester he'd propped against his chair. He would not allow gunplay at the table and certainly not with his mother in the line of fire.

Lowery broke the silence and talked into an atmosphere as fragile as a glass rod. "Howdy, Frank. It's been a while."

"Seems like," Frank said.

"You don't want me here, do you?" Lowery said.

"No, I don't."

"I stayed for the chicken and dumplings," Lowery said. "No other reason."

"Yes, there is another reason," Kate said. "Frank, I asked Mr. Lowery to have supper with us. The decision was mine."

"Was that before or after he told you about Longdale, Kate?" Frank's voice was tight, thin, and menacing. "Ask Lowery about Levi Fry . . . or did he already boast of it?"

"Why don't you ask me, Frank?" Lowery said.

"Damn you, I will. Tell me why, when the old man was down on his hands and knees and coughing up black blood, did you put a bullet in his head?"

"Whoever told you that is a damn liar," Lowery said. "And you were a damn fool to listen to him."

"I won't let you play Kate for a fool!" Frank's chair tipped over as he jumped to his feet, his hand dropping for a gun.

Two things happened quickly. The first was the *clack-clack* of the lever of Trace's Winchester.

The second was Kate's shout of, "Enough!"

"Both of you, back away from my mother," Trace yelled. "By God, Frank, if I have to, I'll kill you both."

"Stay right where you are," Kate said. "Trace, put down the rifle. The other two of you sit down. It's a beautiful evening. We're sitting in my new dining room of my new home and I don't want this occasion spoiled."

"Ma, will the house fall down while we're eating?" Shannon said.

The girl's question made Kate smile and did something to ease the tension.

As Frank picked up his chair, Lowery said, "Mrs. Kerrigan, it was far from my intention to spoil your dinner. Please forgive me."

"There is nothing to forgive, Mr. Lowery," Kate said. "Now unbuckle your gun belt and you, too, Frank. Jazmin, take the revolvers into the cabin before you serve. Trace, you may give Jazmin your Winchester."

"I bet Lowery's got a hideout stashed somewhere, Kate," Frank said. "He's not a man to be trusted."

Kate looked at the man in question. "Mr. Lowery, do you have a second weapon?"

"No." He opened his frockcoat. "Satisfied, Frank?"

"I'll only be satisfied when I see you dead."

"Everyone sit down," Kate said. "I will not have our meal spoiled by bickering." Then after a few moments, "Ah, there is Jazmin with the food at last. A hungry man is an angry man, my grandmother always said. Once we have eaten, we'll all be perfect friends again."

"I doubt it," Frank said under his breath.

Kate chose to ignore that statement.

CHAPTER FOUR

A high-riding full moon bathed the Kerrigan ranch in metallic light and out in the brush country coyotes yipped their hunger. The horses on the corral were restless, usually a sign that they'd caught the scent of a bear or cougar.

As sleepless as the horses, Frank Cobb stood in darkness under the oak outside the cabin, the tiny, scarlet glow of his cigarette rising and falling as he smoked. He turned his head as the cabin door opened and Kate stepped outside. She wore a green robe over her nightdress and her luxuriant mane of red hair was pulled back with a ribbon of the same color. As she stepped closer, Frank saw that she carried a steaming teacup in her hand.

"I brought you this. It will help you sleep," she said, extending the cup and smiling. "It's two o'clock in the morning and you have a full day ahead of you."

Frank took the cup and sniffed. "What is this?"

"Chamomile tea. It's very calming."

Several times on any given day, Frank was struck by what a spectacularly beautiful woman Kate Kerrigan was, and in the moonlight, he was enamored of her yet again. He sipped the tea then said, "I'm sorry about tonight, Kate. I guess I pretty much ruined everybody's supper."

Kate smiled. "Trace and Quinn ate like wolves and so did Moses. Ivy and Shannon always pick at their food, so there's no need to blame yourself for that. Why do you hate Hank Lowery so much, Frank?"

"It's getting late," Frank said. "Best I turn in and grab some shuteye."

"It will take the tea some time to work, so tell me about him. Come into the house. We'll sit in the dining room."

Despite his depressed mood, Frank managed a smile. "Kate, four framed walls and a few roof rafters don't make a house, despite what the pirate tells you."

"It is a house because I say it is a house. Frames and rafters do not make a home. It's the people who live within the walls that do that. Besides, I have my hearthstone in place, so the new Kerrigan home is on a firm foundation, even though it shakes and creaks."

Frank laid his teacup on the dining room table, pulled out a chair for Kate, and then sat.

Kate eased him into his story. "All right, where is Longdale?"

"It's a settlement in the New Mexico Territory, up in the Rio Hondo country. Before the massacre it was a cow town like any other—small, dusty, and drab. Longdale slept six days a week and only woke up on Fridays when the punchers from the surrounding ranches came in to drink and dance with Annie and Bettie. It had a general store with a saloon attached, a blacksmith's shop, some scattered cabins, and not much else."

Kate said, "Who were Annie and Bettie? Need I ask?"

"Working girls, Kate."

"Ah, I see. Were they pretty?"

"The punchers thought they were."

Kate smiled. "Please go on with your story. I ask too many silly questions."

"A waddie shot dead during an argument over water rights started it. The Rocking-J Ranch and the Slim Chance Horse and Cattle Company claimed the same creek that ran off the Rio Hondo and one morning during roundup their hands got into it. It started with fists and then went to guns and during the scrape a feller who rode for the Rocking-J by the name of Shorty Tillett got shot and another man was wounded." Frank drank the last of his tea and built a smoke. "After that, both outfits gunned up and brought in professionals. One of them was a draw fighter out of Amarillo who called himself Stride Lowery."

"He was related to our Mr. Lowery?" Kate asked.

That "our Mr. Lowery" rankled, but Frank let it go. "He was Hank Lowery's twin brother."

"Oh, I see," Kate said, but she really didn't.

Frank lit his cigarette. "The ranchers' war lasted three months. During that time seven men were killed, another crippled for life, and Stride Lowery was one of the dead. Finally a peace conference was called, to be held at the saloon in Longdale. At three in the afternoon Levi Fry, owner of the Slim Chance, rode into town with two punchers. A few minutes later the Rocking-J crew arrived. Jesse George, a careful man, brought along three men. One of them was Mordecai Bishop, an Arizona Territory revolver fighter who'd made a name for himself as a fast gun in the Lee-Peacock feud in the Texas four corners country. Well, the seven men got to cussin' and discussin' and the ranchers poked holes in the air with their forefingers. They got to drinking and then to talking again."

Frank stopped talking and listened into the still, mother-of-pearl night. "Coyotes are hunting close. They're making the horses restless."

"Did the ranchers reach an agreement?" Kate asked.

"We'll never know. Hank Lowery stepped into the saloon and locked the door behind him. He had a Colt in each hand, cut loose, and put a lead period at the end of the last sentence those boys uttered."

"But why?"

"Why? It seemed that he blamed both parties for his brother's death. Whatever the reason, when the smoke cleared seven men lay with their faces in the sawdust, five of them dead and two dying. Later I was told that old Levi Fry was gut-shot and crawled around the floor on his hands and knees coughing blood. Lowery's guns were shot dry, but he drew a .32 hide-out, shoved the muzzle into the back of Levi Fry's head, and pulled the trigger."

Kate drew her nightdress closer around her shoulders. "Frank, why should the Longdale Massacre trouble you? You weren't involved."

"But I was, indirectly anyway. I'd worked a roundup for old man Fry and he'd paid twice what he owed me. I liked that old man and he didn't deserve to die the way he did."

"Hank Lowery says he didn't shoot Mr. Fry while he was on the floor," Kate said.

"And you believe him?"

"Well, no. But I don't disbelieve him, either."

"Kate, Lowery is a cold-blooded killer. He proved it in Longdale."

"Has he killed anyone since?"

"I don't know."

"Well, he may have. He says he has angry men on his back trail."

"Who are they?"

"He wouldn't say." Kate was silent for a while. The moonlight tangled in her hair and turned the fair Celtic skin of her beautiful face to porcelain. Finally she said, "Hank Lowery wants to join our drive. He says he's worked cattle before, and we could use another hand."

It took Frank a few moments to recover before he said, "What did you tell him?"

"I said I'd speak to you. And I told him something else, Frank. I said if he killed a man while he was under my employ, I'd hang him."

"Kate, Lowery is a professional gambler. When was the last time you saw a gambler eating dust? Riding drag? And he's a shootist. I bet you never saw one of them punching cows, either."

"And that's the whole point. Lowery wants to make a fresh start and put his violent past behind him. He thinks he might prosper in Dodge as a merchant, perhaps in the lumber business."

"He wants to be a storekeeper? And pigs will fly." Frank flicked away his cigarette butt. It glowed like a firefly before hitting the ground. "I'll tell you something about the Colt's revolver, Kate. It casts a mighty long shadow. A man who's lived by the gun and made a reputation can run, but he can't hide. Sooner or later the past catches up to him and he's forced to draw the Colt again. John Wesley tried to go straight and so did Dallas Stoudenmire, two men I knew and liked. Now Wes is rotting in Huntsville and five months ago Dallas was shot down in El Paso. Lowery will end up the same way."

"I aim to take a chance on him, Frank," Kate said.

"Then you're making a big mistake."

"I took a chance on you, remember? You turned out all right."

"Have it your own way, Kate. You're the boss. But if Lowery harms or even *threatens* harm to me or anyone I know, I'll kill him. Is that understood?"

"Perfectly," Kate said. "But it will not come to that. I will not let it happen." She rose and walked into the moonlight, her back stiff.

CHAPTER FIVE

By cowboy standards, at forty years old Les Bowes was an old man, but there was not a man in Texas who knew as much as he did about cattle and their ways. He'd gone up the trail for the first time in 1866 with Charlie Goodnight and Oliver Loving and ten years later was a top hand on Goodnight's JA Ranch in the panhandle. In 1880, he became a member of the Panhandle Stockman's Association and had a hand in killing several nesters and rustlers.

Stove-up and hurting, he'd nonetheless let Kate talk him into one more drive before he moved to Philadelphia to live with his widowed sister.

As he spoke to Frank, Bowes's face bore a worried expression. "The cattle are strung out all over the range. Even the yearlings are no longer close to their mamas."

Frank immediately saw the implications for a delay of the roundup. "How scattered, Les?" he asked as the other hands gathered around, their curiosity roused.

"A fair number, maybe five hundred head, drifted

south. That's what I know so far. I suspect we'll find other bunches to the west and north." Bowes dropped his eyes to the cigarette he was building. "I saw hoss tracks, Frank."

"Rustlers?"

"Could be."

Frank nodded. "Your mount is used up. Saddle another horse and we'll go take a look-see." He turned to Trace. "Keep bringing in the yearlings. I'll ride south with Les. Lowery, you'll come with me."

"I got a bad feeling about this scattered herd business. It's making me uneasy," Trace said, the branding iron with its distinctive KK head smoking in his gloved hand.

Frank nodded. "Me, too, Trace. Me, too."

Normally, a grazing herd will spread out in groups of three or four over several acres, but they will keep each other in sight. That wasn't the case with the Kerrigan herd.

"They've been hazed, deliberately scattered." Frank lowered his field glasses. "They're strung out for miles in every direction."

Nobody had asked his opinion, but Hank Lowery said, "That's why the calves have been so slow coming in. The drovers can't find them."

"That would explain it all right," Les Bowes said.

Irritated, Frank said, "Then maybe one of you pundits can tell me why."

"What's a pundit?" Bowes asked, his browned, lined face puzzled.

"It means expert," Lowery said.

"Or know-it-all," Frank said. "Let's ride and see if we can find the rest of the herd."

After two hours of searching through sagebrush and piñon under a burning sun, they found several places where cattle had forded the Pecos. Frank waved the others forward across shallow white water and again picked up cow tracks that headed south and due west.

An hour later, they stumbled on a sight they hadn't reckoned on. The bodies of three dead Mexicans were already buzzing with fat black flies.

All were young men who'd crossed the border in search of work. At least that's what Frank deduced since all three had carried packs on their backs and clothing and scraps of food were scattered around the corpses. A small, framed image of the Madonna of Guadalupe lay near the corpse of the youngest of the three, a boy in his late teens.

Frank swung out of the saddle and examined the dead men one by one, then he rose to his feet. "They were shot at close range. The oldest has a powder burn around the bullet wound in his chest."

"Apaches?" Lowery said.

Les Bowes shook his head. "White men. Boot tracks all over the place."

Lowery walked off a ways.

"The Mexicans saw faces that they could later identify. That's why they were murdered," Frank said. "A bullet can shut a man up real quick."

Lowery returned. "Four riders headed"—he chopped down with a bladed hand—"that way. Due north."

"How long ago?" Frank said.

The gambler shook his head. "I'm not that good a tracker."

"We're going after them," Frank said. "See where the tracks lead us."

"I'm not wearing a gun, Cobb," Lowery said. "If there's killing to be done count me out. I'm all through with that."

Frank turned hard eyes on the man. "Lowery, I think I disliked you less before you got religion."

Lowery smiled. "Very good, Frank. Very funny. Maybe I'll write that in my memoirs."

Bowes spat into the dust at his feet. "Yeah, and make sure you write this, sonny. The pen is mightier than the sword except in a swordfight. The rannies we're going after will shoot you dead as hell in a parson's parlor whether you're heeled or not."

"It's a chance I'm willing to take, Bowes," Lowery said. "Like you, I'm riding for the brand."

"Head back to the ranch, Lowery," Frank said. "If we meet up with those four gunmen, you'd only be a liability and maybe get me or Les killed."

"I could draw some of their fire," Lowery said. "There's always that, huh?"

"I told you to go back to the ranch." Frank's handsome face was stiff with anger. "Maybe you reckon you've already killed more than your fair share or maybe you're yellow and have always been. Either way, I don't want you around."

Hank Lowery looked as though he'd just been slapped. "That's a hell of a thing to say to a man." He turned, mounted his horse, and rode away at a canter. Soon, he was lost in the rippling heat haze.

Bowes used his fingers to wipe the sweatband of his

hat and settled it back on his graying head. "I never seen a man turn coward right before my eyes before. You ride for the brand, you fight for it."

"Despite what I said, I don't think he's a coward, Les," Frank said.

"Then what the hell is he?" Bowes said.

Frank shook his head. "I don't know."

CHAPTER SIX

Frank Cobb and Les Bowes rode north into the southern edge of the timber country. Frank rode with a wary eye on the terrain around him. The notion that he was riding into gun trouble piled up inside him like thunderheads before a storm. Bowes was unnaturally silent for a talking man and the only sounds were the creak of saddle leather and the soft footfalls of their horses.

"I know this country," Bowes said finally. "Tobias Briggs's place is about a mile ahead of us."

"I've never been north this far," Frank said. "It's a ways off my home range. Who's Tobias Briggs?"

"From what folks around here say, Briggs got his start as a slave trader in New Orleans but killed a man and lit a shuck for Texas just ahead of a hanging posse. He worked as an Indian agent for a spell and opened up a trading post. Now that the Apaches are all but gone, he's turned his place into a hog farm and saloon. You want a woman and rotgut whiskey, Tobias Briggs is your man. They say he also sells opium the Chinese bring in from Fort Worth, but I don't know about that."

"You think those four killers might have stopped there?" Frank said.

"Yeah, if they have money to spend. Most times them Mexican peons have a gold peso or two stashed away somewhere."

"It's thin," Frank said. "I want to know why they scattered the Kerrigan cattle and on whose order. Why would they ride so far off our range?"

"I told you, Frank. For women and whiskey. Chances are they'll head out again tomorrow morning and do some more mischief."

Frank drew rein and glanced at the sky. "Be dark soon, Les, and we're needed at the ranch. I don't think those riders headed this far. I reckon we should get back."

Bowles disagreed. "We can take a look at the Briggs place and still be eating Kate's beans by nightfall. Call it what you want, but I got a feeling in my water that right now them boys are whooping it up."

"A mile you say?"

"Yeah. We'll come up on a clearing in the pines and Briggs's place is right in the middle of it."

"I think you're leading me on a wild-goose chase, but I guess it won't hurt to take a look."

Bowes drew his Colt and thumbed a round into the empty chamber that was under the hammer. "We'll find them there. Four horses leave a wide track and the hog farm is right where they're headed."

"Hell, I didn't see any tracks," Frank said.

Bowes smiled. "Mr. Cobb, that's because you don't know how to look."

* * *

The Briggs place consisted of a long, low timber cabin with a slatted door and four small windows facing the hitching rail out front. To the side were a pole corral, a number of outbuildings, and a squeaking waterwheel that turned listlessly in the slight breeze. Hogs and chickens had the run of the yard, including a massive sow that lay on her side and suckled a dozen piglets. Above the door was a crudely lettered sign.

RYE WHISKEY & WILLING WHORES
~ Nothing Less and Nothing More

Frank's eyes flicked to the sign but what caught and held his attention were the four cow ponies at the hitching rail. He drew rein and said to Bowes, "Looks like we came to the right place after all."

"Looks like," Bowes said.

"I want to check the brand on those mounts." Frank swung out of the saddle and led his mount to the hitching rail where Bowes joined him. "Strange-looking brand. What is that? A bird?"

"I've seen that bird before," Bowes said. "It's a raven—the brand of Ezra Raven's outfit. He's got a spread to the southwest of here. Raven is one of them big ranchers who wants to be even bigger. He's got a *segundo* by the name of Poke Hylle—"

"Poke Hylle the draw fighter?"

"I don't know . . . but it's unlikely there's two men in Texas with that name. You heard of him?"

"If he's the same Poke Hylle, then, yes, I've heard of him. He outdrew and shot Bingley Abbott in Wichita that time and nobody considered Abbott a bargain, including me."

"Ol' Poke is that fast, huh?"

"One of the fastest there is."

"Want to call it a day and ride?" Bowes said, his stare measuring Frank, figuring how much sand the *segundo* had in him.

"Hell no." Frank smiled. "Nobody ever considered me a bargain, either."

The saloon consisted of a plank bar resting on empty beer barrels and a couple shelves holding a variety of bottles behind it. A few tables and chairs were the only furnishings. The timber walls were adorned with the heads of long-dead antelope and deer and the place smelled of piss, vomit, ancient sweat, and smoking oil lamps.

The cathouse was cordoned off from the rest of the room by a series of canvas tarps. It was a dark, dreary place, but Tobias Briggs's saloon was no better and no worse than thousands of others scattered across the frontier.

The man himself—tall, lank, and bearded—stood behind the bar and smiled with all the warmth of a cobra at Frank and Bowes as they entered. "Welcome, boys. Make yourself to home and tell me what I can do for you."

After Frank let his eyes grow accustomed to the gloom, he saw four men sitting at a table with a bottle of rotgut and glasses between them. A hefty woman with bleached blond hair stood behind one of the men and massaged his shoulders. The man grunted every now and then and rolled his head back and forth. A second woman, as plump as the first, stood and watched the fall of the cards as the four visitors played poker. Under her blouse, her breasts were as large as flour sacks and an old black top hat with a bullet hole in the crown rested on top of her frizzy yellow curls. Looking worn and tired, the two women studied Frank and Bowes with bold, disinterested eyes.

One of the men at the table stared at Bowes, dismissed him, and let his eyes remain on Frank for a long moment. Then he shifted slightly in his chair and adjusted the lie of his gun belt.

His spurs chiming, Frank stepped to the bar and Briggs, a man with eyes the color of swamp mud, said, "What's your pleasure, big feller?"

"Two of whatever you have that passes as whiskey." Frank waited until Briggs filled glasses from a bottle with no label, then said, "Came across three dead Mexicans south of here. They'd been shot."

Briggs pretended shock. "Well, do tell. Probably tried to lift somebody's cattle and got caught in the act. Well, don't you worry none, mister, I don't allow their kind in here."

Out of the corner of his eye, Frank saw the men at the table lift their heads and take notice. Their conversation died into silence and the man who'd been getting massaged slapped the woman's hands away then turned and stared hard at him and Bowes.

"Well, as you say, they were probably rustlers." Frank laid fifty cents on the bar and watched as Briggs dropped the coins into a tin box he picked up from the shelf behind him. Before the man could put the box back, Frank reached out with the speed of a striking rattler and grabbed it from his hands.

Briggs was shocked. "Hey, what the hell—"

Frank opened the box lid and spilled its contents onto the bar. As coins rang onto the floor, he picked up a couple silver pesos. He held them up where Briggs could see them. "I thought you told me Mexicans weren't allowed into this fine establishment."

"They're not," Briggs said, his eyes sliding to the men at the table.

"Then who paid for their whiskey with pesos?"

"Feller who came in earlier," Briggs said.

"What kind of feller? Describe him. I want to know what he looks like."

"Big man . . . no, wait. He was short . . ." Briggs's tongue got tangled in his mouth and he said nothing more.

But a voice from the table spoke for him. "I paid with the pesos." A man's chair scraped back on the rough floor as he got to his feet. "Briggs is right. Them greasers were rustlers and they got what they deserved."

"Shot in the back and robbed?" Frank said. "They deserved that?"

"Why the hell do you care?" the man said. "You some kind of Mex lover? Or some kind of lawman maybe?"

"Neither. What I care about is that the Kerrigan ranch cattle are scattered all over the range and it could take weeks to round them up," Frank said.

"What's that to me?" The man wore two Colts—a revolver in a holster and another tucked into his waistband—which was unusual at that time in the West.

Frank pegged him for a professional gun hand and not a tyro trying to act tough.

Neither was the youngster with carrion eater's eyes

and a low-slung Remington who stepped next to him and said, "I'm siding you, Poke."

"I think the men who drifted the Kerrigan herd all over God's creation also killed and robbed the Mexicans," Frank said. "And I think those men are standing right in front of me."

"And I reckon you're a damn liar." Poke Hylle went for his gun and learned in that instant that though he'd been faster than Bingley Abbott, he was nowhere near as sudden as the man facing him.

Frank's bullet took out the center of the tobacco tag hanging over Hylle's shirt pocket. The gunman was stunned, horrified, and made ashen-faced by the hit. He staggered back a step, making no attempt to bring up his gun. Standing his ground beside Hylle, it was obvious that the dead-eyed youngster had never encountered a draw fighter before. He took up a duelist's stance, right arm extended in front of him at eye level, but never got a chance to trigger a shot. A gunfight is measured in split seconds, and the young man died knowing that he was way too slow. When Frank's bullet hit him in the center of his chest, the youngster's dreadful bellow came from the terror in his belly. Knowing the man was dead on his feet, Frank again concentrated on Hylle. Game as they come and a hard man to kill, Hylle fired, missed, and fired again. His second bullet tugged at the collar of Frank's shirt. No mercy in him, Frank got his work in coolly and accurately and scored two more body hits. Hylle went down hard, blood in his mouth

"Frank!" Bowes's voice. Behind him.

Frank swung around in time to see Bowes trigger a shot at Tobias Briggs. The tall man was in the process of bringing a shotgun to bear, but Bowes's bullet hit him just under the left ear. A man can't stand and make his fight after a wound like that, and Bowes pumped two more bullets in Briggs as he fell.

The two Raven punchers who remained made a hasty stampede for the door, but Frank shot down the first one. Unable to stop, the second tripped over his fallen companion and stretched his length on the floor. The man immediately rolled onto his back and held his hands up. His face terrified, he yelled, "Don't shoot! I'm not in this fight!"

"Get on your feet," Frank said. "Drop the gun belt and stand over there by the far wall."

The scared puncher did as he was told and Frank looked around the smoke-drifted room at the mayhem he and Bowes had wrought in the space of just a few seconds. Four men were down. Three of them were dead and the dying Briggs was groaning his death dirge.

"There was hell to pay, wasn't there?" Les Bowes said, staring at Briggs. "I never killed a man before."

"He called it. Wouldn't let it trouble you. Just hope that you never have to kill another one." Frank punched the empties out of his Colt, reloaded from his cartridge belt, and lifted his eyes to the man standing against the wall. "You're coming with us."

"Whatever you say, mister. I ain't no gunman."

"You got a name, cowboy?" Bowes said.

"I don't mind putting it out," the puncher said. "Name's Lou Standish, from the Sabine River country."

Frank motioned to the body of one of the men he'd killed. "I heard the name Poke mentioned. Would he be Poke Hylle?"

"He would," Standish said.

Frank nodded. "He was fast on the draw and shoot. And he was game."

"Not fast enough it seems, beggin' your pardon," Standish said.

The whore with the top hat stepped close to Frank. She glanced down at Briggs. "Is he dead yet?"

"Seems like," Frank said.

"Never trust a wolf like Tobias Briggs to be dead until he's skun," the woman said.

"Especially that one, Flossie." The other woman stared at the man. "He's got more lives than a cat."

Flossie hiked up her dress and pulled a Colt .41 cloverleaf revolver from her garter. She bent over, shoved the muzzle into Briggs's temple, and pulled the trigger. In the ringing silence after the racket of the shot, her voice was loud. "Now he's skun."

She moved behind the bar, found a whiskey bottle and a glass, poured herself a shot and downed it, then poured another. Taking a knee beside Briggs, she poured the whiskey into the dead man's open mouth. "Drink that in hell, Tobias," she said as amber liquid trickled down the man's ashen chin.

When the woman rose to her feet, Frank said, "Not one to hold a grudge, are you, ma'am?"

"You know what that piece of human filth did to Flossie? You know what he did to me?" the other woman said. "Tobias Briggs was a monster and we've both got the scars to prove it."

"Flora, save your breath," Flossie said. "He's a man and he won't understand."

"My mother worked the line to keep me fed and put clothes on my back," Frank said. "I think I understand. The day I turned fourteen she killed herself."

Les Bowes glanced out the window. "Shading into dark, Frank. What do we do with the dead men?"

"We'll take care of it," Flossie said. "We've buried the dead out of here before."

"Ladies, there are four saddled horses outside," Frank said. "They're yours. Get the hell away from here and sell them somewhere. God knows you deserve it."

"What's your name, mister?" Flossie said.

"Frank Cobb."

"Thank you, Frank Cobb. Ain't nobody ever gave us anything like that before."

"There's a first time for everything, I guess," Frank said.

"Hell, I need my hoss," Lou Standish said.

"No, you don't," Frank said. "You're walking."

CHAPTER SEVEN

"He's half dead, Frank," Kate Kerrigan said. "How far did you walk him?"

"A fair piece, Kate, most of it in the dark. I guess he regrets getting his boots sewn on a narrow Texas last, huh?"

"He won't need any kind of last ever again. I reckon his feet are worn down to nubbins."

"Well, now we don't have to hang him. He swore on his mother's grave that he didn't kill any of the Mexicans, so maybe he's suffered enough."

"I'll be the judge of that. Even if you believe him about the Mexicans, it was my cattle he helped scatter all over the range."

"Yeah, well, there's always that," Frank said. "I reckon it's a hanging offense."

Kate poured more coffee into Frank's cup and said, "I know you've had no sleep and are all used up, but do you feel like riding?"

"I'll ride. I'll catch up on sleep later."

"Good." Kate turned to Moses, who held a plate under his chin and was scraping up the last of his breakfast eggs. "Mose, make me a hangman's rope with thirteen coils on the noose. Unlucky for some."

Frank smiled. "Who you going to hang, Kate?"

"Hopefully nobody, but I'm keeping my options open. Do have that last slice of bacon and help yourself to another biscuit, Frank."

Black Barrie Delaney delicately dabbed his mouth with his napkin. "What course are you laying, Miz Kate?"

"I'm headed for Ezra Raven's spread," Kate said.

"That damn rogue," Delaney said. "I'll come with my cutlass and split him from skull to chin."

"You'll do no such thing, Barrie Delaney. You and your shiftless crew will get to work on my house, and if I don't see progress by the time I get back, I'll find another place to stick your cutlass. Oh, I do declare, the coffee is getting cold." Kate stood then turned. "Mr. Delaney, why are you still in my presence?"

"I'm just going, Miz Kate, and thank 'ee kindly for breakfast." The man rose to his feet and winked at Frank. "A poor sailorman's work is never done."

"Barrie Delaney, you wouldn't know a hard day's work if you tripped over it," Kate said. "You're more used to cutting throats than cutting lumber, I'll be bound."

Delaney left the cabin and waved to his crew, who'd filled up on coffee and Jazmin's flapjacks and were lounging under the shade tree. "Come on, you damn lubbers," the captain yelled. "Let's build the nice lady a house."

Kate shook her head. "How did Black Barrie Delaney and his pirates ever escape the gallows? It's a mystery to me."

* * *

Kate ordered four of the hired hands to mount up. In addition, she planned for Frank and her son Trace, a first-rate rifleman, to ride with her.

Hank Lowery volunteered, but Frank would not hear of it. "Lowery won't carry a gun, and an unarmed man will be of no account when we brace Ezra Raven."

"Then he can stay behind with Quinn and the others and help brand whatever calves we can find." Kate stared at Frank. "I won't argue the point with you, but I admire Hank Lowery for trying to change and leave his guns behind."

"I won't argue, either, Kate. A man has the right to choose to be unarmed and defenseless if he wishes," Frank said. "I just don't want him anywhere around me."

Kate was silent for a moment, trying to come up with the last word. After a few attempts, she said finally, "Well, I think Mr. Lowery is to be commended, so there." She turned and walked to her horse, her slender back stiff.

A couple miles south of the Raven ranch house the trail divided. One branch led straight ahead and the other made a sharp turn toward a collapsed soddy so old that no one knew who built it, when, or why. Frank took the straightaway and after a few minutes they came on a dozen fat cattle grazing on both banks of a narrow stream. All of them bore the KK brand.

Trace said, "I would never have trespassed this far onto the Raven range to hunt our cattle."

"I think that's the whole idea," Kate said. "Raven expects us to obey the rules."

Frank Cobb nodded in agreement and poked Lou Standish in the ribs with his rifle. "Were you a party to this?"

The man winced and jerked in the saddle. "Yeah, following Mr. Raven's orders." His hands were tied behind his back and to keep him honest, he rode bareback on a gray mustang. "See up ahead, the dead cottonwood that fell into the stream one time?"

"I see it," Frank said.

"Mr. Raven ranged his Big Fifty on that there tree."

"And you're riding point, Standish." Frank grinned. "The thought that a Sharps rifle could be aimed right at your belly must be a tad worrisome."

"I'll holler when we get closer to the cabin," Standish said. "Mr. Raven will recognize me."

"You sure?" Frank said.

The puncher shook his head. "Hell, mister, I'm not sure of anything."

"Well you can be certain of this," Kate said. "Make a fancy move and I'll shoot you right off that pony."

Standish grimaced and shifted his weight on the little gray's bony back. "Lady, you'd be doing me a kindness."

CHAPTER EIGHT

The Raven ranch house was a large, two-story edifice set among pines and wild oak. It had been recently painted white and the door, like the one to Kate's cabin, complete with brass knocker and handle, had been imported from back east. But there the resemblance to the Kerrigan place ended. Flower boxes hung under all four lower-story windows, but all they held were a few stems that stuck up like dead twigs. A small flower and vegetable garden to the left of the house had gone to weed and cactus. The brass on the door was dull and had not been polished in a long time.

Kate read the signs.

A woman had once lived there but no longer. It seemed that she'd left suddenly and bequeathed to Ezra Raven a fine house without a soul. It was a fine house, one Kate could only dream about, but sadness— a darkness and a sense of loss—surrounded the place. She felt it deeply.

Beside her, Frank Cobb yelled, "Ezra Raven, if you're to home, show yourself."

A few tense moments passed. A window curtain flickered and then the door opened. Ezra Raven, big, bearded, and commanding, filled the doorway. "Have you finally come to your senses and are ready to sell, Mrs. Kerrigan?"

"No, but I'm here to ask you to come to yours, Mr. Raven," Kate said.

"What the hell?" Raven's black eyes burned on Standish. "Lou, what are you doing with them?" To Kate, he asked, "Why does my puncher have a noose around his neck?"

Before Kate could answer, Standish said, "They're going to hang me, Mr. Raven, for drifting the Kerrigan cattle."

Raven looked at Frank. "Damn. Are you Cobb?"

"I'm Cobb."

"Is the hangman's noose your doing?"

"No, it's mine," Kate said. "And right now I'm inclined to use the same rope on you, Mr. Raven. Why did you scatter my cattle?"

"I didn't drift your herd, and anybody who says I did is a damn liar," Raven said.

"I say it, Raven," Frank said.

"Big talk, Cobb," Raven said. "If Poke Hylle was here, he'd make you sing a different tune."

"Boss, Poke is dead," Standish said. "And so are Dave Brisk and Verne McCoy." He nodded in Frank's direction. "He killed all three of them in Tobias Briggs's place. Briggs is dead, as well."

That news hit Ezra Raven hard and he gasped as though he'd just been punched in the gut. "No, that ain't true. Not Poke."

Misery written large on his face, Standish said, "But

it is true, boss. Poke drew down on Cobb an' got shot. Cobb shot Dave and then Verne. And Briggs got shot. Hell, everybody got shot excepting me."

Raven stared at Frank, his mouth slack. "Poke drew first, but you had time to haul iron and gun him?"

"Yeah, that's how it happened, Raven," Frank said. "Poke Hylle was good with the Colt, real fast on the draw and shoot. And he had sand. But I was more than a shade faster and I got sand of my own."

The conversation cut off there as two of Raven's punchers rode in from the range, dusty, dirty, and on the hunt for coffee. The *clack-clack* of levered Winchesters from Kate's party welcomed them.

After looking from Raven to Kate Kerrigan and back again, one of the riders summed things up in his mind then said, "Is there trouble here, boss?"

"No trouble," Kate said. "If Mr. Raven agrees to my terms."

The rancher was almost apoplectic with rage. "Terms! What are you talking about, lady? Terms? You don't give Ezra Raven terms."

"It's quite simple, really," Kate said. "You will use your men to help me round up my herd—the one you scattered, Mr. Raven. Remember? Only after that job is completed will you carry out your own gather."

"Damned if I will!" the big rancher said.

"Kate, do you want me to hang Raven as a rustler and murderer now or later?" Frank said.

"Not yet. Let's hope we won't need that unpleasantness. Mr. Raven, you willfully scattered my cows all over the range. It's only right that you gather them up again."

"I'm no rustler," Raven said. "And where do you get this murderer nonsense, Cobb?"

"Your *segundo* Poke Hylle and four of your hands, including Standish here, killed and robbed three Mexicans just south of the Briggs place," Frank said. "They may have been acting on your orders, Raven, but even if they were not, they were your men and that makes you responsible and just as guilty."

"Lou, is he telling the truth?" Raven said.

"I had no hand in the killing, boss," Standish said. "It was all Poke's idea. You know how he hated Mexicans . . . and everybody else who wasn't white, come to that."

"I gave no such order," Raven said.

"You're guilty nonetheless," Frank said. "You deserve to hang, Raven. Anybody ever tell you that you got a neck made for a rope?"

One of the Raven punchers, a kid with a round face as freckled as a robin's egg, lowered his hand toward his holstered gun.

"Esau, leave the iron be. Cobb will kill you." After the cowboy pulled his hand away, the rancher said, "The last thing I need is another dead drover." He glared at Kate Kerrigan. "And if I don't round up your herd?"

"Then I'll hang you, Raven," Frank said. "Today or another day, it doesn't make any difference to me, but depend on it. You'll swing and soon."

"You gonna let your hired man talk to me like that, Mrs. Kerrigan?" Raven said.

It could have been a statement of defiance but wasn't. Coming from a man who normally cut a wide path and had a history of riding roughshod over lesser men, it sounded like weakness.

"Yes I am, Mr. Raven," Kate said. "And I'll let Frank Cobb hang you with my blessing. You have a choice to make. For your sake, I hope it's the right and honorable one."

"Damn it, lady. Do you have balls under that skirt?" Raven said.

Kate's beautiful face hardened. "Mr. Raven, push me hard enough and you'll sure find out."

Raven had lost Poke Hylle, his ace in the hole. When he looked into Frank Cobb's eyes, he saw resolve and a readiness to kill. He saw the way of his own death and made up his mind. His hands were no match for Frank Cobb. It went against the grain, but he had to eat crow. "All right, Mrs. Kerrigan, I'll round up your herd . . . but when the work is done, I expect your hands to help gather mine."

"Apologize to Mrs. Kerrigan for the remark you just made," Frank said, his eyes hard. "A gentlemen doesn't speak that way to a lady. Not in my presence he doesn't."

"I apologize," Raven said. "I'm a rough-mannered man and not often in the company of ladies."

Kate let the man save face. "Your apology is accepted, Mr. Raven. I have already forgotten the matter. As to helping you with your cattle, that sounds perfectly agreeable to me. I'm sure working together in perfect harmony we can get the job done."

Frank Cobb took his foot out of the stirrup and used it to shove Standish off the mustang. He fell so hard the loud thump made Kate's horse start. "Raven, I guess you'll need this one for the roundup."

The rancher turned to his riders. "Help Lou to his feet. Untie his hands and get the damn noose off him." He looked at Kate. "Would you really have hanged me, Mrs. Kerrigan?"

"Oh yes, most assuredly." Kate smiled. "Here's an invitation, Mr. Raven. After the gather is finished and before we take to the trail, you must come to my place for afternoon tea and we'll have sponge cake. Have you ever eaten sponge cake before?"

The big rancher seemed at a loss for words, but finally he managed, "No. I guess not."

"You will like it very much," Kate said. "It's Queen Victoria's favorite, you know."

Ezra Raven was as good as his word, and the Kerrigan hands rode with his own to complete the gather and get the yearlings branded. A month later, he and Kate were ready to take to the Chisholm, but he never did show up for afternoon tea.

CHAPTER NINE

A cattle drive could run into a lot of problems before the cows got to where they were supposed to be. Stampedes, drought, floods, and sickness were common. As Kate Kerrigan drove her three thousand head north, the prairie grass was fresh and the Canadian and Cimarron rivers were wet and so were their streams.

After two months on the trail and only a couple days before they reached the cattle pens at the railhead one of Kate's drovers was thrown by a mustang and busted up his leg. He rode into Dodge City in some style in the back of the chuck wagon.

Kate took one look at the bustling, roaring cow town and decided she had never seen the like. Even the wild Five Points district of New York couldn't compare to the dusty, smelly, fly-ridden Gomorrah of the Plains. Everything and everybody in Dodge was "full up and raring to go" as the eastern newspapers said. Everybody lived for the day and to hell with tomorrow.

Most frontiersmen considered Dodge the finest city

in the West, a seductive, beckoning utopia where a man could get anything he wanted—for a price. But some citizens of the more respectable sort believed the devil had carelessly allowed a chunk of hell to slip though his scaly hands and it had landed smack dab in the middle of the Kansas prairie.

Kate rode past dozens of saloons, brothels, and dance halls. Among the finest were the Long Branch Saloon and the China Doll cathouse. But the establishment that was causing the most stir that hot summer day was a newly constructed false-fronted building named the Top Hat. A sign hung outside the glass doors.

GRAND OPENING TODAY

GIRLS! GIRLS! GIRLS!

*The Finest Spirits, Cigars, and Games of Chance
for the Sporting Gentleman*
~Maddox Franklin, Prop.

To get Mr. Franklin's message across, a pretty woman, naked as a seal, paraded up and down outside the establishment on a white horse led by a small black boy dressed like a Moor in scarlet tunic and feathered turban. The young lady's long blond hair was strategically arranged to cover her nudity but it was, as Kate would say later, "at best, a hit-and-miss arrangement."

"Dodge is quite a place, huh, Ma?" Trace said, grinning. "And that there gal is Lady Godiva right from the history book."

Ignoring Frank's grin, Kate said, "You stay away

from that den of iniquity, Trace. Girls, girls, girls indeed. Better you remain in your hotel room and read the Holy Bible and better Lady Godiva found herself some decent, modest clothes."

"You listen to your ma, Trace," Frank said. "Reading scripture sure as hell beats whiskey, cigars, and naked women."

Kate glared at him, but Frank's face was empty as he studiously looked straight ahead.

Once the Kerrigan herd had been penned, Kate sought out the cattle buyers and arranged for a count. Because of the easy trail conditions, the beeves had put on weight and were in prime condition. She expected top dollar and was paid thirty-five dollars a head for her twenty-eight hundred steers for a total of ninety-eight thousand dollars.

After paying off the hands, Kate took rooms for herself, Trace, Frank, and Hank Lowery at the respectable and whisper-quiet Drover's Rest Hotel. Despite making a huge profit, Kate insisted that Frank and Trace share a room. Lowery, still a pariah despite having done a man's part on the trail, had a room by himself.

That evening after dinner, Kate lingered to drink coffee and bade the others to do the same. The sounds of Dodge City drifted into the dining room— the roars of whiskey-drinking men, the brassy laughter of painted women, and the constant tinpan cacophony of competing pianos and banjos. "I told Ollie Bligh to set out for home tomorrow morning with the chuck wagon."

"I hope he's a better driver than he is a cook," Frank said.

Kate nodded. "That may be so." Having some empathy for bad cooks, she added, "But he does try, bless him. Trace, you will accompany the wagon and see that Ollie stays away from the bottle."

Trace was crestfallen. "But Ma—"

"No buts, Trace, and no maybes. Do you remember what happened the last time you were here?"

"I remember."

"You were wounded and forced to kill a man," Kate said.

"Ma, I said I remember."

"I'll feel better when I know you're on the trail back to Texas. And first thing after breakfast tomorrow you will be."

"Why don't we all head back?" Frank said. "There's nothing in Dodge I need to do that I haven't done many times before."

"Yes, I'm quite sure that is the case, Frank," Kate said. "And please spare me the details of what you've done before. I'll stay in Dodge until I can arrange a bank transfer and discuss a few business details with my cattle buyers. That will only take until the day after tomorrow and then we'll leave. Trace, you'll be slowed by the wagon so I'm sure we'll catch up with you on the trail." Kate looked around the table. "Well, are we all in agreement?"

"Would it make any difference if we were not?" Trace said.

Kate shook her head. "Not a bit."

Before leaving Texas, Hank Lowery had traded his gambler's finery for range clothes, but he still managed to look elegant as he rose to his feet. He was still unarmed. "I'm off in search of a friendly poker game. The sixty dollars you paid me, Mrs. Kerrigan, is burning a hole in my pocket."

"Mr. Lowery, you're a grown man and may do as you please, but I wish you would reconsider. The gambling houses in this town are rough and dangerous places, and I wouldn't want to see you come to harm." Kate's beautiful face brightened. "I know, we can order a deck of cards and play Loo. I'm told it's all the rage of the British aristocracy."

"I'm afraid I've never heard of that game." Lowery looked anxious to leave.

"Loo is very simple, really. The dealer deals each player five cards and he or she is given the opportunity to stay in or drop out. Any player who stays in takes a share of the pot for every trick he takes, but he must pay an amount equal to the whole pot if he fails to take any tricks." Kate smiled. "Isn't that a hoot?"

"What are the stakes?" Lowery said.

"Since we're in Dodge and all feeling a little reckless, I think we can go as high as two pennies a trick," Kate said.

"Loo promises to be a sweet distraction for a future time, dear lady," Lowery said. "But the poker table beckons and I must heed its siren call."

"Then do be careful, Mr. Lowery. Don't stay up too late and do avoid the ladies of the night who are all too willing to part the unwary gentleman from his hard earned money."

"I'll be careful," Lowery said. "I've been in cow towns before."

"Want me to hold his hand, Kate?" Frank said.

Kate said, "That will be quite unnecessary, Frank."

After Lowery left she stopped a waiter and ordered

a pack of cards. "Now we'll play Loo. And we'll have more tea and some scones with strawberry jam and clotted cream. Isn't that better than frequenting some hot, smelly saloon, Trace?" She smiled as the waiter returned. "Ah, and here are the cards at last. I'll deal."

Outside, as the evening shaded into darkness, Dodge was ablaze with light—a glittering beacon in the darkness of the plains. The saloons, dance halls, and gambling dens were doing a roaring, boozy trade and somewhere close a drunken rooster took potshots at the rising moon.

CHAPTER TEN

Hank Lowery chose the newly opened Top Hat Saloon, figuring his guise as an over-the-hill puncher would stand him in good stead with the high rollers. They'd peg him as just another hayseed to be fleeced.

He had been around and had gambled on the riverboats and in some fancy places, but the Top Hat, still smelling of raw timber, impressed him as a pleasure palace where a man could commit every mortal sin in the book had he the time, money, and inclination.

A large dance floor, a massive mahogany bar, and an elevated stage dominated the vast interior space and seemed designed to make a tall man feel small, as well as awed by the brass and red velvet splendor. A balcony shaped like a horseshoe was compartmentalized into small rooms closed by violet-colored curtains. Paintings of naked women in suggestive poses hung above each crib, advertising the varied pleasures to be had within. Tables and chairs surrounded the dance floor, each with its own small oil lamp, and from the timber ceiling, illuminating all, hung a great crystal chandelier.

But it was the score of saloon girls who doubled as dance partners and waitresses that took Lowery, a man of some sophistication, aback. He found himself staring like a slack-jawed rube just off the farm at glorious girls who had obviously been chosen for their dazzling looks. They wore laced and buckled boned corsets in every color of the rainbow, gauzy little skirts that served no useful purpose, fishnet stockings with embroidered tops that came to mid-thigh, and high-heeled ankle boots. A tiny top hat dyed to match the color of the corset perched on each girl's upswept curls, and their painted, scarlet mouths never ceased to smile.

Lowery feared that surely their faces must hurt. He summed the place up by deciding that, depending on a man's religious point of view, the Top Hat Saloon was either a heaven or a hell.

In snowy white shirts and brocade vests, eight magnificent bartenders with slicked-down hair complete with kiss curls stood behind the bar jammed with patrons. They were mostly big-hatted Texas punchers, but also prosperous merchants in broadcloth, drummers of all kinds, cattle buyers, and the usual assortment of gamblers, goldbrick artists, dance hall loungers, and smart young men on the make.

The man who caught Lowery's attention stood at the end of the bar in the place of honor beside the serving hatch. He was very tall, close to seven feet. His shoulders were ax-handle wide and he had a broad powerful chest. He was dressed like a sporting gent in white linen trousers and a pearl gray frockcoat and like the saloon girls, he wore a top hat. The hat was full size and matched the gray of his coat. He had a wide, handsome face as stoical and watchful as that of a cigar store Indian, but there was a hint of bemusement about his wide, thick, and sensual mouth. It was as though he found the antics of his patrons droll and his restless green eyes moved constantly, seeing everything.

Standing next to him was a man Lowery recognized from a back trail. Drugo Odell was the essence of evil condensed into a five-foot-five, hundred-and-twenty-pound frame. Odell was a killer for hire, a man who notched his fast guns, and as far as was known, he had no conscience. That the big man was his boss Lowery had no doubt.

A five-piece orchestra walked on stage, settled themselves onto folding chairs, and launched into a lively version of "Poor Nellie from Cork."

Lowery looked around. His gaze settled on a table to the right of the stage where the stakes seemed to be high but not out of his reach, and he stepped in that direction.

His way was blocked by a huge bouncer with a broken nose and an attitude. "We'll have no loungers here. Show me your coin."

Lowery reached into his pocket and produced three gold eagles.

The man nodded. "Enjoy your evening, sir."

Classy place, Lowery thought.

After three hours of playing careful poker, Hank Lowery stepped away from the table fifty-three dollars richer and had made no enemies. When he bellied up to the bar and ordered a whiskey, he caught Drugo

Odell watching him. He saw the little gunman's eyes flicker with recognition but then dismiss him and slide away, leaving a snail track across Lowery's face. Drugo had no interest in the man he'd met only once in passing down El Paso way. He wore a blue ditto suit with a high-button coat, a celluloid collar, a red and black striped tie, and a bowler hat. He disdained gun belts as cumbersome and uncomfortable, but Lowery knew he'd have a revolver about him someplace. Odell was bad news and a man to step around.

A pretty brunette with huge brown eyes looked at Lowery like a startled fawn when he refused her offer to dance. "Would you like me to send over another girl more to your taste?" She wore a shiny black patent leather corset done up on both sides with a dozen silver buckles.

Lowery said, "How long does it take you to get into that thing?"

"A lot longer than it takes to get it off."

"It must be hot."

"You'd be surprised how many men like sweat." She turned on her heel and left, her heels clacking like castanets on the wood floor.

Lowery finished his drink and stepped outside into bustling Front Street. Reluctant to seek his bed, he decided to take a stroll around town and take in the sights. Dressed like any other cowboy, he attracted little attention as he made his way along the crowded boardwalk, stopping to read the banner hung between two posts in a vacant lot. Dodge was full of signs, advertising everything from dyspepsia pills to lawyers and land agents, but he figured this one was king of them all.

GOLEM—THE AMAZING MECHANICAL MAN
☞ The Wonder of the Age

He walks! He talks! He bows to the ladies!
For 50 cents he'll tell your fortune!

A barker in a striped shirt, a bandana tied tightly around his thick neck, stood under the sign and yelled in the voice of God, "Come one, come all. Come no one at all! Returned to these shores after his triumphal tour entertaining the crowned heads of Europe and the pashas of the Orient, we present Golem, the amazing mechanical man."

A fair-sized crowd had gathered, but the barker picked out a young couple. The girl was plain and respectable, and her pale beau looked like an accounting clerk. "Come right up, young lady and gentleman, soon to be Mr. and Mrs., I'll be bound."

That drew a laugh from the crowd and a couple ribald comments from its more inebriated members.

Emboldened, the barker said, "Come, sir, don't be shy. Introduce your ladylove to the amazing Golem, who kissed, not a three month ago, the hand of the Empress of China."

The clerk was shy, blushing, and bashful, but he led his equally coy girl into the lot to meet the Wonder of the Age.

Golem stood about eight foot tall, an automaton made of steel, brass, and copper piping. His round head was large as a nail keg. Covered over with iron mesh, his red eyes, false nose, and O of a mouth gave the impression of a human face. His chest was large as a beer barrel and covered in copper pipes and brass valves, several leaking jets of steam. His arms and legs were of also of metal, somewhat patterned on the limbs of a suit of late medieval armor.

The barker yelled, "And now, without any further ado, I present Professor Abraham Woodmancey, the creator of the mighty Golem and his master!"

The growing crowd cheered apart from one whiskey-sodden rooster who eyed the blushing bride-to-be and shouted, "Do 'er!"

Professor Woodmancey was a small man, wrinkled as an overripe pippin. He wore a long canvas coat, much oil stained, and a battered top hat with a pair of goggles parked above the brim. He bowed to the crowd and then placed his hand on the mechanical man's back. "Bow to the ladies and gentlemen, Golem."

The automaton bowed stiffly and raised his top hat at the same time. This drew many huzzahs.

When Golem straightened, the professor said, "Now say how-de-do to the pretty young lady."

In a tinny voice, the mechanical man said, "Hello young lady."

More cheering, except from the rooster who'd yelled, "Do 'er!"

The barker said to the clerk, "I know you want to learn what fortune awaits you and the young lady. Cross my palm with silver. Fifty cents' worth."

The young man, who looked as though getting his fortune had been the least of his intentions, nonetheless paid the money, a considerable sum for a lowly clerk.

Professor Woodmancey placed his hand on Golem's back. "Now, tell the nice couple their fortune, Golem."

"Happy marriage," the mechanical man said.

The girl blushed, the young man grinned, the crowd cheered, and the rooster yelled, "Do 'er!"

Woodmancey escorted the clerk and his girl off the lot.

The barker again turned his attention to the crowd. "Who will step right up and meet the Mechanical Man, the Wonder of the Age? Why, Golem just recently had tea with Queen Victoria and advised the Czar of Russia that there was a poisoner in his midst. Saved the Czar's life, Golem did, and was awarded"— with considerable drama and flourish the barker waved a hand in the professor's direction— "*this!*"

Professor Woodmancey withdrew from his coat pocket a round medal the size of a clock dial and held it up to the crowd.

The barker yelled, "Solid gold, encrusted with precious jewels, made for Golem by a famous French jeweler on the express orders of the Czar of all the Russias. Ladies and gentlemen, in his hand Professor Woodmancey holds a fortune, enough to buy the entire town of Dodge City with all its cattle and fine buildings. Now, who will step up and meet Golem, the hero of all the Russias? Perhaps he will order the professor to surrender his medal to one lucky member of the audience. In Golem's world, stranger things have happened."

Hank Lowery suspected the medal was made of base metal and paste stones, but the mechanical man fascinated him, and he stayed to watch as a score of people happily paid their fifty cents to meet Golem and have him tell them their fortunes . . . if *Good luck . . . More money . . . Happy home . . .* or *New romance* could be considered fortunes.

Lowery was about to move on when the barker

spotted him and yelled, "Ah, there is one of the booted and spurred gentry come to visit our fair city. Cowboy, will you speak to Golem, the Wonder of the Age, and perhaps be able to call his coveted medal your own?"

Lowery smiled and shook his head, but the crowd cheered him on until he finally relented.

The mechanical man lifted his hat and said "Howdy" in a tone convincing enough to please the crowd.

"Now our Texan friend would like to hear his fortune," the barker said. "What great perils or pleasures await him on the trail to home? I'm sure he wishes to know."

The crowd gave a loud huzzah. Eager to get the thing over with, Lowery paid his fifty cents. He saw Professor Woodmancey put his hand on Golem's back and was sure the man was manipulating the automaton's speech and actions.

"Now Golem, tell the handsome cowboy what lies on the long trail ahead," the professor said.

The mechanical man's eyes glowed red and he rocked back and forth on his massive feet. A crackling sound came from his mouth and a blue spark flashed across his brass chest.

"Tell the cowboy his fortune, Golem." The professor sounded puzzled and irritated.

Finally the automaton spoke . . . one word. *"Death."*

The crowd was shocked. A few of the woman shrank back in alarm and an angry man yelled, "Here, that won't do!"

"Death . . . death . . . death . . ." Golem said, his voice as hollow as a drum.

Forcing a smile, the flustered barker yelled, "No,

Golem, that's not the cowboy's fortune. Now tell him his real one." He held up his hands. "Hold on, ladies and gentlemen. I think Golem was just having a little fun."

"He's got a strange sense of humor," the angry man said.

"*Death.*" Golem gave a great sigh and collapsed in a heap with a sound like tin cans being thrown down a coal chute.

Professor Woodmancey rushed to the front of the lot where the crowd was dispersing and threw up his hands. "Wait, wait. Ladies and gentlemen, this has never happened before."

"That was a mean trick to play on the cowboy," a stiff-faced woman said. "He wasn't doing you any harm."

"It wasn't a trick! No trick," the barker yelled, but he was talking to empty space. He turned, reached into his pocket, and withdrew several dollars. "Here, cowboy, take this. We didn't try to trick you. Something happened to the machine."

"Breath. It said *breath*, not *death*. See, cowboy, Golem means that you'll keep on drawing breaths for many, many years to come." Then to the barker, Professor Woodmancey said, "Isn't that so, Charlie?"

"As sure as shootin', that's what he said all right. I heard *breath* as clear as day."

Hank Lowery grinned. "I don't know why you boys are getting so worked up about a tin man and a cheap carnival trick. Professor, I think you pulled the wrong lever."

"That's it," Charlie said. "It was just the wrong lever."

"Thanks for returning my money." Lowery's grin widened as he shook his head. "You pair of crooks."

After Lowery walked away, Charlie said, "It was *death* all right."

Professor Woodmancey said, "Here, you don't think Golem can really tell the future, do you?"

"Damned if I know," Charlie said. "Just don't ask him to tell mine."

CHAPTER ELEVEN

The night was warm and humid. Heat lightning flashed without sound in a starless sky as Hank Lowery walked along Front Street in the direction of the Drover's Rest Hotel. The air smelled of penned-up cattle, horse dung, crowded, sweating humanity, and the ever-present odors of spilled beer, overused outhouses, and vomit. The boardwalks and streets were still thronged. For the cowboys and sporting crowd, the night was young and getting younger.

His spurs chimed on the boardwalk as he walked closer to the hotel. After he passed the Bonnie Blue Pool & Dance Hall, the crush of people thinned and he found himself alone except for a drunk wearing a dark suit and necktie who buttoned up his pants as he stepped out of an alley and then lurched across the street.

The floor of the alley had been raised with dirt and then covered over with crushed rock, an attempt to prevent the mud of Front Street from entering when it rained. To the right stood the blank wall of a furniture warehouse and opposite it was a series of five shacks that shared adjoining walls. Lowery had been in enough cow towns to know those were the abodes of women who worked the line. They were too old, too plain, or too drunk or drugged to grace the saloons and dance halls. He'd been told that in San Francisco's Barbary Coast the average life expectancy of the Chinese girls who worked the line was two years, and he didn't think the white girls doing the same in Dodge would fare any better.

Lowery was about to walk on when a woman's piercing shriek knifed through the night, stopping him in his tracks. A moment later, another, just as loud, came from a girl down at one of the saloons. He recognized the difference. A drunk had probably grabbed the saloon girl as she'd sashayed by and she'd screamed. It often made a drunk feel good and was excellent for business. The first wasn't that kind of scream. It was a strangled cry of terror and pain and it came from one of the line shacks.

Instinctively, Hank Lowery's hand dropped for his gun. Then he remembered . . . oiled and wrapped in sailcloth, it lay in the bunkhouse back at the Kerrigan ranch. And there it would remain.

His boots crunched on gravel as he stepped slowly to the shacks. The first was dark. A dim oil lamp glowed in the second, but the third cabin's door was ajar. He detected the odor of whiskey and cigar smoke coming from inside.

"Anybody to home?" he called.

Silence.

A crowd of men roared in a nearby saloon. Above the din, a tinny piano and a banjo played "The Ballad of Jesse James," a song that was all the rage in Dodge.

From the second shack in the row a man grunted and an iron cot squealed.

Lowery pushed the door of the silent shack open with his foot and stepped inside . . . into a scene of horror.

A slender blond girl lay sprawled across a brass bed that took up half of the room. The front of her pale blue corset was stained red from the blood that ran from the huge bowie knife embedded between her pushed-up breasts. Her pretty face showed no fear or pain but bore a startled expression as though the knife in her chest had come as a complete surprise. Lowery leaned over the body and looked into the girl's wide-open brown eyes. He saw no sign of life. The girl's eyes were as dead as she was.

Gravel crunched and a woman's voice yelled, "Sarah! Are you all right, sugar?" A few moments later, she shouted, "Oh, my God!"

A tall, thin black woman stood in the doorway. She wore a gauzy pink robe cinched tight at the waist. Staring over her shoulder, his big hat tipped back on his head, stood a freckled puncher who looked to be all of fifteen.

"She's been stabbed," Lowery said. "I found her—"

The woman screamed and ran, the young drover right on her heels. Even in Dodge City a black woman and a white puncher running out of an alley yelling, "Murder! Murder!" was not a sight folks saw every day and it tended to attract attention. Within a couple minutes, the alley was crowded with onlookers. Several men dragged Lowery outside and slammed him against the wall of the warehouse.

A saloon girl shrieked and pointed, "Look at him! He's covered in blood!"

One ranny, drunker than most, tried to break through the cordon of men around Lowery. "Poor Sarah! Let me take a punch at him!"

"No," said a big, bearded man in a plaid shirt. "Wait until Sheriff Hinkle gets here."

George T. Hinkle arrived a few minutes later, a nondescript man in his mid-thirties who had no reputation as a man killer. He was more local politician than lawman and had defeated Bat Masterson in the election for sheriff. Bat was said to be good with a gun, was a sharp dresser, and cut a dash with the ladies. Hinkle, sour and businesslike, had none of Masterson's charm, but he did his difficult job well and kept the Texas cowboys in line.

Hinkle examined the body of the dead girl, took stock of Hank Lowery's bloodstained shirt, and summed matters up in his mind. "Why did you kill her? Sarah Hollis was only a two-dollar screw. What harm did she do you? Did she laugh at your little pecker pole?"

The crowd giggled.

Lowery said, "I didn't kill her. I heard a scream and that's how I found her. I never saw the girl before in my life."

"You saw her once and that was enough," Hinkle said. "Mister, I'm arresting you for the murder of Sarah Ann Hollis, a known prostitute of this city." He stared into Lowery's eyes. "You'll get a fair trial and I'll supervise your hanging myself. I can't say fairer than that." Always the politician, he turned to the crowd and said, "Can I say fairer than that?"

The eager throng, most of them half drunk, yelled, agreeing that fairer words had never been spoken.

One sentimental whore said to Lowery, "Did you have a good mother?"

Hinkle poked his shotgun into Lowery's belly. "Right, move. You're headed for the lockup."

"Sheriff, I never touched that girl. You're making a big mistake," Lowery said.

"I've made plenty of those in my time, but I never yet hung a man by mistake."

The Dodge City jail was a small, timber building that was mostly used to house drunken revelers overnight. In the morning, they were hosed off and sent home. A rope hung across the room, dividing it. Several drunks snored on the jail floor behind the rope and a couple more hung over the rope, having suspended themselves by their armpits. A single, barred cell with an iron cot and a corncob mattress was reserved for more serious offenders.

Hinkle pushed Hank Lowery into the cell, slammed the cell door shut, and turned the key in the lock. "I guess I should know your name, huh?"

"Hank Lowery."

The sheriff frowned and took time to light a cigar. "Where have I heard that name before."

Lowery watched the blue smoke curl around the lawman's face, then said, "The Longdale Massacre."

"Damn, that's right. You were the one. Two Colts, twelve shots, and twelve dead men I was told. How come you don't carry a gun?"

"Because I've already killed more than my share," Lowery said, echoing what Frank Cobb had said to him.

"I'd say that. Twelve in one go is a fair number."

Hinkle said. "First time I've had somebody famous in my jail, and just so you know how proud that makes me, I'll bring you steak and eggs for breakfast."

"I'm touched."

"You should be. I don't do that for everybody."

"Then maybe you could do me another favor, Sheriff."

"Name it. Damn, it's going to be such an honor hanging you, Lowery. You being so important an' all."

"There's a woman by the name of Mrs. Kate Kerrigan at the Drover's Rest Hotel. Would you tell her I'm here?"

"A sweetheart, huh?"

"No, my boss."

Hinkle was surprised. "You got a woman boss?"

"She's quite a woman. And quite a boss."

The sheriff nodded. "Well then, sure. Sure I'll tell her. She purty?"

"Kate is a rare beauty," Lowery said. "Red hair and green eyes and skin like ivory."

"Then I'll most certainly tell her."

"I thought you might," Lowery said.

He lay down on the smelly mattress, fell into restless sleep to the snores and mutterings of his fellow prisoners, and dreamed of clockwork men and the murder of young ladies of the night.

CHAPTER TWELVE

Sheriff George T. Hinkle stood outside hotel room Number 17, adjusted his celluloid collar and tie, and tapped politely. A few moments passed. A key turned in the lock, the door swung inward, and Hinkle found himself looking into the black eye of a Colt .45.

"Do you always greet your gentlemen callers like this?" he asked.

"It depends on who's calling," Kate Kerrigan said. "State your business."

"Name's George Hinkle, Mrs. Kerrigan. I'm the sheriff of this town. Do you have a hired hand who calls himself Hank Lowery?"

"Yes I do," Kate said, alarmed. "He's not in any trouble, is he?"

"The worst kind, ma'am. I arrested him this evening for the murder of the prostitute Sarah Ann Hollis." As though he thought it important, he added, "She worked the line. That means—"

"I know what it means, Sheriff. You'd better come inside." Kate opened the door farther.

Hinkle stepped into the room, removed his hat,

and stood awkwardly just inside the doorway, acutely aware of the gorgeous flame-haired beauty who wore night attire of clinging silk yet seemed to be completely unaware of the effect she had on him.

Kate sat on the corner of the bed. "Tell me what happened, Sheriff."

"Not much to tell, ma'am." Hinkle turned his bowler in his hands and looked everywhere except at Kate.

"For heaven's sake, man, sit down. Have you never been in a woman's bedroom before?"

"Not a woman who looked like you, ma'am."

"Then I'll do my best not to distract you, Sheriff. Now, please tell me what you allege Mr. Lowery did."

"Ma'am, he was found bending over the dead girl's body," Hinkle said. "And there was blood on his shirt and hands."

"How was the girl killed?" Kate asked.

"She was stabbed, ma'am. A bowie knife in the chest between her— Uh, I mean, a bowie knife in the chest, ma'am."

Kate's eyes closed and then opened again. "Who saw him bending over the girl?"

"Two people. A woman of color by the name of Alva Cranley and a puncher called Godalming McGuire. They came to Sarah Hollis's shack after they heard her scream."

Kate said, "Godalming?"

"The kid swears that's his given name, ma'am."

"Did the witnesses see Hank Lowery stab the girl?"

"No ma'am. But they'll swear in court that Lowery was bending over her body, and him all covered in gore."

Kate was silent for a few moments, then said,

"Sheriff Hinkle, Hank Lowery is incapable of such a crime. He's a gentleman and not one to seek the company of fancy women."

"Was he a gentleman when he killed all them folks in the Longdale Massacre? I wondered where I'd heard the name before, but then I remembered. Twelve men dead in as many seconds."

"He was a young man avenging the murder of his brother," Kate said. "I would expect him to do the same for me."

"That may be the case, Mrs. Kerrigan, but I believe Lowery murdered Sarah Hollis for a reason I have not yet established. I plan to hang him, ma'am."

"And I tell you again that Hank Lowery could not commit such a crime," Kate said.

Hinkle rose to his feet. "Ma'am, when I was a boy there was a man in our town who was a church deacon, read his Bible every day, sheltered the poor, and fed the hungry. Everybody agreed he was a fine man and an upstanding member of the community. Well, one night something snapped inside him and he took a wood ax and murdered his wife, her elderly mother, and his three children. Then he cut his own throat."

The sheriff stepped to the door. "What I mean by all that, Mrs. Kerrigan, is this. Any man is capable of murder, no matter who he is or what people think he is."

"Can I see him?" Kate asked.

"Certainly ma'am. Any time between now and the hanging."

"He won't hang, Sheriff Hinkle. I can assure you of that."

"Whatever you say, Mrs. Kerrigan. Whatever you say."

Hinkle stepped into the hallway and closed the door behind him.

"I never trusted him, Kate, and now you know why." Frank Cobb tried the morning coffee and made a face. "Is there anyone in Dodge who knows how to make a decent cup of coffee?"

"The coffee is fine. Tobacco and whiskey have burned out your taste buds, Frank." Kate set her cup on the saucer. She wore a tightly fitted sky blue dress with a bustle of the largest kind that had made the trip from the Kerrigan ranch carefully folded in a trunk behind the seat of the chuck wagon. Her red hair was swept up and pinned, set off by a tiny hat in the current fashion of the well-to-do Texas belles. "Though I will admit that I've tasted better. Jazmin Salas has spoiled us."

Trace said, "Did the sheriff say why Hank murdered the girl, Ma?"

"Get this through your head, Trace, and you, too, Frank. Hank Lowery didn't murder anyone. Right now someone else is laughing up his sleeve, happy to let someone else take the blame."

"You sound mighty certain, Kate," Frank said, looking around the crowded hotel dining room. "When it comes to rannies like Hank Lowery, you can't be certain of anything."

"As certain as a person can be," Kate said. "I plan to talk to Hank this morning and ask him what happened. I'll go on from there."

"We know what happened, Ma," Trace said.

"All right then, I'll ask him how and why it happened," Kate said.

Frank said, "Kate, you won't get a straight answer from Lowery. He's yet to tell the truth about the Longdale Massacre and the killing of old Levi Fry. Lies on top of lies, that's all you'll get."

"Then how do you explain it, Frank?" Kate smiled and poured him more coffee. She was never more dangerous than when she was being nice.

Frank treaded warily. "Kate, I don't know why a man like Lowery would murder a woman. Such a question has never before entered into my thinking."

"Well, let's go and find an answer to that question, shall we?" Kate turned to her son. "Trace, you're not going back with the chuck wagon. Now I may need your rifle right here in Dodge."

Trace grinned. "Suits me fine, Ma."

Despite the crowded dining room, Frank had spotted a tall, slender man he'd pegged as a prime example of arrogant gun bullies that had plagued the frontier the last two decades. Since the shootist was eating breakfast and minding his own business, Frank dismissed him and paid him no further attention.

When the man rose to his feet just as Kate left her chair, her silk dress rustling, Frank stepped beside her, putting himself between them. He was conscious of Trace at his side, relaxed and unaware, chewing on a half-eaten biscuit.

Sporting a wide-brimmed hat of a tan color, the tall man wore a beaded and fringed buckskin jacket that covered his hips, and under that a white shirt set off by the red puff tie at his throat. His checked pants were shoved into expensive leather boots adorned with yellow butterflies. Two ivory-handled Colts rode butt forward in a tooled gun rig that showed evidence of wear. A fastidiously trimmed imperial and long black hair cascading over his shoulders gave the man a rakish look. In all, he cut a handsome, dashing figure and he knew it.

As Kate attempted to step past him, the man stretched out a blocking arm and grabbed her by the upper arm. "Not so fast, little gal. I got five dollars burning a hole in my pocket. Catch my drift?"

Before Kate could speak, Frank said, "The lady is with me."

The gunman turned his head slowly . . . slowly . . . taking his time. He stared at Frank like a man looking at cow dung on his boots as he's about to step into church. "Go away, cowboy."

Frank didn't move. "I said, the lady is with me."

"And she's my mother," Trace said, his eyes angry.

As heads turned in their direction, the man grinned. "And what do you say, little lady?"

"I say get your dirty hand off me," Kate said.

"Five dollars," the gunman said. "Hell, that's more money than you make in a week."

As Frank moved closer to Kate, the man made a bad mistake—a serious mistake a less arrogant man would not have made. He said, "I told you to git, cowboy," and he pushed Frank hard in the chest.

Frank Cobb had been around gunmen most of his life and he wasn't in the least bashful. His hand dropped to his revolver, and the Colt came up very fast and slammed into the man's head just above his left ear. As the buffalo went, Frank's was one of the best. The thud of blue steel against bone was heard all over the dining room. The gunman groaned and dropped like a felled oak, his eyes rolling in their sockets.

Frank bent, stripped off the man's gun belt, and hung it over his shoulder.

"Here, that won't do." The hotel manager, a balding, harried-looking man named Featherstone stepped beside Frank and glanced at the unconscious man stretched out on the rug. "What happened here?"

"The . . . um . . . gentleman insulted Mrs. Kerrigan," Frank said. "He offered her money to prostitute herself. As a Texas gentleman myself, I could not let such an insult stand."

Featherstone knew Kate was a rancher, a guest of the hotel, and paying plenty for that privilege, but he hesitated a moment.

It wasn't until a respectable-looking man yelled, "The cowboy is right. He was defending the lady's honor," that Featherstone made up his mind.

"That is an outrage, madam," he said to Kate. "Such a thing has never happened in this hotel before and I assure you that it won't happen again."

Kate decided to let the squirming manager off the hook. "These things happen in the best-run places. Mr. Featherstone, I am convinced that your management skills are perfectly adequate and I am prepared to testify to that fact, even to the Texas Cattlemen's Association."

Featherstone, justifiably worried about the damage liquored-up and angry Texas cowboys might do to a hotel where one of their number—a lady—was insulted and manhandled, gladly agreed to let the matter drop. He looked at the unconscious man and said to Trace, "Help me get him into a chair, young fellow."

"He does look a tad poorly," Trace said.

"Who is he?" Frank asked Featherstone, then

stomped on the gunman's fancy Stetson and rammed the battered hat onto the groaning man's head.

"I don't know his name, but he goes by the Buckskin Kid," the manager said. "He told one of my waiters that he's killed a dozen men."

Frank smiled and nodded. "Rannies like this one are always a Kid of some kind and they've always killed a dozen men. When he comes to, tell him he can pick up his guns at my room."

"Do you think he'll do that?" Featherstone looked worried. "I don't want a shooting scrape in my place."

"He'll need to buy a revolver first, so I wouldn't worry about it too much," Frank said. "He says he's got five dollars in his pocket and he can't buy a Colt in Dodge for that."

"Frank, I hope you didn't hurt him too much," Kate said. "That blow to the head made such a terrible clunk."

"No, I didn't hurt him too much. Enough to get his attention was all."

"Anyway, tonight I'll say a rosary for him, just to be sure," Kate said.

Frank nodded. "That will make the Kid feel much better, I'm sure."

Chapter Thirteen

"And then the black woman screamed and the next thing I knew the sheriff had a scattergun rammed into my belly."

"Hank, you didn't see anyone enter or leave the cabin?" Kate said.

"No, no I didn't," Lowery said.

"Does the cabin have a back door or window?"

"I don't know. I was too busy noticing other things."

"Like the knife in the young lady's chest, for instance?" Frank eyes were hard and blue and devoid of sympathy.

Lowery nodded. "Yes. Mostly the knife."

"Hank, did you kill her?" Kate asked.

"I swear to God I didn't, Mrs. Kerrigan."

"And I believe you. Frank, what do you say?"

"What do you want me to say, Kate? That I think he's telling the truth?"

"Yes, something like that."

"I can't say it. I think Lowery is a cold-blooded murderer. He proved it at Longdale. Anyone who's capable of killing an old man for no reason can kill a young girl who maybe said a cross word to him."

"I'm sorry you think that way, Frank," Lowery said. "You're badly mistaken about Levi Fry."

"No, Lowery. Killing Levi was your mistake and now you're paying for it."

"I didn't kill Fry and I didn't kill Sarah Hollis."

"Then both times, who did?"

"The girl, I don't know. Fry, well, you wouldn't believe me."

"No, I guess I wouldn't."

"I'll tell you anyway. A stray bullet killed Levi Fry, and it was fired by one of his own men." Lowery's knuckles were white on the cell bars. Bloated blue flies from the stock pens buzzed in the shaft of light from a high rectangular window.

"That's not how I heard it." Frank said.

"You're hearing the right of it now. The truth," Lowery said.

"You're a damned liar."

"Frank! Please go and wait outside," Kate said. "You need some fresh air. Trace, go with him."

Without another word, Frank turned and walked away and Trace Kerrigan followed him.

Kate and Lowery watched them leave.

"Mrs. Kerrigan, the mechanical man—"

"Under the circumstances, please call me Kate."

"You're my boss. I'd prefer to call you Mrs. Kerrigan," Lowery said.

"As you wish. What about the mechanical man?"

"He's a kind of carnival sideshow, a man made of metal who will bow to the ladies and talk pretties."

"Better mannered than some human men I've known," Kate said.

Lowery allowed himself a smile and then said, "His name is Golem, and if you give him fifty cents he'll tell your fortune. He told me mine."

"The mechanical man did?"

"Yes. He said just one word. *Death.* Did he mean the death of Sarah Hollis or the death of me for a crime I didn't commit?"

Kate said, "Hank, the word *golem* appears in the Old Testament, in Psalms I believe. In Biblical times it meant a strange creature that was not quite human in the eyes of God. Today, in these modern times, it describes a person who is not too clever. And, Hank, you'd be a golem to believe a word a clockwork man said. Where was this wonder may I ask?"

"Here, in Dodge, at a vacant lot off Front Street. I think he's powered by steam, but I'm not sure."

"And he was operated by a pair of hucksters, I'm sure."

"Yes. How did you know that?"

"Because hucksters always operate in pairs, one to bring in the mark and the other to work the swindle. I watched bunco artists do the hundred-dollar prize in the soap wrapper scam many times in New York when I was a child. A fortune-telling mechanical man is no different, even if he's powered by steam."

"Golem said 'Death' only to me, Mrs. Kerrigan, not to anyone else. It could mean I'm going to hang."

"It means no such thing. I will not permit it. I plan to investigate this murder and bring the real culprit to justice. Now, is there anything you need?"

"Cigars and something to read to take my mind off things. A bottle of bourbon would be good if Sheriff Hinkle will allow it."

"He might, but I won't, Hank. You need to keep

your wits about you. You're fighting for your life and your brain can't be befuddled by alcohol."

Kate left the jail area and swept into Sheriff Hinkle's office like a forty-gun frigate on the prod. The lawman was sitting back in his chair reading a newspaper, his feet on the desk.

When he saw Kate, he quickly scrambled to his feet. "You had a nice talk with the condemned, Mrs. Kerrigan?"

"*Condemned,* Sheriff Hinkle? Surely you mean *accused*?"

"Yes, yes, of course," Hinkle said, intimidated by Kate's frown. "Just a slip of the tongue, you understand."

"I understand perfectly, Sheriff. Let's not allow such a slip to happen again, shall we? Now, first, do you have any wholesome reading material for Mr. Lowery? I would prefer that he not have novels of the more risqué sort since the last thing a prisoner needs is his dormant ardor inflamed." Kate looked around the small office. "Of course anything by Mr. Dickens or Sir Walter Scott would be quite acceptable."

"Mrs. Kerrigan, all I have is the 1879 edition of the Revised Statutes of Texas, and it makes for some mighty ponderous reading," Hinkle said. "A man spends an hour trying to make sense of that book and all he gets for it is a headache."

"I suppose it will have to do for now," Kate said. "See that Mr. Lowery gets it. Do you have any cigars, Sheriff Hinkle?"

"For the prisoner?"

"For Mr. Lowery."

"I don't smoke."

"Then get him some. A box of the best kind, mind. I'll reimburse you later."

"Mrs. Kerrigan, Lowery is my prisoner. I'm not his servant," Hinkle said.

"And now on to the second thing, Sheriff," Kate said as though she hadn't heard. "I want to see the cabin where Sarah Hollis died. My son Trace and my *segundo* Mr. Frank Cobb will accompany me."

"All right. I can tell you how to get there."

"No. You will also accompany me. I want you to be there."

"Mrs. Kerrigan, I—"

"I will brook no refusal, Sheriff. You said you're not Mr. Lowery's servant, but you are indeed a *public* servant. Now come along with me and start serving."

"Ma'am, have you been sent to Dodge to be a trial and tribulation to me?"

"Possibly," Kate said. "God works in mysterious ways."

His shoulders slumped in defeat, Hinkle said, "Now God is on your side. All right. Let's go."

"Aren't you forgetting something, Sheriff?" Kate asked.

"Now what?"

"The law book for Mr. Lowery. Please give it to him and tell him he will get more suitable reading material and a box of cigars as soon as possible."

"When do you plan to return to Texas, Mrs. Kerrigan?" Hinkle said.

"Quite soon, I hope."

"Not soon enough for me, lady."

CHAPTER FOURTEEN

"She didn't have much room, did she?" Trace Kerrigan said, looking around the tiny cabin furnished only with a cot, a dresser, and a pole nailed into a wall to hang clothes.

"Gals who work the line don't live in palaces, young feller," Sheriff George Hinkle said. "This place is a sight better than some I've seen."

"This is where the body was found." Kate used her arms to indicate the space. "Her back on the cot and her legs on the floor."

"That's right, Mrs. Kerrigan," Hinkle said. "Seems to me she was stabbed and then fell backward."

Kate shook her head. "She didn't fall. Her killer held her and let her down on the bed gently."

"How do you figure that?" the sheriff said.

"The cot is several inches from the wall," Kate said. "If she'd fallen, her weight would have driven it against the partition."

"Maybe," Hinkle said. "What does that tell us?"

"It tells me that her killer cared for her enough to support her as she collapsed backwards." Kate stared at the lawman. "I think Sarah Hollis knew the man who murdered her, perhaps knew him very well."

"Mighty flimsy, Mrs. Kerrigan," Hinkle said. "He could have held her because he didn't want the noise of her falling on the cot to carry next door."

"Yes, the shack next door was being used at the time by the black lady and a cowboy," Kate said. "Sarah's murderer would have known that."

"And Hank Lowery would have known that as well," Hinkle said. "He was new in town, remember. He wouldn't have cared about someone he didn't know. After he stabbed her, he let her down gently so not to alarm Alva Cranley and her cowboy."

"I still think the girl and her murderer had some kind of close relationship," Kate said. "A strange one though it may be. The back door, Sheriff, where does it lead?"

"A couple outhouses back there, that's all."

"Was the door locked the night Sarah Hollis was killed?"

Hinkle shrugged. "I don't know."

"You mean you didn't try it?"

"I didn't have to. I had my killer."

Kate stepped to the door and tried the handle. "It's unlocked." She opened the door, stuck her head outside and looked around. "Frank, come and take a look at this."

When Frank Cobb stepped beside her, she said, "It rained a little the night Sarah Hollis was killed." She pointed to tracks in the thin mud outside the door. "What do you make of those?"

Frank kneeled and studied the ground for a while and then rose to his feet.

"Well?" Kate said, trying to read his face.

"The prints are of a man's shoe who left the shack sometime after the rain ended. He has small feet and judging by the depth of the tracks, he is not heavy."

Kate turned to Hinkle. "Well, Sheriff, are those the tracks of the man who murdered Sarah Hollis and then left when he heard Hank Lowery's steps crunching on the gravel outside?"

"Mrs. Kerrigan, Sarah was a prostitute," Hinkle said. "All kinds of men came here and some, especially married ones, might leave by the back door so they wouldn't be seen. The tracks prove nothing."

"Frank, what do you think?" Kate said.

"Kate, I have to agree with the sheriff. Anyone could have left those shoeprints."

"Not anyone," Kate said. "The real killer of Sarah Hollis left them."

Hinkle sighed. "Can I go now, Mrs. Kerrigan?"

"Not yet, Sheriff. There's one more thing you can do for me."

"And what's that, may I ask?" Hinkle managed to make himself look like a martyred saint, like St. Sebastian pierced by arrows.

"We will interview a mechanical man and his cohorts and you will throw all of them out of Dodge City," Kate said.

Hinkle and Frank Cobb's eyes met and Frank gave an almost imperceptible shrug.

Hinkle said, "What if the mechanical man gives me sass, Mrs. Kerrigan? You want me to arrest him?"

Kate frowned. "Now you're giving me sass, Sheriff. Come, let me take your arm. We have police work to do, you and I."

* * *

Sheriff George Hinkle said, "And you claim this . . . whatever it is . . . said, *Breath*, not *Death*."

"As sure as my name is Charlie Finch, Sheriff. Finch by name, Finch by nature I always say. A man bred to the truth, that's me." The barker looked at Professor Woodmancey. "Have Golem say howdy to the lady, Professor."

Woodmancey placed his hand on the automaton's back and it bowed, lifted its top hat, and said, "How do you do, ma'am?"

"Now tell the nice lady her fortune, Golem," Finch said.

The mechanical man's meshed eyes glowed red but its round, startled mouth remained silent.

"Tell the lady her fortune," Finch said again. "Come now, Golem, be a sport."

The automaton said nothing, but its eyes continued to glow.

"That thing is an abomination," Kate said. "It already upset poor Mr. Lowery, who's now rotting in the city jail, and it's trying to do the same to me. Frank, your revolver, if you please."

Frank Cobb, knowing how Kate was when her mind was set on a thing, passed over his Colt without a word.

Professor Woodmancey looked alarmed and Charlie Finch took a step back.

"Hey, be careful with that hogleg, lady."

Kate raised the Colt and pumped three fast shots into the mechanical man. The automaton shrieked an unearthly squeal like pressurized steam escaping from a boiler. It staggered around like a drunken man, its arms flailing, and then it collapsed, twitched like a dying insect, and then lay still.

"My God, was that thing alive?" Hinkle said, his face shocked.

"Yes, it was, Sheriff." Kate handed Frank his Colt and then pushed out her hands. "Now do your duty and manacle me, Sheriff. Throw me into your darkest dungeon."

"Finch," Hinkle said, alarmed, "was a real man inside that damn tin suit?"

Woodmancey answered for Finch. "No, Sheriff. Golem is an automaton, a machine powered by steam and electric coils. He's the future, Sheriff, a sign of things to come, but he's not alive. He's not a man. Not yet."

"Well, if he ain't a man I can't charge you with murder, Mrs. Kerrigan. Can I?"

"You've already charged a man with murder on even less evidence, Sheriff," Kate said.

Hinkle shook his head. "Mrs. Kerrigan, I'm leaving now. My business with you is finished."

"Only for today, Sheriff. You will hear from me very soon." Kate noticed a tiny animal nearby. "Oh dear, what is that?"

Charlie Finch said, "It's been hanging around here for a few days. I plan to get rid of it."

Kate shook her head. "You'll do no such thing. The poor little thing is probably starving."

"Nothing skinnier than a lizard-eating cat," Finch said.

"She's only a kitten." Kate scooped up the little calico and held her close in her arms. The kitten mewed. "Hear that? She really is hungry. Frank, Trace, we'll take her back to Texas with us."

"Cats make me sneeze," Frank said.

"Nonetheless, we can't leave her here," Kate said.

"I swear, she'd starve to death or"—her eyes moved to Finch—"get murdered by some ruffian. And speaking of ruffians, Professor Woodmancey, can your mechanical man be repaired?"

"He can, but it will take time."

"Then let's hope it will take until after the cattle season," Kate said.

"Will you be gone by then, ma'am?"

"Yes, I will."

Professor Woodmancey nodded. "Then that's how long it will take."

CHAPTER FIFTEEN

"What did they talk about when they were in Sarah Hollis's shack," Drugo Odell said. "What are you worried about? You can talk to me."

Alva Cranley, her mahogany face shiny with sweat from the afternoon heat trapped inside her own tiny cabin, shook her head. "I don't know what they talked about, sugar. I wasn't there."

"But you saw them leave, huh? I got a man says you watched them leave."

"Yeah, a real pretty woman with two young men and Sheriff Hinkle."

"Did they stay in the shack long?"

"Long enough, sugar. Why you asking a poor black lady all these questions? You a detective of some kind?"

"No. Just call me an interested party. You scared of me?"

"Hell, no. Should I be?"

"Yeah, you should," Drugo said. "I'm down on people like you."

"Man in a ditto suit and a celluloid collar got to be

a preacher," Alva said. "You come here to preach to me or screw a black woman?"

"Neither. I don't preach and I'd rather screw a rat than a black woman."

Alva rose from the edge of her cot, a large imposing woman with a massive bust and a broad face with high cheekbones. "Get out of here. I don't want you in my house."

"House? You call this hovel a house?"

"Will you get out of here or do I have to yell for help?"

"Try that and I'll kill you," Odell said.

Alva Cranley smiled, showing fine white teeth. One of the central incisors was crowned with gold. "I've beaten up bigger men than you, little feller."

Odell reached under his high-button coat and suddenly a short-barreled Colt was in his hand. Alva's eyes opened wide. The motion had been quick, so amazingly rapid it defied reality. No one could move that fast . . . like a lightning strike. The triple click of the Colt's cocking hammer sounded like a death knell.

The big woman collapsed onto the rusty iron cot and it squealed under her like a piglet caught under a gate. "What do you want from me, mister?"

Odell pointed the gun at her head. "Who killed Sarah Hollis?"

"Not the man Hinkle arrested," Alva said.

"Who do you think killed her?"

"I don't know."

"You don't think it was the man the sheriff arrested?"

"Maybe I don't."

"You pretended you'd never seen me before."

Alva said, "I never seen you before. I figured you come here to lie with a black woman."

"Why don't you tell me the truth? Are white men rough with you?" Drugo Odell waited.

"Sometimes. All right. Maybe I seen you here. Sarah had all kinds of gentleman callers."

"She tell you about any of them, what they wanted, what they did to her?"

"Sometimes she'd tell me things."

"She ever speak about me? Drugo Odell. She ever mention that name?"

"No."

"You're a liar."

"Could be she did one time. I don't remember."

"Remember this, I'll kill you if you don't tell me." Sweat beaded on Odell's forehead under the rim of his bowler hat and a mad light filled his feline eyes

Alva was scared, very afraid. Sarah had told her about Drugo Odell, what he did to her and she'd said, "One day he'll kill me or I'll kill him." And Alva had seen the little gunman before, on the night Sarah had died. That fact scared her most of all.

Alma took a deep breath. "She said you beat her, stuffed her mouth with cotton, and whipped her with a leather belt."

"And what else?"

"She said you always held a knife to her throat when you screwed her. She said you told her that one time you'd use the knife, but she'd never know when. You said you'd ram it between her tits and hold her so you could watch her die. She said you were loco, wrong in the head, and that she'd bought a .32 for protection. She said you scared her worse than the devil himself and that after this cattle season she was going to run away, head out on a train for Chicago. I asked her to leave right then, but she needed money for her fare and to live in Chicago for a while. She said the Colt she'd bought would protect her if you cut up rough again. I told her that if she shot you, I'd help her dump the body somewhere. And Sarah said, 'Alva, maybe it won't come to that. I know a gentleman who'll protect me from Drugo.' Well, I guess when the chips were down that gentleman didn't protect her worth a damn."

Odell shoved his gun back into the shoulder holster, stared at the woman for long moments, and then backhanded her across the face. "Why didn't you tell me all this earlier? What kind of person are you?"

A trickle of blood ran from the corner of Alva's mouth. "I was afraid to tell you."

Odell's hand moved up the slope of the woman's shoulder and then to her neck. He gently placed his thumb on her throat and said, "Tell me about the night Sarah Hollis died. Tell me what you saw when you came out back to show the cowboy the outhouse." The gunman smiled. "Tell me about that, Alva. I promise, if you do I won't hurt you real bad."

"I didn't see anything. It was dark. Too dark."

Odell increased his thumb pressure and the woman made a small, gagging sound in her throat.

"What did you see, Alva?"

"You . . . I saw you. I didn't tell the sheriff. I knew if I told the sheriff you'd come around here and kill me."

"Well that's bad news, Alva. For you, I mean. I can't let you live. You could put a noose around my neck."

"I won't tell, Drugo." The woman was terrified and it showed in her eyes. "Honest, I won't sell you out. I'll leave Dodge today, go far away, to the Indian Territory maybe. I got kinfolk live with the Choctaw and they'll take me in."

"Way too thin, Alva. I can't take the chance."

"Drugo, you can depend on me." Alva placed her hand on Odell's cheek. "You can trust me to carry the gate key."

Odell smiled. "Trust a black? Not in this lifetime."

The gunman was small and looked almost frail, but that was deceptive. He had considerable strength in his gun hand, the one that squeezed Alva's throat. The woman was big and robust and she struggled, but Odell's hand was like a vise. He throttled the life out of her and when it was done, he looked down at her sprawled body and smiled.

"Dead women tell no tales, Alva. The Choctaw would have told you that." Odell giggled. He enjoyed killing. It made him feel good inside. Like vanilla ice cream.

CHAPTER SIXTEEN

"Shall we take a stroll and see the sights?" Kate said.

Her son Trace pushed his plate away. "After finishing every scrap of this porterhouse I could use a walk."

She looked at her *segundo*. "What about you, Frank?"

"Sets fine with me." Frank smiled at Trace. "I'd rather clothe you for a year than feed you for a month."

"He's a growing boy, Frank," Kate said. "And you did all right yourself."

"Good grub in this hotel, Kate. Surprised me."

"Then shall we go?" Kate dabbed her mouth with her napkin and rose to her feet. "It sounds quite lively outside tonight."

When she and the others stepped out of the hotel into Front Street she was proved correct. Every saloon and dance hall was bursting at the seams and the melodies from competing pianos tangled in the air like strands of silver barbed wire. Brightly lit windows cast rectangles of orange light onto the boardwalks and gleamed on the muddy street like wet paint. Cowboys were everywhere, the huge rowels of their Texas spurs chiming like bells.

Kate stopped to talk with a street vendor, an elderly woman with black, Gypsy eyes. She wore an embroidered shawl and said she hailed from County Cork and had lived in the United States since the Great Famine.

"And what are those you're selling?" Kate said.

The old woman said they were called butterfly cakes and were a great favorite of old Queen Vic.

"Now that's a coincidence. I bake a sponge cake that's also one of her favorites."

The old woman nodded. "Milk, butter, flour, and eggs. That's what you need for a sponge cake."

"And fresh cream and jam for the filling."

"Indeed that is so," the old woman said. "You're a beautiful woman, lady, but you've had sorrow in your life. I can see it in your eyes. Well, here's a cure for sorrow. Have one of my butterfly cakes with my compliments and for the sake of the auld country."

The little cake had two arcs of pastry placed into the cream topping and Kate ate it delicately and declared it wonderful. She insisted on paying the woman and then she bowed her head as the old lady made the sign of the cross over her and said her blessing would protect Kate from harm.

As they continued their stroll along the boardwalk Frank said, "I guess I should tell you that you've got a blob of cream at the tip of your nose."

"I'll get it, Ma." Trace stood in front of Kate and used a corner of his bandana to get the cream off her nose . . . and in doing so, he took the bullet intended for his mother.

* * *

Trace Kerrigan cried out as the bullet burned across his shoulder blades and shattered an oil lamp burning outside an apothecary. A river of flame immediately ran down the wall and spread across the boardwalk. Illuminated by fire, Trace ignored his wound and pulled his mother to a crouching position. Colt in hand, Frank had already sprinted across Front Street to an alley opposite. The sound of gunfire was not rare in Dodge City, but a curious crowd gathered on the boardwalk and surrounded Kate and her wounded son. Calls for Sheriff Hinkle and a doctor rang out and a man and woman from the apothecary beat at the oil lamp flames with straw brooms.

Frank knew better than to run into an alley where an armed would-be assassin lurked. He slowed to a walk and entered on cat feet, his eyes reaching into the darkness. The moon splashed an opalescent light on the top half of the store wall to his left, but the end of the alley was shadowed. He moved forward slowly, his gun up and ready.

From behind him, a man yelled, "Hey, what's going on there?"

Immediately, a rifle roared like rolling thunder in the narrow confines of the alley and chips of wood splintered from the timber wall inches above Frank's right shoulder. He was dazzled by the flash of the rifle but he fired, fired again. Ahead of him, a man cried out in pain and shock, followed by the sound of dragging feet.

Frank went after him, his boots clanking on the empty whiskey bottles that littered the alley floor.

The man at the entrance to the alley yelled again. "Here, stop the shooting!"

Frank thought he sounded drunk and ignored him.

The alley ended at the blank wall of a warehouse of some kind. Passageways led to the left and right, but a rickety tower of packing cases blocked the one to the right. Frank moved to his left. Between the rear of the store and the wall of the warehouse, the passageway was narrow, only a few feet wide. Ahead of him he heard a curse and a shadow moved awkwardly, as though a man had tripped and stumbled forward. Frank snapped off a shot, aware that he could have fired on some drunk who'd wandered onto the scene. He heard a grunt.

A man's voice said, "For God's sake, mister, don't shoot me no more."

"State your intentions."

"Damn it, I'm shot through and through. I don't have any intentions."

"Drop the rifle and step forward," Frank said. "And I warn you, I can drill ya from here."

"Hell, I can't walk. I'm dying here. I need a priest." The man's voice was weak, barely a whisper heard in darkness. "You've done for me."

"Stay right where you are. I see any sign of a fancy move from you, pardner, I'll cut loose."

A louder voice came from behind him. "Don't shoot, Cobb. It's Sheriff Hinkle."

Footsteps sounded as the lawman emerged from the gloom. He held a scattergun in his hands. "Mrs. Kerrigan said somebody took a pot at her son. He got burned across the back, but he'll be all right."

"I think the shot was intended for Kate," Frank said. "She's been prying into Sarah Hollis's murder and somebody in this town wants her dead. I plugged the shooter and he's laying wounded right there ahead of us. Maybe he'll tell us something."

"Is he out of it?" Hinkle said.

"He says so."

"Never trust a wolf till it's skun, Cobb. You ever hear that before?"

"Yeah, I have. All right. Let's take a look. Keep the Greener handy."

As Hinkle walked forward, his hands opening and closing on the shotgun, he said, "Any chance Mrs. Kerrigan might consider leaving Dodge real soon? And if that sounds hopeful, it is."

"She's got the bit in her teeth over Hank Lowery," Frank said. "Once she proves him innocent, she'll leave."

"Then I'll hang him sooner than I planned." Hinkle turned and yelled, "One of you men bring a lantern up here." And then to Frank, "Then we'll go see who the hell you shot and hope he ain't a friend of mine."

Reaching the wounded man, Hinkle took a knee beside him and held the lantern high.

"Recognize him?" Frank said.

"Uh-uh. Never seen him before. What's your name, feller?"

"Am I gonna die, Sheriff?" the man said.

"Seems like," Hinkle said. "You got two chest wounds and one of your lungs is sucking air. Best you make your peace with God."

"My name is Adam Cook. I was born and raised on a farm north of here before I fell in with low companions and came to this pass."

"Who told you to shoot Kate Kerrigan," Frank said.

"Man paid me fifty dollars to do for her. I followed her from the hotel and got my chance when she stopped to buy a cake. But the light was so bad in this alley I couldn't rightly see the gun sights."

"Who paid you to kill a woman?" Frank said.

"A man . . . Sheriff. My name is Adam Cook. Will you remember it? Say it sometimes so I'm not forgotten like I never even was?"

"I'll see there's a marker on your grave with your name on it," Hinkle said. "I'll have the undertaker carve it twice. Now who paid you to kill Mrs. Kerrigan?"

"Man . . . big man . . . fifty dollars . . ."

After a few moments of silence, Hinkle said, "He's gone." He rose to his feet and his knees cracked. "You shot a rube, Cobb. Seems a shame to bury him in them rags he's wearing. It ain't decent."

Frank looked around him and found the dead man's rifle. It was a model 1876 Winchester in .45-70 caliber that would cost a puncher a month's wages.

"He's wearing rags, but he carried an expensive rifle," Frank said. "Find out who gave him this rifle and you'll discover the ranny who paid to have Kate murdered. I reckon it's the same man who killed Sarah Hollis."

"Hell, Cobb, now you sound like Mrs. Kerrigan," Hinkle said.

"Yeah, I do because after tonight I'm inclined to agree with her. You'll do what you promised for Adam Cook?"

"Hell no, Cobb. A promise to a dead man doesn't mean a thing. You know what a marker costs in Dodge?"

"How much?"

"With his name on it twice, at least twenty dollars."

Frank reached into his pocket and by the light of Hinkle's lantern counted out a twenty and a ten. "That will pay for it. If there's any left over, put some flowers on the grave, huh?"

"You sure put stock in a dead man," Hinkle said.

"Hell, he was only a rube."

CHAPTER SEVENTEEN

"How many big men are there in Dodge right now?" Frank already knew what the answer would be and Trace Kerrigan supplied it.

"A lot, I reckon." He winced as Kate dabbed something that stung on the bullet burn across his shoulders. "And plenty with fifty dollars to pay for a killing."

"Trace, I'm still alive," Kate said.

Trace grimaced. "Well, I mean attempted killing."

Kate said, "Frank, if the man you shot—"

"Adam Cook," said Frank, going out of his way to say the name.

"Yes, Adam Cook. He really made an effort to say *big man,* don't you think? Why would he use his dying breath to say that unless the man who paid him was, well . . . exceptionally big?"

"More than a few of those in town, Kate," Frank said.

"Then that's where our investigation must begin. When we find the big man we will solve the mystery of Sarah Hollis's murder and the attempt on my life. I was getting too close to the truth and he panicked. He may panic again."

"Kate, Hinkle is set on hanging Hank Lowery," Frank said. "We can expect no help from him."

"No, but we can expect his help to find the man who tried to kill me. My son came within an inch of dying tonight. That ought to spur Sheriff Hinkle into action."

Frank smiled. "You'll be setting spurs to a dead horse, Kate."

"No, I won't. I will make my voice heard and force Hinkle to do his job. He won't hang an innocent man on my watch, Frank."

Trace flexed his muscular young shoulders. "Damn, that hurts."

"I know it hurts, Trace, but we will have no profanity. Leave Frank to handle that side of the business since he does it so very well." Kate picked up the calico kitten. "Isn't that so, snookums?" The little animal purred and kneaded the front of Kate's dress.

"Snookums? Is that what you plan to call the cat?" Frank said.

"No. I thought Gertrude, but I haven't made up my mind yet."

"Back home we have a barn full of cats," Trace said.

"But none of them is a calico," Kate said. "Do you know what they call calicos? Well, I'll tell you. They're called money cats because they attract good financial fortune to your home."

"Cats make me sneeze," Frank said. "I think I'll turn in, Kate. It's been a long day and a longer night."

She looked up. "Killing that man is wearing on you. Isn't it, Frank?"

"Seems like. He was a rube. He knew nothing about gun fighting."

"He was a rube who tried his best to kill me, Frank . . . and you," she said. "Just look at Trace's back . . . another inch . . ."

"Yeah, I know. But killing a man like him—a pumpkin roller—doesn't set right with me."

"A killing never sets right with any normal person," Kate said. "And I speak from experience. Frank, tonight I'll say a rosary for the soul of Adam Cook, and I'll say one for you, too."

Frank, not a churchgoing man, seemed a little taken aback by Kate's piety and Trace stepped into the awkward silence that followed. "Frank, before you turn in, I have an idea."

"We can use all the ideas we can get," Frank said, jumping on the young man's words. He seemed glad to talk.

"Well, it's more of a suggestion than an idea."

"Then let's hear it."

"The only one of us from the KK ranch who has seen anything of the town is Hank Lowery. Maybe we should ask him if he saw any exceptionally big men . . ." Realizing how weak that sounded, Trace's voice petered out into a whisper. "I mean in the saloons."

"He saw a tin man," Frank said, smiling. "He was big."

Kate said, "Frank, don't tease. Trace is right. We should talk to Hank. I know it's a long shot, but we're all here and willing enough to clutch at straws.

"Hinkle is the one to talk to," Frank said. "But I don't think he's much inclined to help Lowery escape the noose."

"When we question Hank we'll also talk to the sheriff," Kate said. "Who knows, between them both we might learn something."

"Like you said, Kate, clutching at straws."

Kate nodded, her lovely face unnaturally pale and still. "Yes, a wispy little straw . . . all that stands between Hank Lowery and the gallows."

CHAPTER EIGHTEEN

"There hasn't been a whore murder in Dodge for the past three years," Sheriff George Hinkle said. "Now I got two in the same week."

"George, why am I here?" Bat Masterson said.

"Because I need your help."

"You beat me out for sheriff in the last election and I hold a grudge forever," Bat said. "Nobody ever tell you that? Why should I help you?"

"Because I'm a politician, not a lawman like you, and I'm not gun handy. I need your help, Bat. Want me to put it in writing?"

"It wouldn't be a bad idea, at that. Hey, good citizens of Dodge, the man you elected sheriff now needs help from the man he defeated. That would look real good in the newspapers."

"Then do you want me to beg?" Hinkle said.

"No, I guess not. I can't stand to see a grown man cry. I'll help you, George, but only until the cards start to fall my way again. I've been trying to outrun a losing streak since Luke Short quit town and took my luck with him." Bat wore a bowler hat, a caped

Inverness coat over his long nightshirt and carpet slippers. It was two in the morning and Hinkle had wakened him from a sound sleep. Bat turned and said to an older man who wore a deputy's star, "Bring the lamp closer."

In flickering amber light that cast shadows in the corners of Alva Cranley's tiny room, Bat Masterson lifted the dead woman's skirt and petticoats. "Rape wasn't the reason she was strangled. She's still wearing her drawers and her corset is laced. How was the other girl killed?"

"Knife," Hinkle felt no need to elaborate.

"Was she raped?"

"I don't think so."

"You should determine these things."

"Sarah Hollis was a harlot."

"What was the state of her clothing?"

Hinkle nodded to Alva's body. "Like hers."

"You told me you'd arrested somebody for Sarah Hollis's murder," Bat said.

"Yeah. I aim to hang him for Sarah's murder. Man by the name of Hank Lowery. Remember the Longdale Massacre?"

Bat nodded. "I've heard of that. He handled himself well if it's the same Lowery."

"It is."

"Did he escape from your jail, George?"

"Nope. He's still there."

"Then Lowery didn't kill Alva Cranley," Bat said.

"No, I guess not . . ." Hinkle didn't sound like he was sure of anything.

"Maybe the man who murdered Sarah Hollis also killed this woman."

"I don't think so."

"You asked for my help, George."

"I know I did, but Hank Lowery killed Sarah Hollis and there's an end to it. I told the same thing to that Kate Kerrigan woman. She thinks he's innocent and says she aims to prove it. "

"I heard some cowboys in the Long Branch talking about her earlier tonight," Bat said. "Seems she's a rancher and somebody took a shot at her and hit her son."

"Before he died, a rube by the name of Adam Cook said he was paid fifty dollars to kill Mrs. Kerrigan. Her son was burned by the bullet intended for her but his wound is nothing serious."

"Did you kill Cook?"

"No. Mrs. Kerrigan's *segundo* done for him. A man named Cobb."

"Would that be Frank Cobb out of the Texas Brazos Valley country?"

"His name is Frank. That's all I know about him."

"If he's Brazos Frank Cobb he ran with some wild ones back in the day."

"He's a hand with a gun. I can tell you that much."

"Did Kate Kerrigan let it be known that she thinks Hank Lowery is an innocent man?"

"Let it be known? Hell, Bat, she was here while the impression of Sarah's body still lay on the bed. She said she plans to find the girl's real killer. Mrs. Kerrigan is a strong-willed woman, and by now I reckon everybody in Dodge knows that she's on the scout. Her and her son and Frank Cobb."

"Don't you think it strange that an attempt would be made on Mrs. Kerrigan's life right after she announces to the world that she's planning to find Sarah Hollis's killer?"

"Bat, it was a coincidence. You know Texans. They're born to the feud. Some other rancher may have it in for her and paid the rube to do his dirty work."

A rising wind rustled around the cabin. The lamp flame fluttered and caused the dark shadows of the two men to move back and forth on the wall. Somewhere a door banged and a dog barked once and then fell silent.

"You're a hardheaded man, George," Bat said. "You got your heart set on hanging Hank Lowery and nothing will make you change your mind."

"Evidence will. I mean when real, tangible evidence is presented to me that the murder was done by somebody else or a person or persons unknown."

Outside, footsteps crunched on the gravel path and then stopped.

Hinkle and Bat exchanged glances.

"Give me your gun," Bat said.

"You don't carry one?"

"Hell, man, I'm in my nightshirt."

Hinkle passed over his Colt, a large revolver with rubber grips and a seven-and-a-half-inch barrel. The barrel and cylinder were specked all over with rust.

"Don't you ever clean this thing?" Bat said. "How old is the ammunition?"

"I don't know. Maybe a couple years."

"Damned politician. How did you ever beat me in the election? It's a mystery known only to the citizens of Dodge and God." Bat swung open the cabin door and rushed quickly outside, the Colt up and ready. In the gloom, he saw a man rapidly walk away from him.

"Hey you!" Bat yelled. "Hold up there!" Barely visible, the man turned and snapped off a shot, his gun flaring in darkness. Bat heard the bullet *zzzip* an inch past his head.

Sweet Jesus! The ranny could shoot.

Bat did not return fire. He'd be shooting into Front Street where the late-night sporting crowd still walked. He watched the man disappear into the darkness.

Hinkle stepped beside Bat. "Are you hurt? Did he get a bullet into you?"

"He missed. Just missed."

"Did you get a good look at him?"

"Too dark. But he can shoot, I can tell you that. He scared the hell out of me. Here, take your gun. Damn thing probably wouldn't have worked anyway."

"Who was that man?" Hinkle said. "What was he doing here?"

"George, I'd say it was the feller who murdered Alva Cranley and probably the one who murdered Sarah Hollis. I know you don't want to hear that, but it's what I think."

"Where do we go from here?" Hinkle said miserably, a man who knew he was way out of his depth.

"Me, I'm going back to bed. You're going to clean and oil your revolver and load it with new ammunition. And leave an empty chamber under the hammer, George. Less chance of shooting off your damn toes that way."

CHAPTER NINETEEN

Kate and Frank entered the sheriff's office. Sheriff George T. Hinkle, sitting behind his desk, said, "Alva Cranley was murdered last night. Strangled. I think her killer took a pot at Bat Masterson out there in the lane."

"Masterson get hurt?" Frank Cobb asked.

"No. But he says the bullet came close enough to scare the hell out of him."

"The man who killed Alva also murdered Sarah Hollis," Kate said. "Sheriff Hinkle, that fact will be the basis for your new line of investigation, and you must act quickly."

"Mrs. Kerrigan, Hank Lowery was found in Sarah's shack, the bloody knife that killed her in his hand," Hinkle said. "You know what that is? I'll tell you. It's a fact, and facts are what get a man hung."

"Sheriff, I'm getting extremely irritated with your pigheadedness," Kate said.

"And I with yours, madam."

"The murderer who killed the two women also paid

an assassin to kill me," Kate said. "That fact should be obvious to even the most dense of men."

Frank saw Hinkle's face redden and he stepped in to calm the situation. "Sheriff, I have a question for you. Adam Cook told us a big man paid him to kill Mrs. Kerrigan. How many really big men are in town?"

"Dozens." Hinkle still glared at Kate. "Some of them beef-fed Texas boys grow to size."

"How about permanent residents?" Frank said.

"Well, there's Reuben Mattock—"

"Write this down in your tally book, Frank," Kate said.

"There's Reuben Mattock," Hinkle said as though Kate hadn't spoken. "He owns the Cake and Cookie Bakery. Reuben probably dresses out at around four hundred pounds."

"How tall is he?" Frank said.

"Not tall. He's just fat."

"Not quite what we had in mind," Kate said. "Is there anyone else?"

"Tom Bender the blacksmith is big. So is Harry Cord, who owns the lumber company, and then there's the Methodist parson Lafayette Hooks. He stands maybe five inches over six feet, but he's as skinny as the shadow of a barbed-wire fence."

"To the best of your knowledge, do any of these men regularly seek the company of loose women?" Frank could have said it in plainer English, but Kate might disapprove.

"Bender and Cord are both God-fearing family men," Hinkle said. "I don't know about Parson Hooks, but he's walking out with Miss Maude Depham, the piano teacher. Maude reads scripture every day, drinks prune juice, and she and Hooks are reckoned to be a perfectly suited couple. I doubt the parson chases after fancy women."

"Not much to go on, is there?" Kate said.

"Best I can do, Mrs. Kerrigan. That's all the big men I know." Hinkle smiled. "With the exception of Mr. Cobb here."

Kate looked at her *segundo*. "Do you wish to assassinate me, Frank?"

He shook his head. "Never even crossed my mind."

"Well, there you have it, Sheriff Hinkle. Now I'll talk to Mr. Lowery, if you please. Did you get him his cigars and some books?"

"The best five-cent cigars in town, Mrs. Kerrigan. And some works of Sir Woody Scott."

"Sir Walter Scott," Kate said.

"Yeah," Hinkle said, brightening. "That's the feller."

Standing outside the cell, Kate and Frank told Hank Lowery about the murder of Alva Cranley and the attempt on Kate's life.

"All we know is that a big man wanted Kate dead," Frank said. "Do you recollect seeing any really big men in town before you were arrested?"

Lowery shook his head. "I saw a lot of big men, but didn't pay them much mind." Suddenly, a stored memory gleamed in his eyes. "Wait. I did see a tall, well-built man. His name is Maddox Franklin and he's the owner of the Top Hat." Lowery shrugged. "But why would Maddox be involved with a gal on the line? Seems to me he has all the women he wants right there in his saloon."

"He's worth talking to, though," Kate said. "He's obviously around women a lot."

Hank Lowery shook his head. "Mrs. Kerrigan, you're flogging a dead horse. Hinkle means to hang me. He's made that clear, and I have nothing to bargain with."

Frank said, "If it's any consolation, Lowery, when Hinkle hangs you, I think he'll have strung up the wrong man."

"Well, I'll hold on to that. Thanks."

"Don't mention it.

Only a handful of customers were in the Top Hat when Kate swept inside and demanded to see the proprietor, Maddox Franklin.

The duty bartender polished a glass and laid it on the gantry behind him before he answered. "Mr. Franklin never gets up before dusk, ma'am." He looked Kate up and down and added, "If you want a job, go talk to Caddy Early in the booth over there by the stage. She does Mr. Franklin's hiring."

To Frank's surprise Kate showed no offense.

"Not that I wouldn't be good at it, but I'm not here to find a job. I need a few questions answered."

"Then ask away," the bartender said, picking up another glass. "It ain't like I'm real busy or nothing."

"What is your name?" Kate said.

"Ed Fetter. What's yours?"

"Kate Kerrigan."

"Sure you don't want to work here? You'd look kinda cute in one of them little top hats."

"I am not here to discuss millinery, Mr. Fetter, though it's a subject dear to my heart. Now answer this and please be frank. Does Mr. Maddox Franklin avail himself of the services of prostitutes?"

Fetter lifted the glass he was polishing to the light and studied it closely before he answered. "Look around you, lady. What do you think this place is? A nunnery?"

"Let me rephrase what I said, Mr. Fetter: Did Mr. Franklin ever visit a prostitute by the name of Sarah Hollis?"

"No."

"You seem very certain."

"I am certain."

"Tell me why. Come now, don't be reticent."

Fetter exchanged glances with Frank and thought he saw a shadow of sympathy in the big man's eyes. "Mrs. Kerrigan, Sarah Hollis would come in here some nights when her business was slow. I liked her and didn't charge her for drinks or the crackers and cheese we put out on the bar. She had been pretty once but not any longer. Laudanum had aged her and one time she told me that a client had introduced her to opium smoking."

Fetter leaned across the bar, closer to Kate. "Mrs. Kerrigan, Sarah Hollis worked the line. Her next step down, and she could only go lower, would be a hog farm. After that, she'd die. Laudanum could kill her or she'd kill herself." The bartender straightened. "Mr. Franklin will take in at least ten thousand dollars tonight. Men like him don't use line girls. Now, does that answer your question?"

"Perhaps, but it leads to another question, Mr. Fetter. What kind of men frequent the line shacks?"

"All kinds, but mainly down-and-outs, the dirty and diseased, the scum of the earth with two dollars to spend. There are others—men who like to use and abuse women. I think Sarah knew one or two of them judging by her face."

"Oh dear God, the poor woman," Kate said.

Fetter nodded. "Sarah had a hard life, Mrs. Kerrigan. She sure didn't deserve the end she got. I'm all done talking about her." He called out to a passing waiter. "Hey, Andy, bring me some rum and a few bottles of champagne for the flips. Here, I'll help you . . ." And then he was gone.

Kate looked at Frank as though she expected him to throw her a lifeline. But there was none forthcoming, forcing her to ask, "Well, Frank, where do we go from here?"

"Back to the hotel, I guess, and check on the invalid."

"That's not what I meant."

"I know what you meant, Kate, and the answer is that I've no idea."

"We need to come up with something if we're to save Hank Lowery."

"We could always bust him out of jail and light a shuck for Texas." He saw the frown on Kate's face and said, "All right, that was a bad idea."

"No, it's not a bad idea and I'm taking it seriously. If worse comes to worst I may be tempted to try it."

"Hinkle would send out wires and the moment we left the Indian Territory and crossed the Canadian we'd find ourselves up to our armpits in Texas Rangers. Lowery would still get hung, and we'd face years in a federal penitentiary."

"You don't paint a pretty picture, Frank."

"You're right. It's not a pretty picture, but it's the truth."

CHAPTER TWENTY

When he was full of Kansas sheep dip, the Texas cowboy was a bad man to handle. Usually lawmen stayed in the background and allowed him to blow off steam until he called it a night and crawled into the nearest hollow log to sleep it off.

But a much more dangerous caste of men was in Dodge City, quieter men with careful eyes who looked at nothing directly, but were aware of everything. Called shootists, pistoleros, or gunmen, some were of the new breed of Texas draw fighters that made the newspaper headlines and the covers of the dime novels. Like all the other two-legged predators in town, their only reason for being there was to prey on the cowboys. Their weapons were cards and dice. In a wild violent town, their gun reputations were sufficient to keep most of them alive.

Such a man was Morgan Braddock.

Some said he'd killed twenty men, others half that number, but when he was in his cups and maudlin, Braddock admitted to only nine, all of them kills-for-hire. So when a big man, rough as a cob, approached

him in the Long Branch and offered him a contract
kill, Braddock jumped at the chance. He'd been losing
big at the tables and a fast five hundred, just like that,
would put him back in the game.

"Can you handle Frank Cobb?" the big man said.

"Never heard of him, but I can handle anybody you
care to mention," Braddock said.

"He's a tall, good-looking—"

"No need to spell it out. If he's a gun, I'll peg him."

"Because of the murders the whores are staying
away from the line, but Cobb and a woman will be
there tonight at ten. I sent a boy to deliver a message
to their hotel that will draw them out. It's the woman
I'm most interested in. Red hair, expensive clothes,
real pretty. I mean a looker. I want her dead, dead,
dead, Braddock. Dead as hell in a parson's parlor. The
five hundred is for both, but you give me clean kills,
no maybes, and I'll add another hundred."

"You got it," Braddock said, counting the five hundred, all in federal bills. "When the job is over and the
killing is done, I'll come back for the other hundred."

The big man studied the gunman's duds, black
shirt, pants, boots, hat, gun, holster, and cartridge
belt. "You always dress like that, all in black like an
undertaker?"

"Yeah. I'm always in mourning for the men I've
killed."

"And now you'll mourn a woman."

"There's a first time for everything."

"Cobb's fast. Killed a man only last night."

"Men are always getting themselves killed," Braddock said. "Now get the hell away from me. I like to
think when I'm drinking."

"Remember, I want it clean. No slipups."

"Beat it."

After the big man left, Braddock stared at the painting of a nude woman above the bar. To the bartender he said, "Who is she?"

The bartender glanced at the painting. "Bat Masterson says—hey—do you know him?"

"By sight. What does he say?"

"Well, he says the gal's name is Mattie Blaylock, one time the common-law wife of an Arizona lawman by the name of Earp. Masterson says she was facing hard times when she posed for the picture for fifty dollars."

"She isn't pretty," Braddock said.

"Mister, nobody who comes into the Long Branch looks at her face."

"Big ass."

"Yeah. I guess from her ass alone the painter got his fifty dollars' worth," The bartender flipped a towel over his shoulder and stepped away.

Braddock continued to study the nude, his intense sky blue eyes moving over her shoulders, breasts, slightly rounded belly, and then to her hips again. Soft, all of her soft. He drained his whiskey glass. *Damn!* He'd never thought about it before—where do you shoot a woman?

Drugo Odell studied himself in the full-length mirror in his hotel room. What a pity no one ever saw him without his coat. The oxblood shoulder holster he wore had been made and hand-tooled by an Austrian craftsman, the carving done in the ancient Celtic style, and it fitted his Colt like a glove. So pleased had Odell been by the work, it crossed his mind to kill the Austrian so that he'd never make another quite like it.

But when the old man declared it his masterpiece, sadly swearing that as he entered his dotage he would never surpass its beauty and function, Odell let him off the hook. The old fool would die soon enough anyway.

Odell sighed and covered up the beautiful gun rig with his high-button coat. Sarah Hollis had long admired his holster and that had pleased him. Of course, she'd had to die and that was unfortunate. Telling him that she was running away with an eighteen-year-old Texas puncher—to get married, or so she said—was an insult not to be borne. That was why she got the bowie knife in her chest. The cowboy, his name was Rusty Rhodes for God's sake, left Dodge with his outfit and Odell never knew if he planned to marry her or not. Probably not. Under the spell of whiskey and the heat of lust, a cowboy would pretty much tell a woman like Sarah anything she wanted to hear.

After donning his bowler and adjusting the fall of his coat around his gun, Odell admired himself at length. No wonder the whores loved him. Bat Masterson was in town and the dude could certainly cut a dash, but he'd nothing on the man smiling so confidently at Drugo Odell in the mirror . . . himself, of course.

He had urgent business to attend to that evening, an affair of the heart. He needed to find a woman to dominate, to use and abuse, and satisfy his sadistic urges.

He smiled at himself in the mirror. It was time to begin the hunt.

CHAPTER TWENTY-ONE

"We could walk right into a trap, Kate," Frank said. "There's something about the setup that makes me feel uneasy."

"I'm aware of that, Frank." For the second time that evening, Kate read aloud the note the boy had delivered. "'Come to the line shacks at ten tonight. I have information. Bring a hundred dollars.' Just that. No signature."

"The boy handed it to me and then ran away," Trace said. "I didn't get a chance to question him."

"The fact that the informant, he or she, is doing this for a hundred dollars might indicate that it's genuine," Kate said.

"Or someone is being mighty clever," Frank said.

"Ma, we could show the note to Sheriff Hinkle and let him handle it."

Kate shook her head. "No. If this note is genuine Hinkle would only mess things up. Whoever the informant is, he'd take one look at the sheriff and run."

"Then how do you want to play this?" Frank said.

"And I might as well tell you that I dread your answer, Kate."

She was silent for a few moments as she stared in concentration at the sepia brown hotel room wall. "We'll go there, Frank. A man's life is at stake and we can't ignore anything that could save him. I guess we'll have to take a chance."

"Then we'll all go," Trace said.

"No, Trace. You need to rest and heal." Kate smiled. "But I'll take your Winchester. I'm not that trusting."

"I got a burn across my shoulders, that's all, Ma. You're trying to keep me out of harm's way, but I'm going with you."

"And I say you're not."

"Kate, Trace is man-grown and he's good with a rifle. I'd like him with us."

Kate Kerrigan looked from Frank to her son. Two men, both of them big, capable, and confident. Her son wasn't a boy any longer. He'd killed a man on his first trail drive and after that he'd grown up fast. From boy to man almost overnight. It had been that quick.

"Very well, Trace, you can come with us," Kate said, knowing full well that she was surrendering. "But if you get shot again don't blame me."

Frank and Trace exchanged amused looks, but neither said a word.

Morgan Braddock lifted his eyes to the railroad clock on the saloon wall. It was nine-thirty. Time to move. He finished his whiskey, stepped away from the bar, and walked outside into the crowded, clamorous night.

* * *

She was perfect.

After the girl finished a fifty-cent dance with a puncher, Drugo Odell called her over to his table. "Can I buy you a drink, little lady?"

The girl had hennaed hair and a pout. She sat and said that the Top Hat was very busy and yes, she'd like a drink. A bottle of Mumm's Brut Cordon Rouge would be perfect if the gent felt inclined to be generous.

Odell grinned and began to reel in his prey. "For you, anything your little heart desires." He ordered the overpriced champagne and said, "What's your name?"

Her name was Nellie, Nellie Wilde from Liverpool, England. She'd gotten off the boat just a year before and had made her way to Kansas, selling her favors to gents along the way, but only to cover expenses, mind. Now she was much more choosy and preferred to sell them only to well-bred gentlemen like the one she was sitting with.

"Isn't the champagne just too-too delicious?" With her luxuriant red hair and big brown eyes, she was a pretty girl. She was slightly plump and she knew how to fill out the scarlet corset she wore. Her moist, pouty mouth was always slightly open as though she found it difficult to breathe. When she laughed at Odell's dirty jokes, her small teeth, even and white, were visible.

Watching her, he had a wonderful idea. He'd invite Nellie to take a stroll with him and begin her education in Sarah Hollis's shack. How droll. It was a plan so elegant, so exquisite, he could barely contain his excitement. The girl was pliable. Once she was broken in, she'd learn quickly.

Odell consulted his watch. It was fifteen minutes until ten. It was stuffy in the saloon and he suggested a stroll. "We'll take the bottle with us."

Nellie was fine with that, but there would be an additional charge on top of . . . well, whatever the gent might want. Mr. Franklin didn't like the girls leaving the Top Hat with clients, but he made exceptions if a walking-out fee was paid.

Odell said she was worth every penny and the two walked out of the Top Hat arm in arm, laughing.

Placed so it could be seen from Front Street, a red lantern was attached to the gable wall of the first of the line cabins. Morgan Braddock took it down, thumbed a match into flame, and lit the wick. The lamp flared into scarlet life and he hung it on its hook again. The lit lantern would attract the attention of anyone walking up the alley, if only for a few moments. He was a man who believed in getting an edge, no matter how slight. His boots crunched across the gravel lane away from the shacks and he faded into the darkness opposite where a few struggling soap-berry trees grew.

He drew his Colt and let the revolver hang by his side. Somewhere along Front Street a male tenor sang "A Maiden Fair to See" from *H.M.S. Pinafore* and made a nice job of it. The moon was up but hidden behind clouds and Braddock thought it might rain. He'd killed a gambler named Lawson Beaudry in New Orleans during a thunderstorm and hadn't cared for it much. His damn gun hand had gotten wet and slippery and had slowed him on the draw and shoot. He'd still been too fast for Beaudry, but it had been a close-run thing.

Ten o'clock, the big man had told him. Well, it was closing in on that time. Braddock breathed easily, consciously slowing his heartbeat for the draw as his eyes and ears reached out into the sights and sounds of the Dodge City night.

He had not much longer to wait.

Kate buttoned the split canvas riding skirt she'd worn on the trail, put on a white shirt, and pulled on her boots. She piled up her hair and pinned it in place and then slipped a .450 caliber Webley Bull Dog revolver into her skirt pocket, a present from Captain Delaney, who assured her it had once been the property of the gallant Custer.

Trace and Frank were waiting for her in the lobby. It was time to go.

Odell thought the girl seemed eager since she was already a little bit sweaty, a desirable trait in a whore. As they left Front Street and turned into the alley, Nellie became more professional, outlining her services and the price list. He wanted them all, and Nellie said that many gents went that route. It was cheaper in the long run because of the ten percent discount.

Odell reckoned that he would take great pleasure in breaking her to his will. At first, he'd use a combination of fear and occasional displays of affection and generosity, but once he had her completely dependent on opium, he would own her—body and soul.

The lit red lantern at the gable end of the line shacks troubled him. He'd been told that the working girls had abandoned the place out of fear. He wondered if they had moved back, driven by necessity.

Nellie said, "Seems that some of the girls are already working." A wind had sprung up and the air smelled of rain. "Oh, there's a client, but I don't see a girl with him."

Odell pushed her away from him and she shrieked and fell. The bullet that would have taken her life split the air two feet above her recumbent body. He had spotted the danger the moment the man stepped out of the shadows and was already drawing as he stepped to his left and fired. Illuminated only by the red mist of the lantern light, he thought he saw the man stagger as though he'd taken a hard hit. The man steadied and swung his gun on Odell, holding it in both hands. Closer to the scarlet lantern, Odell looked as though he was splashed in blood. He and his assailant fired at the same time. The girl was screaming and scrambling around on all fours.

Odell, a fine marksman, scored another hit, then fired again, believing that would be his bluebird shot. But the big gunman staggered forward on dragging feet and moved in the direction of the redheaded girl, who was facedown on the ground, her head covered by her arms.

Odell lowered his Colt to waist level, his eyes on the gunman. *What the hell?* Why was he so determined to shoot Nellie? Had she given him a dose of the clap? He wondered as the big man stopped, and again two-handed his revolver as though it had suddenly become too heavy for him.

Odell shook his head, took up a duelist's stance—his right arm straight and extended—and shot Morgan Braddock in the left temple. Braddock fell like a puppet that had its strings cut. At the same time, Nellie scrambled to her feet, her face frantic. She ran for Front Street as fast as her short, shapely legs could carry her yelling "Murder!" at the top of her lungs.

Intrigued, Odell stepped to Braddock's sprawled body. The man laid on his back, staring at the black sky with open, dead eyes. Odell had never seen him before. The gunman had been hit four times, three bullets in the chest and one in the head. He earned Odell's grudging admiration. Whoever the hell he was, he'd been a hard man to kill.

CHAPTER TWENTY-TWO

It gave Kate a strange feeling to be once again standing outside Sarah Hollis's shack, stepping around yet another corpse.

"Anyone recognize him?" Sheriff George Hinkle said.

His question drew a shake of the head or a blank expression from the onlookers until a puncher in a black-and-white cowhide vest said, "Yeah, I recollect him now. I seen him gambling in the Top Hat."

"Anybody call him by name?" Hinkle said.

"Not that I heard, but then I was only drifting past the poker table. I noticed him because he was a big feller and kinda looked like a hardcase."

"Well, he don't look like a hardcase any longer," Hinkle said.

"No, he don't," the puncher said.

Rain driven by the rising wind pattered along the lane and the crowd began to fade away.

Hinkle turned his attention to Drugo Odell. "Tell me about it. After you put out your name."

The dapper little man in a ditto suit and bowler hat kept his gun hidden. His smile was open and forthright, a practiced, reassuring facial gesture with all the warmth of an alligator's grin. "My name is Drugo Odell, Sheriff."

"Drugo? What the hell kind of handle is that for a Christian man?" Yet another killing at the line cabins had irritated the sheriff.

"My pa named me for a favorite coonhound of his," Odell said. "He never told me why."

"What happened?" Hinkle said.

"I was walking out with my new lady friend—"

"Who?" Hinkle said.

"Her name is Nellie Wilde."

"Nellie ain't a lady friend. She's a prostitute."

"I wasn't aware of that."

"She's selling it at the Top Hat, wearing a corset with her bosoms hanging out, and you didn't know what she was?"

"Sheriff, my father was a clergyman and I was raised to think the best of people."

"So you were strolling with Nellie in a place where two murders had been committed," Hinkle continued. "Very romantic."

"Curiosity. A sense of adventure, I guess," Odell said. "People in love do strange things."

"How long have you known Nellie Wilde?"

"I just met her tonight."

"Love at first sight, huh?"

"It happens, Sheriff."

"Never happened for me," Hinkle said. "Go on. You were walking and . . . ?"

"This man stepped out of the shadows with a

gun," Odell said. "I threw Miss Wilde aside just as he fired at her."

"He fired at the girl, not you?"

"Yes. And even when he was dying on his feet, he still tried to kill her."

"After you plugged him."

"Three rounds to the chest. He was a hard man to kill."

"Was the girl wounded?"

"No. She ran away."

Kate spoke up for the first time. "Mr. Odell, what color hair does Nellie Wilde have?"

Odell looked at her. "Same as you, lady. Red. But I think she dyes hers."

Hinkle stared at Kate in the gloom. "Coincidence, Mrs. Kerrigan. Lot of redheaded gals in Dodge right now."

"Is this a coincidence, Sheriff?" She handed him the note she'd received and studied his face while he read it.

The lawman didn't disappoint. "Hell, no, it ain't happenstance. You were lured here."

"I was to be murdered by the dead man, whoever he is," Kate said. "He saw Nellie Wilde and mistook her for me."

"If that's the case, he wanted to kill you real bad, ma'am," Odell said, donning his sympathy mask. He looked over Kate's shapely body and wanted more than anything to do her in Sarah Hollis's shack.

Hinkle rubbed his temples. "Damn, I've got a headache."

"Because you're so set on hanging an innocent man, Sheriff," Kate said. "I'm getting close to identifying the real killer and he wants to be rid of me."

An alarm bell went off in Odell's head, but then he relaxed. He could have been killed tonight escorting the woman's lookalike and was hardly a suspect."

"Mrs. Kerrigan," Hinkle said, "What I got here is two murders and two murderers. I know who killed Sarah Hollis and now I want to find the other killer, the murderer of Alva Cranley. I will concede that Alva's killer wants you dead. You saw her body and investigated the ground around the shack and now the man who strangled Alva is after you. He thinks you know something and he's running scared."

"And so he should be," Kate said. "Because he's the same man who murdered Sarah Hollis. And don't you dare to tell me otherwise, Sheriff."

Driven by the wind, the rain fell heavier and Drugo Odell decided it was time he left. The redheaded woman's talk was making him uneasy and the two punchers with her looked like hardcases, especially the older one, who had the look of a Texas gun. Anyway, it seemed that Hinkle was ready to call it a night. The lawman was already talking about getting an undertaker to pick up the body.

Bat Masterson arrived on the scene and everything in Odell's world took a turn for the worse.

"Why are you here, Bat?" Hinkle said.

Masterson wore his usual bowler hat and a black opera cape closed at the neck with a bright silver clasp in the shape of a dragon. The handle of the cane he carried in his left hand was also in the form of a silver dragon. "This latest murder is the talk of the Top Hat, George. Little gal in there is hysterical, telling everybody that someone wants to kill her."

"He did," Hinkle said, nodding in the direction of

the corpse. "We think he mistook Nellie Wilde for Mrs. Kerrigan here."

"We don't think, Sheriff, we *know*," Kate said.

Despite the dark, the wind, and the rain, Masterson gave an elegant bow to Kate. "I do not believe I've had the pleasure."

Kate said her name, dropped a curtsey, and then extended her hand for Masterson to kiss.

After he did, Bat straightened and said, "You are very beautiful, Mrs. Kerrigan."

"And you, sir, are very gallant," Kate said.

Watching the exchange, Trace grinned and Frank suddenly felt like a bumpkin. He'd always heard that the sophisticated Masterson could set female hearts aflutter when he cut a dash.

Then Bat surprised him and everyone else. "Don't slink away into the darkness like a Louisiana alligator, Drugo. I want to talk to you."

"I told the sheriff all I know." Odell looked uncomfortable.

"You killed a man tonight, Drugo," Masterson said. "Are you going to the Top Hat to boast of it?"

"No, I'm planning to get out of this rain and console my poor Nellie."

"Poor Nellie, is it? Why did you bring her to this place where two women had been murdered?"

"It was only a lark, Bat. A pair of young people looking for adventure."

"And I'd say you found it."

"Yes. I suppose we did."

Hinkle said, "Bat, it's pouring rain. Can't we talk about this later? Odell is not a suspect here."

"He was sparking Sarah Hollis, George. That makes him a suspect. I heard about it no later than this afternoon." Masterson smiled. "From one of my more low and disreputable friends."

"You don't spark Sarah's kind," Odell said. "She had something to sell and I bought it. I didn't bring her flowers."

Driven away by the rain and the beckoning pleasures of Front Street, the crowd had dispersed. Only six people stood in the scarlet hell-light of the lantern, the body of the man at their feet silent and unmoving in death.

Masterson broke the silence. "Drugo, you're leaving?"

"I'm through here," Odell said.

"Pity. I thought we could talk about Dora Redberry down Tombstone way. The poor girl is dead. Did you know that? I seem to recall that you jumped a Butterfield out of town just after it happened."

Odell turned and faced Masterson full on. "Don't push me, Bat."

"Nobody's pushing you, Drugo. I wondered if you wanted to talk about Dora was all."

"You don't like me, Bat. Not liking me can be dangerous for a man."

Masterson nodded, rain dripping from the narrow brim of his hat. "I know that, Drugo. Well? Be off with you. I'm sure Nellie Wilde is pining for you to comfort her."

It seemed to Frank that Odell hesitated for just a moment, maybe thinking about the draw. Then he turned on his heel and walked away, and soon the rain and darkness closed around him.

Masterson smiled and echoed Frank's thought. "Ol' Drugo might have skinned it." His Colt came out from under his cape. "I had my gun in my hand. I might have shaded him."

"We've had enough killing around here, Bat," Hinkle said. "Put the iron away and get out of the rain."

Masterson looked at Kate. "Mrs. Kerrigan, there's a Chinese teahouse not far from here where they serve the most delicious little cakes. Would you and your friends care to join me?" And then to Hinkle, "Sorry, George, you're not invited since you have to stand guard over the dead man."

"I'd love a cup of tea," Kate said. "Mr. Masterson, this is my son, Trace, and Frank Cobb, my *segundo*."

"From time to time I heard about you, Frank," Bat said, his face expressionless.

"And I you," Frank said. "Small world."

Masterson nodded. "The West is vast, but there's a certain breed of men who are few in number though we tend to hear much about them." He unbuckled his cloak and, with a fine flourish, draped it around Kate's shoulders." "This will keep you dry, dear lady."

"Thank you, Mr. Masterson. Indeed, you are very gracious."

"Ah, but how easy it is to be gracious to a beautiful woman. And please call me Bat. Everyone else does."

CHAPTER TWENTY-THREE

"Is the tea to your liking, Mrs. Kerrigan?" Masterson said.

"It's excellent, Bat. And the little cakes are delicious, so delicately flavored. If you ever get down to Texas, you must visit my ranch and I'll bake a sponge cake for you. Sponge cake with a cream and jam filling is a favorite of Queen Victoria, you know."

"How interesting. Now I am really looking forward to your baking."

"I only bake sponge cake, I'm afraid, nothing else," Kate said.

"Then that will more than suffice, I'm sure."

Frank envied Masterson's easy way with women. Kate seemed to enjoy his charm and fine manners, of which Frank had neither. Even holding the china teacup in his big, work-hardened hand was a chore, and he was sure if he held the little cup too firmly it would shatter like an eggshell. To his embarrassment, he'd already tried to pick up one of the tiny, delicate rice cakes and left it a crumbled mess on the plate.

Beside him, Trace seemed totally at ease, enjoying Masterson's company.

Frank's misery increased. For the first time in his life he was actually jealous of another man. Bat Masterson would be an easy ranny to hate . . . if he wasn't so all-fired charming.

"I've always been much enamored of the Chinese," Bat said. "Look around you, Mrs. Kerrigan. Lanterns of all colors and shapes, paintings of birds and pretty ladies on the walls, delicate, lacquered furniture. We might well be in a teashop in Cathay itself."

"The chimes and tinkling bells are so soothing," Kate said. "And the scent of incense is divine."

"Sandalwood, I think," Masterson said. "But there is also a hint of jasmine. More tea, Frank?"

Rather than let the cup beat him, Frank laid it on the table and Masterson poured from a blue and white teapot with a painting of a man and a woman crossing a wooden bridge.

"Rice cake?" Bat said.

"No thanks," Frank said.

"They're very good, Frank," Kate said. "Do try a pink one. They have a rosewater flavor."

Bat Masterson's smile was the equivalent of an amused wink and Frank wasn't about to let him win. Using his thumb and forefinger, he gingerly picked up a cake about as big around as a silver dollar, but before he could transfer it to his mouth, it slipped from his fingers and landed somewhere on his crotch. "Damn."

Bat grinned, but covered his mouth with his hand.

Kate was watching Frank. She smiled and said that hands accustomed to ropes, reins, and branding irons were not made for rice cakes. She took a pink one from the plate and said, "Frank, open your mouth and close your eyes and you will get a big surprise."

Frank's misery and embarrassment could get no worse, so he did as Kate said and she popped the cake into his mouth. After she watched him chew, she asked if it was good.

Frank thought that it tasted like newsprint, but he smiled and said, "It's real good, Kate."

A bell jangled as the front door opened and Sheriff George Hinkle stepped inside.

"Thank God," Frank said under his breath.

Hinkle made his way to the table. Rain ran down his black oilskin and his hat brim ticked water onto the table. Irritated, Masterson quickly moved the cakes away from the cascade.

"The dead man's name was Morgan Braddock and he's been in town only a few days." Hinkle picked up a rice cake and effortlessly tossed it into his mouth. He ate another before Bat glared at him, scowled, and slid the plate away from him and in front of Kate.

"How do you know this?" Frank said.

"Old wanted dodger in the sheriff's office." Hinkle didn't bother to explain further. He didn't need to hear himself talk. "He was a hired gun."

"Who hired him?" Kate said.

"Hell if I know, Mrs. Kerrigan."

"Then you must find out, Sheriff. Now there are two lives at stake—Hank Lowery's and mine."

Hinkle nodded and water poured off his hat onto the table. "Strange things happening in Dodge this cattle season. Did you know the tin man is back up and running? Saw him earlier tonight." He looked around and saw blank faces. "Ah well, I thought it was interesting." To Masterson, he said, "Tell me about Dora Blueberry."

"Redberry," Bat said.

"All right. Tell me about her instead."

"She worked as a prostitute in Tombstone in the Arizona Territory. She claimed to be descended from Russian aristocracy and in fact she could speak Russian fluently . . . or what sounded like Russian to me."

"Not much call for a Russian speaker in Tombstone," Hinkle said.

"No, I reckon not," Masterson said. "She was a pretty girl though—yellow hair and blue eyes—and she could sing and dance."

"Cut to the chase, Bat," Hinkle said.

A small thin Chinese man wearing a round black hat bustled up to the table, glared at Hinkle, and said to Kate, "This man bothering you, missy?"

Kate smiled. "No, he's not, but thank you for asking."

Hinkle was less polite. "Beat it, Chinaman, or you'll be eating chop suey in my jail."

"Big bully man," the Chinese said before he glided away, muttering to himself.

"Cutting to the chase, George, Dora spent a lot of time in the company of Drugo Odell. Maybe it was a love thing, but I doubt it. Sheriff Johnny Behan, a congenital idiot, found Dora's body behind the Birdcage Theater. She'd been stabbed between her—" He stopped speaking and looked at Kate. "I mean, she'd been stabbed in the chest and had been dead for some time. Behan decided to wait for the doctor's report as though the cause of death wasn't pretty damn obvious, and by that time, Odell had lit a shuck for places unknown."

"Bat, do you think Odell murdered Dora what's-her-name?" Hinkle asked.

"Redberry. Yeah, I think he did."

"Thinking ain't proving," Hinkle said.

"Sarah Hollis was killed in the same manner, Sheriff." Then with a mischievous smile, Kate added, "A knife between her tits."

Hinkle's eyes widened. "Yes, yes she was, Mrs. Kerrigan. I'll talk with Odell and hear what he has to say."

"He'll deny Dora's murder," Masterson said.

"What did Behan think about the girl's death?" Hinkle said.

"He didn't think anything. Dora was a whore and he let her murderer go. He was dealing with the Earp boys at the time and had more important things on his mind."

Talking amid a rumble of distant thunder, Kate said, "Sheriff, is it possible that Odell murdered Dora Redberry, Sarah Hollis, and Alva Cranley?"

For the first time Hinkle revealed some doubt. "It's possible, Mrs. Kerrigan. Anything is possible. But now I ask myself the question, who is trying to kill you? Drugo Odell would hardly have walked into his own ambush."

Kate said, "But it can only be Odell . . . somehow. There's no one else."

"Sheriff, are you going to release Hank Lowery?" Trace said.

"No, not yet. Not until I get this thing settled."

"When will that be?" Trace said.

"Young man, your guess is as good as mine."

"But in the meantime, Hank Lowery could hang."

Hinkle said. "I guess he'll have to take his chances like the rest of us."

After Hinkle left, Frank Cobb said, "I reckon if we want to save Hank Lowery's life we'll have to bust him out of the juzgado."

"Bad idea," Masterson said. "As lawmen go, George Hinkle isn't much of a sheriff, but he's never lost a prisoner and I've never known him to back down. If he has to, he'll kill Lowery without a moment's hesitation. And there's another thing. If you want Lowery, you'll have to step over George's dead body."

"No, no, we don't want that," Kate said.

"No you don't," Bat said. "I told the sheriff that I'd help him with this investigation and I plan to keep my word. Kate, I think we forget your puncher for a spell and concentrate on Drugo Odell . . . and hope to God that our guns don't jam."

CHAPTER TWENTY-FOUR

Bat Masterson's talk about Dora Redberry had shaken Drugo Odell to the core. He dropped all his plans regarding the taming of Nelly Wilde since he could no longer take the chance on drawing some unwelcome attention, especially if he chose to kill her. Too nervous to eat, he settled for coffee in the crowded Dodge House Restaurant, where he could take refuge behind his newspaper.

The *Dodge Times* had the story of last night's shooting scrape on their front page, and as usual got it all wrong.

DEADLY DOINGS IN DODGE

THE READY REVOLVER DOES ITS WORK

*Robber Hurled Into Eternity
In a Moment*

Sheriff Hinkle Praises Valor
of Armed Citizen

Drake Ordell, a well-known sporting gent of this town, shot down a would-be

robber as the gallant Mr. Ordell and his
schoolteacher sweetheart promenaded along
Front Street.

A few mangled details of the shooting followed and
the piece ended with, "The dead man was identified
by Sheriff Hinkle as Morton Bradshaw, a desperate
character, much given to whiskey and rowdy behavior.
The *Times'* only comment is to wish the rogue's sable
shade a hearty good riddance."

Odell smiled behind his newsprint barricade, the
thought of Nellie Wilde as a schoolteacher amusing
him greatly. What would she teach? Her occupation?
Plus whiskey and wantonness probably. He had no
time to ponder his questions because someone sat
heavily on the chair opposite and flicked his newspaper with a finger. Odell lowered the paper.

A big, rough-hewn, and unshaven man scowled at
him. "Me and you need to talk."

Kate dabbed her mouth with her napkin. "The
scrambled eggs were quite acceptable, the overcooked
bacon was not. Has it occurred to you, Mr. Masterson,
as it has to me, that perhaps Morgan Braddock was
acting on his own?"

"You mean that he murdered the two women?"

"Yes, and possibly Dora Redberry."

Bat shook his head. "The word around town is that
Braddock was a hired killer. His only other interest
seemed to be gambling and he wasn't very good at it.
Braddock was a professional and he didn't kill those
women. There was no profit in it." He forked a piece
of bacon into his mouth and said around a chew,

"Hired assassins don't draw attention to themselves. They drift into a town like ghosts, make the kill, and drift out again."

"Then again that leaves only Drugo Odell."

"Sticks out like a bandaged thumb, don't he?"

"You'll have a fast horse and five hundred dollars traveling money," the big man said.

"If I make the Kerrigan kill I want a fast horse and fifteen hundred traveling money," Odell negotiated. "Pretty woman like that should be kept around, barefoot and naked most of the time. Why do you want her dead?"

"I have my reasons," the big man said. "Right now they're none of your concern."

"You hired Morgan Braddock to kill Kate Kerrigan," Odell said. "The damn idiot tried to kill me and a redheaded whore."

"Mistaken identity," the big man said. "It happens."

"I won't make the same mistake," Odell said. "That is . . . if I accept the contract."

"You'll accept the contract. I agree to the fifteen hundred." The big man looked around him and leaned closer to Odell. "Don't mess with Bat Masterson, Odell. He's got a nose like a bloodhound. I got a feeling the feller in the jail ain't gonna hang for killing the whores, but there's a good chance somebody else will. Maybe a ranny who least expects it. Maybe that somebody should think about putting a heap of git between himself and Dodge while the gittin's good."

"I didn't kill them," Odell said.

"Yes, you did, but I don't give a damn," the big man

said. "I need Kate Kerrigan dead. Do you want the job or no?"

"Two thousand and I want the horse ready at the livery when the job is done."

"You come high."

"Kate Kerrigan isn't a two-dollar prostitute."

"No, she's a rancher and she's got powerful friends. Odell, make it look good, and be damn sure the killing can't be traced back to me."

"I've contract killed before. Protecting the client's identity comes with the job."

"Good. Now listen up. Go to the front desk of the Dodge House at four this afternoon and ask for the package someone left for you. Inside you'll find a thousand dollars. When it's over and Kate Kerrigan is dead, the other thousand will be in the saddlebags of a roan horse at the livery."

"And then?"

"And then you get the hell out of Dodge and don't ever come back."

"Your terms are acceptable. I don't know your name."

"And you don't need to know it." The big man rose to his feet. "Just take care of business, you hear?"

"You can depend on me," Drugo Odell said.

CHAPTER TWENTY-FIVE

Maddox Franklin left his post at the end of the Top Hat bar and stepped to the table where Bat Masterson was in conversation with Nellie Wilde.

The girl had recovered from her experience but had prevailed upon Bat to buy her a brandy. "For my nerves, like." She couldn't tell him much about Drugo Odell that he didn't already know, but she was pretty enough and smelled nice.

He lingered longer than he'd intended.

"Hey, Bat, seems like your friend George Hinkle's got himself some trouble," Franklin said.

"What kind of trouble?" Masterson said.

"Look out the window."

Bat excused himself to Nellie, who didn't seem to care overly much, and stepped to the window where he had a clear view of the sheriff's office. He'd seen a lynch mob before and it looked just like the one on the street.

"Seems like they intend to string up that jasper you've taken an interest in," Franklin said. "What's his name?"

"Hank Lowery."

"Looks like he'll soon be Hung Lowery," Franklin said.

"I'd better get over there," Masterson said. "Hinkle is sure to make a bad situation worse."

"Wait. I'll come with you. Let me get my gun."

Bat was surprised. "You don't need to take a hand in this, Maddox."

"I know. But I'm bored. Being a saloonkeeper isn't as exciting as I thought it would be. A lot of standing around mostly."

"Not like being a Texas Ranger, huh?"

"That job was ninety percent boredom, as well."

Maddox said something to the bartender and the man passed him his holstered Colt and a scattergun. He handed the Greener to Bat and then buckled his gun belt around his hips and grinned. "Right. Let's go raise some hell in Dodge City and be somebody."

Kate had said her rosary and was about to get into bed when someone knocked on her door. She picked up the Colt from the nightstand and said, "Who is it?"

"Kate, it's me, Frank. We got ourselves some trouble."

"Hold on." Kate put on her dressing gown and opened the door. "Come in, Frank. What's happened?"

He stepped into the room. "Lynch mob outside the jail. The desk clerk is waking everybody so they can come join in the fun."

"Oh sweet Jesus preserve us! Is Hank all right?"

"I don't know."

Trace stepped into the room and looked at Frank. "I see you've already been told."

Kate tightened her robe around her, slipped her feet into slippers, and picked up the Colt again. "Let's go."

"But Ma, you aren't decent."

"No I'm not decent. And my hair is tied back for war."

"There speaks the Irish warrior princess," Frank said, grinning.

"Damn right," said Kate.

Sheriff Hinkle tried to placate the crowd of two score men who faced him outside the jail, half of them Texas punchers nearly drunk and up for any diversion. "Whoever told you I was releasing Hank Lowery is a damn liar. Where is he? Show yourself."

"We were told you'd say something like that," a gray-haired man said. "Now get that woman-killer out here or we'll come in after him."

A half-drunk puncher yelled, "That jasper ain't goin' nowhere except the nearest crossbeam. We all know about what he done in Longdale . . . all them women and children he murdered an' scalped."

That drew cheers and the mob surged forward, one man waving a noosed rope above his head.

"Damn you. I'll kill the first man who tries to enter this jail." Hinkle's Colt was holstered, but he carried a shotgun.

"And I'll kill the second."

It was a woman's voice, loud enough to make men stop in their tracks and look in Kate's direction. She stepped onto the boardwalk in front of the sheriff's office, Frank and Trace flanking her.

She stepped to the edge of the walk. "Hank Lowery will not be released until the real killer of Sarah Hollis and Alva Cranley is found. Who told you otherwise?"

"Lady, there's a lot of talk going around," a man said.

"Who started the talk?" Kate said. "And was he the one who told you that Hank murdered women and children in Longdale? That's a lie and he knows it."

Men looked at each other until finally a puncher said, "We heard Hinkle is taking Lowery out of Dodge on the midnight train. We're here to see that ain't gonna happen."

Muttered agreement passed among the crowd and again voices were raised in anger. A larger group of onlookers had gathered to watch the lynch mob and at least a hundred people stood in the street, eager for some action.

Kate realized she was losing them, and she placed her back against the office door. "Then you'll have to hang me, as well." Her robe had slipped, revealing her shoulder and the top of her right breast. With her flaming red hair tied back in a green ribbon, she did look like a Celtic princess at bay.

"We can do that, lady," a man yelled. "We can hang you next to Lowery."

Angrier than Kate had ever seen him, Frank roared, "Damn you for a bunch of lily-livered skunks to threaten a woman like that. You want Lowery? All right. That's fine by me, but you'll have to step over your own dead to get him." Frank drew his Colt. "Now have at it. My pistol is ready and my talking is done."

No one in the street wanted to walk into Frank's revolver, and for a moment the mob hesitated. Then a shotgun blast tore through the air above their heads, giving them further pause.

His Greener smoking, Bat Masterson studied the crowd from the boardwalk. "I still got one barrel left. I want the bravest of you to step up, a volunteer willing to get his guts blown out as an encouragement to the others. Come now, where is there such a man?"

Beside him, the tall, elegant Maddox Franklin, gun in hand, smiled. "Make your play, boys, and deal me a hand. I already got five aces in this here iron."

"Damn you, we're ready," Frank Cobb yelled to the crowd. "Come and take the man you want to hang."

Some of the men in the lynch mob were sobering fast. The prospect of rushing two shotguns, three Colts, and a Winchester in the hands of a young man who looked as though he knew how to use it was not a pleasant one. Besides, the federal authorities might not easily forgive the hanging of a beautiful woman in the streets of Dodge by a drunken hemp posse.

Calmer voices in the crowd, mostly merchants, urged the mob to disperse, promising that they would make sure justice was done and that no guilty person would escape the rope.

When she looked back on the incident, Kate was certain that a few of the hotter or drunker heads might have tried it, but the summer rain that had threatened all day came down in earnest, a Kansas frog-strangler that immediately spoiled the crowd's evening. It was no fun to hang a man in the rain. The ground turns muddy and everybody gets wet. The crowd quickly melted away under the guns of Kate and the others.

Hinkle spoke for everyone when he whispered, "My God, I hope I never have to go through that again."

"We were lucky," Masterson said. "The spark to light the fuse never came. It happens that way sometimes and sometimes it doesn't. When the fuse does get lit you end up with dead men on the street and a hanging."

Hinkle took Kate's arm. "Mrs. Kerrigan, let's get you inside out of this rain."

"Who started the rumor that Lowery was getting released?" Hinkle said.

"Drugo Odell?" Kate stood at the office window staring at the downpour that looked like steel needles angling into the street.

"Doubtful. What does he care if Lowery hangs or not?" The sheriff's face frowned in concentration. "I think whoever spread the rumor and worked up the crowd hoped it would draw you out from the hotel."

A moment's silence followed that statement.

Then Frank Cobb yelled, "Oh my God!" He ran across the floor and dived at Kate.

They hit the floor hard even as a bullet shattered the window and thudded into the wall opposite. Masterson immediately blew out the lamp and rushed outside. Maddox Franklin was right behind him.

"There!" Franklin yelled and thumbed off a shot.

"Where?" Bat said.

"In the alley. I caught a glimpse of a man with a rifle."

Bat was already running, the rain falling around him, mud kicking up from his pounding feet. He fired and fired again then vanished into the alley's gloom.

A few tense moments passed without a sound from the alley, then the roar of two revolver shots sounded . . . evenly spaced apart. Then silence again.

Bat reappeared, his Colt hanging loosely by his side, a disappointed scowl on his face.

"Did you get him?" Franklin said. The shoulders of his blue frockcoat were black with rain.

"I fired at shadows. I hit nobody." Masterson slid his Colt back into the shoulder holster. "Whoever he was, he's long gone."

Franklin starred into the darkness. "I reckon so. But I sure don't want to grope my way down a dark alley to put it to the test."

"Me neither," Masterson said. "Damn, I'm soaking wet."

"That makes two of us."

"Did you get him?" Sheriff Hinkle asked as the former lawman entered the office.

"Scared an alley cat or two," Masterson said. "No, I didn't get him. I didn't want to walk any farther into the alley, that's for damn sure."

Kate studied a bruise on her left arm. "You saved my life, Frank. And not for the first time."

"Kate, somebody wants you dead real bad," Frank said. "Apart from Drugo Odell, is there anyone you can think of in Dodge who hates you bad enough to kill you?"

Without a moment's hesitation, Kate shook her head. "No. There's no one."

"You shot the tin man, ma," Trace said, smiling. "Maybe it was him."

"It wasn't a tin man I saw run into the alley," Bat said. "You can take that to the bank."

Frank said, "Kate, we'd better get you to the hotel. You took a bad tumble."

"Is that what you call it, Frank? A tumble?" Kate said. Frank looked flustered.

She smiled. "I call it saving my life."

"I reckon we're all agreed on that." Masterson slapped Frank on the shoulder. "Well done, old fellow."

Frank said nothing but proved to all present that he could still blush.

CHAPTER TWENTY-SIX

Drugo Odell sat in his hotel room and seethed. He'd had a clear shot and that damn meddler Frank Cobb had robbed him of the kill. Because of Cobb, Kate Kerrigan was alive and well instead of lying on an undertaker's table with embalming fluid feeding into her body.

Odell poured himself a whiskey from the bottle on the dresser and stepped to the window, where rain still tapped on the glass. Outside, Front Street was deserted, everyone having taken refuge from the downpour, but the saloon crowds were raucous and pianos, banjos, and the few trumpets played unceasingly. The sheriff's office was in darkness. Shuttered, its door was closed and padlocked tight as an orphanage matron's mouth.

Odell turned as someone thumped on his door. He laid down his glass and picked up a Colt from the nightstand. "Who's there?"

"Me."

It was the voice of the big man, no doubt there to find out why his thousand-dollar investment had been so uselessly spent. Odell turned the key in the lock and stepped back, his revolver up and ready.

The big man barged inside and got right to the point. "You missed."

"Frank Cobb meddled." Odell studied his client and wondered how many shots it would take to drop a man that size. More than a few, probably.

The big man looked around and sat on the corner of the brass bed that shrieked under his weight.

"I won't miss the next time," Odell said.

"Shut the hell up and give me some of that whiskey." The big man grimaced, grabbed the front of his shirt, and wadded it into a wrinkled ball. He watched Odell pour bourbon into a glass and said, "Fill it, damn you."

The big man's bearded face was ashen and his bloodshot eyes revealed his pain. He reached into his shirt pocket, took out a small tin box, and removed a white pill that he shoved into his mouth with a trembling hand. Odell handed him the whiskey and the man emptied the glass in a gulp.

After a while some color returned to his face and his breathing became easier. He tapped his chest. "Bad ticker."

"You should see a doctor," Odell said.

"I have a doctor. Every time he comes to the ranch my houseplants die." The big man's eyes got mean. "I'll feel a sight better when Kate Kerrigan is dead."

"I won't miss the next time," Odell said again. "Why do you hate her so much?"

The man worked his left arm, bending and straightening it and then he flexed his fingers. "She made me look small in front of my hired hands. Cut me down to size, you might say. She forced me to eat her dust all along the trail from Texas and then got a better price for her cattle than I did. Sure I hate her, but I want something from her. I want her land, and I can claim it real easy when she's under the ground."

Odell refilled the rancher's glass. "What's your name, mister? I like to know who I'm working for."

"Name's Ezra Raven out of the West Texas Pecos River country. And I ain't going home until the Kerrigan witch is dead." Raven grimaced and rubbed his arm, his face black with anger. "Even if I have to kill her myself."

Odell shook his head. "Mr. Raven, you're a sick man. I suggest you catch a train and ride the cushions back to Texas. I'll let you know when the job is done."

"I'm staying right where I am," Raven said. "I'll head back to my ranch after I see Kate Kerrigan's dead face in the dirt. You do what I paid you to do Odell. If you fail me again . . . well, I hired one killer and I can hire another."

"Are you threatening me, Mr. Raven? I don't like to be threatened."

"Damn right I'm threatening you, Odell. When I pay a man for a job, I expect that job to get done."

"It will get done," Odell said, his face stiff.

Raven got wearily to his feet. "See that you don't miss again."

The rank smell of Raven's sweat lingered after he left and Odell opened the window wide. He brought up a chair, sat down, and stared into the relentless rain.

During the next hour, he left his place by the window only once . . . to refill his whiskey glass. For the rest of the time he sat deep in thought. Finally, as the grandfather clock in the lobby struck midnight, he rose to his feet, grinning, and raised his hands above his head in triumph.

It was all too simple . . . a foolproof plan that would make him a hero and end the black cloud of suspicion that hung over his head. Damn it all, he was a genius. One more killing, that's all it would take. Just one more useless life to end with a bang. Drugo Odell smiled.

End with a bang . . . "Damn, that was funny."

Kate Kerrigan lay in bed on her back and let the pain of her bruises melt into the down mattress. She was sleepless, her open eyes staring at the shadowed ceiling and its dark corners where the spiders lived. Frank had asked her if she knew anyone who hated her enough to kill her, but try as she might, she could think of no one. All Kate's enemies were dead, some of them buried on the rise behind her cabin. She tried harder, remembering angry faces, shouted threats, vile curses . . . but still came up with no living enemy.

She closed her eyes, inviting sleep. She'd think on this again tomorrow.

Frank's only suspect was Drugo Odell. There could be no other. But why did he want to kill her so badly? All he needed to do was saddle—

"My God!" Frank sat upright in bed. What about Ezra Raven? Was he still in Dodge? Did he hate Kate for the humiliation she'd forced on him back in Texas? Was Raven a vindictive man? He wanted the KK grazing land. Was that reason enough to kill? It had been for others of his breed. That's why range wars were fought. Greedy and power-hungry men going to the gun over land or water rights.

Frank made a decision. Tomorrow he'd find out if Raven had not yet left Dodge and talk to him if he hadn't. And if Raven were the one, he'd kill him.

CHAPTER TWENTY-SEVEN

The Golden Garter cathouse was located in a dim area between two warehouses in a narrow rectangular space that had forced the brothel to build upward. It had two stories plus an attic for the three housemaids and the same number of maintenance workers. The place was high-priced, discreet, and stocked only the best champagne, booze, and cigars. The girls were prettier than the norm, and they lasted about two years before their looks began to fade and they were shown the door.

The proprietress was a large-bosomed woman with white, store-bought teeth who called herself Dolly Mop, the current slang for a lady of loose morals. She ruled the Golden Garter with an iron hand and the girls were terrified of her, but toward her customers Dolly was as solicitous as a fond mama and listened to every problem with the undivided attention of a priest in a confessional . . . as long as they had money, of course.

"Poor Mr. Raven. She needs cut down to size, that strumpet," Dolly said.

"She shamed me," Ezra Raven said, his head on the woman's plump shoulder. "And in front of my men. I can't forgive her for that."

"Nor should you." Dolly was feeling poorly. Just three weeks before a disgruntled customer had put three .22 short rounds into her back from a Remington Elliot Pepperbox revolver. A doctor had dug out the bullets from Dolly's fat like buckshot, but for a woman who'd spent most of her working life lying flat on her back, sleeping on her side was proving to be a chore. "What you need is a nice girl and a bottle of champagne to make you feel better, Ezra."

Raven had a catch in his voice as he said, "I have a weak ticker, Dolly. Kate Kerrigan brought it on me."

"Then Caddy Moods is who you need," Dolly said with an air of great finality. "She's a quiet girl, not given to strenuous exertions in bed. She's a perfect match. And don't forget the champagne. It can be had from the bartender at just ten dollars a bottle. It's genuine French, you know."

Raven rose to his feet, looking enormous in Dolly's small parlor. "I plan to kill her," Raven said. "Kate Kerrigan, I mean."

In the lamplight, a stuffed bobcat watched with beady eyes from its glass dome and a woman's ribald laugh rang from a room upstairs.

"And no wonder, after what you've suffered at her hands," Dolly said. "Now stop by the bar and buy the champagne and then go upstairs to room eight, the Presidential Suite. I'll send Caddy up by and by. At the moment she's helping an elderly gentleman"— Dolly smiled sweetly—"with a little problem."

* * *

The desk clerk at the Alamo Hotel looked up and shook his head as Drugo Odell stepped through the door. "We're full. Not a room to be had for love nor money."

Odell smiled, playing it nice. "I don't need a room. I'm here to visit Mr. Ezra Raven."

"I saw Mr. Raven go out. I don't think he's returned yet."

"Then I'll wait for him. I'm one of his friends up from Texas and he told me he'd keep his door unlocked."

"Room twenty at the top of the stairs," the clerk said.

"Every room occupied, huh?" Odell said as though making small talk. He really didn't have much interest.

"They sure are. And apart from Mr. Raven, I think all our guests are in bed. Seems like the rain drove everybody inside." The man smiled. "Good for the farmers though."

"Get many farmers in Dodge?" Odell asked. As he knew it would, that opened up a conversation about farms and farming.

The clerk had obviously been raised on a farm, and he talked at length about seed and plowing and other stuff that didn't interest Odell in the least. When the clock in the hallway struck three he called a halt. "Well, I'd better get upstairs and wait for ol' Ezra. Do you have a spare key? He's a crackerjack fellow, but he can be forgetful by times—cattleman, you know."

The clerk smiled, already pleased that the little man in the bowler hat was obviously sympathetic to the plight of the Kansas farmer. "Yes, I have a spare. Do you want me to tell Mr. Raven that you're waiting?"

"No, I'd like to surprise him."

The clerk smiled again. "I thought that might be the case. Don't you just love it when old friends drop in out of the blue?"

Odell smiled back. "Oh yes, I do. I surely do."

Drugo Odell sat in darkness but rose to his feet when he heard the heavy fall of boots on the stairs. He pulled his Colt and stood to the side of the door. It had to be Ezra Raven. It was after four in the morning and the big rancher was finally seeking his bed with the rest of the sporting crowd.

Rain ticked on the window as a key rattled in the lock and the huge bulk of Ezra Raven stepped inside. Odell waited until the man closed the door behind him before he shoved the muzzle of his revolver into Raven's temple. "Do as I say, Ezra, or I'll scatter your brains."

"What is this?" Raven said, his voice edged with anger, but he stood stock still, ground-hitched to the floor.

"Throw your gun on the bed," Odell said.

"I'm not carrying a pistol."

Odell reached out and felt around the man's waist. "You've been lying with a woman. I can smell her on you."

"Is that you, Odell? Mind your own damn business."

"That's hardly the way to greet a friend, Ezra."

"Why do you have a gun pointed at my head?"

"Because we need to talk."

"You don't need a gun to talk."

"In this case I do," Odell said. "Now light the lamp. Slowly." He stepped back.

Raven crossed the floor, thumbed a match into

flame and lit the oil lamp, bathing the hotel room in a mustard yellow light.

"Sit on the chair over there by the corner, Ezra," Odell said.

"Damn you, Odell, is this a robbery?"

"Sit." Odell's eyes looked like chipped flints.

"What the hell are you doing?" Raven said.

"Shut up and let me handle this. Where's your pistol?"

"I don't have one."

Odell waved his gun around. "Where's your pistol?"

Raven said, "In the carpetbag in the corner."

Odell found a long-barreled Colt in the bag and tossed it onto the bed. He smiled. "Ezra, have you ever done any acting, you know, on stage like Edwin Booth and Billy Chatterley and them?"

"What the hell are you talking about, Odell? Damn you, you're giving me chest pains. I want my money back and then to get the hell out of here."

"No to both, Ezra. But I will give you an acting lesson. You'd like that, wouldn't you?"

Odell backed to the door and pulled it open a few inches. And then he took a deep breath and yelled at the top of his lungs. *"No! I will not kill a woman for you! That's a terrible thing to ask of a friend!"* He smiled and asked in a whisper, "You like that? Good acting, huh?"

Raven was too thunderstruck to speak, mouth open, eyes popping out of his head.

"You've already murdered two women in cold blood, Raven. I won't let you murder another. Get back! Get back or I'll shoot!!" A whisper again. "So long, Ezra." Odell pumped three shots into Raven's chest. The big man didn't even have time to cry out before death took him and he slumped back in the chair.

"No, Ezra, not that." Odell quickly crossed the room, dragged the dead man out of the chair, and left him sprawled on the floor. He got the revolver from the bed and dropped it beside the body.

The door slammed open and a small, skinny man in a white gown and tasseled nightcap barged inside, half a dozen other residents, their faces concerned, crowding after him.

"Here, this won't do," the small man said. "Christian people are sleeping." His eyes went to the body on the floor. "My God, what happened?"

Odell managed to make himself look shaken. "He already murdered two women and he planned on murdering me if I didn't do what he wanted."

"We heard every word, didn't we, Mabel?" The woman was well past middle age with wispy gray hair, her breasts slack and flat under her nightgown.

Mabel, her spitting image, said, "Yes we did. My sister and I heard him threaten you if you didn't kill a woman."

"You heard him say that?" Odell said, surprised. "Oh, you poor ladies."

"I heard him, too," the nightcap man said. "I heard you tell him to get back, but it did no good."

"He told me he'd murdered two unfortunate women of loose morals," Odell said.

"Yes, we heard him say that as well. Isn't that so, Lily?" Mabel said. "What a beast. Those poor girls."

Drugo Odell almost laughed out loud. This was going even better than he'd hoped. The two crazy old ladies and the man in the nightcap with the bare feet and long toenails would back his story all the way.

When Sheriff George Hinkle arrived, bleary-eyed

and irritated at being wakened from sleep, that proved to be the case.

Mabel, Lily, and Nightcap Man maneuvered Hinkle into a corner and cut loose with a hand-waving torrent of talk. They said they were asleep in the adjoining rooms and were wakened by a man yelling at dear Mr. Odell, ordering him to kill a woman. Mr. Odell yelled back that he would do no such thing and then the horrible man said he'd already killed two women and, with a terrible curse, he said he would kill Mr. Odell. And then Mr. Odell said he would not let the man murder another woman, and then he told the killer to step back.

"Step back! Step back! He must have called out three or four times and then came the shots. At first we thought Mr. Odell had been killed and we were so relieved to see that it was the murderer," Lily said.

Nightcap Man, warming to the idea of presenting evidence, went further, stating that the dead man, always in a considerable state of drunkenness, often cursed at him when they met on the stairs and would brandish a "murderous revolver" in his face, leaving him afraid and trembling and him under the care of a doctor.

Several more people testified that they heard Mr. Odell yelling at the man to get away from him before they heard the shots and they advised Hinkle that the killing was a clear-cut case of self-defense.

Hinkle listened to what everybody had to say. One timid lady declared the possibility that the dead man was in fact the notorious Jack the Ripper come from London to terrorize Dodge City. Mabel and Lily and the others went back to bed in a considerable state of nervous fear over that.

* * *

Sheriff Hinkle waited until the undertaker and his assistants had removed Raven's body before he sat at the end of Odell's bed and accepted the whiskey the man handed him.

"Well, Sheriff, you heard what the folks said. Ezra Raven murdered Sarah Hollis and Alva Cranley and he conspired to have Kate Kerrigan murdered." Odell waited until he lit a cigar then said, "I guess now I'm on nobody's list of suspects."

Hinkle stared at Odell for a long time and then said, "You planned it well, Drugo, and carried it off with style. It took a lot of sand."

"You don't believe Raven wanted to kill me?"

"Not a chance in hell."

"It could have happened that way. Who says it didn't happen that way?"

"But it didn't." With the whiskey taste sweet and smoky in his mouth, Hinkle added, "Drugo, you murdered Sarah Hollis and Alva Cranley, and tonight you murdered Ezra Raven, a Texas rancher. You had some kind of a relationship with Raven. Maybe he paid you to kill Kate Kerrigan. How am I doing?"

"Fine. But you couldn't prove all that before, and you sure as hell can't prove it now."

"But look on the good side, Drugo. I don't have to hang an innocent man for your crimes."

"Whoopee, Sheriff. What is he? A drover? Who cares if a drover lives or dies?"

"I do . . . and I guess he does. Maybe I can prove that you tried to kill Mrs. Kerrigan. In Dodge City, that's a hanging offense."

"Good luck with that, Hinkle. You'll never prove

that, either, especially after my heroics of tonight. And now, if you'll excuse me. The events of this busy evening have quite tired me out."

The bed creaked as Hinkle rose to his feet. "Know what I think of you, Drugo?"

The little gunman smiled. "No. But do tell."

"You're a piece of human filth. You should live in an outhouse with the rats."

"I've killed men for saying less."

"You won't kill me, not tonight. Another murder, especially of a lawman, would be hard to explain."

"Just don't push me any further, Hinkle." Odell smiled. "But here's more good news. I'm blowing this burg on the noon train tomorrow, going where my gun talent will be appreciated. Up Montana way maybe. I hear they're looking for range detectives to rid the range of nesters."

Hinkle stepped to the door. "This world will be a better place when your shadow no longer falls on the ground, Drugo. I hope I'm still around to hear where you're buried so I can piss on your grave."

"Trust me, Hinkle, you won't live that long."

CHAPTER TWENTY-EIGHT

"So that's it?" Kate said, her anger on the simmer.

"Yes, Mrs. Kerrigan, that's it," Sheriff George Hinkle said.

Kate said, "Suppose I shoot him myself?"

"Then I'd arrest you for murder."

"For killing a sewer rat?"

"The current penalty for killing a sewer rat is fifteen to twenty in a male penitentiary, Mrs. Kerrigan. The federal government makes no provision for the fairer sex," Hinkle said. "You got your puncher back alive, so let it be. Odell is leaving Dodge tomorrow on the noon train and he'll be out of your life forever."

"Isn't it about time you released Mr. Lowery?" Kate said, trembling as she tried to control her redheaded Irish temper.

Hinkle jangled his keys. "Of course."

Kate looked out the window. "When they planned to lynch Hank there was a big crowd. Now there's nobody."

Hinkle shrugged. "What do you want, Mrs. Kerrigan? A brass band? It ain't going to happen. Dodge doesn't want to be reminded that it tried to hang an innocent man." The sheriff stepped away and returned with Hank Lowery.

The man looked pale and he'd lost weight, but his blue eyes shone when he saw Kate and he smiled for the first time in days. "Thank you. Thank you for having faith in me, Mrs. Kerrigan."

He extended his hand, but Kate ignored that and hugged him. "Welcome back to the land of the living. Now we can all head home."

"Home. It has a fine ring to it," Lowery said.

Frank stuck out his hand and said a little stiffly, "Good to have you back."

Trace did the same, then said, "Hank, you look hungry. Did you have breakfast?"

Lowery looked at Hinkle. "No. Not even coffee."

Kate finally let her anger boil over. "Sheriff, you didn't even bring him coffee?"

"Mrs. Kerrigan, Lowery is a free man. I don't need to feed him at city expense any longer."

"He was still locked up in your darkest dungeon," Kate said.

"Yeah, but he was free to go and buy his own coffee."

"He was locked up, Sheriff," Kate said, her green eyes snapping.

"Please don't bandy words with me, Mrs. Kerrigan." Then, dropping his gaze to the floor, he added, "Truth is, I forgot all about him this morning. I had other things on my mind."

Kate opened her mouth to speak again, but Frank grinned and said, "Trace, we'd better get your mother out of here before she gets fifteen to twenty for assaulting an officer of the law."

"Forgot him indeed! Sheriff Hinkle, how could you?" She grabbed Lowery by the hand and stormed out the door, her high-heeled ankle boots thudding.

Hinkle looked at Frank. "Real purty gal, but I'll be glad to see the last of her."

Frank nodded. "A lot of men have said that very thing, Sheriff." He smiled. "I can't say as I blame you."

Fate will always find a way to intrude, for better or worse, on human existence. It did that morning in the steamy warmth of the Chop House restaurant in Dodge City, Kansas.

After leaving the sheriff's office, Frank and Trace had gone to the livery to check on the horses before the long trip to Texas. Kate, eager to make sure that Hank Lowery was fed, had accompanied him to the restaurant. She waited until he finished his steak and eggs and was drinking his third cup of coffee before she said, "So the man is getting away with murder."

"Seems like," Lowery said. "He would have stood by and let me hang. That's hard to take."

"Sheriff Hinkle told me that Odell said the life of a drover doesn't matter. It's what a killer would say, isn't it?" She sighed. "Odell is leaving Dodge on the noon train tomorrow, and we'll be well rid of him."

As Lowery smoked his morning cigar, the door opened . . . and Drugo Odell stepped inside.

The man hesitated and slowly looked around the restaurant, as is the way of the gunman. His gaze stopped at Kate Kerrigan, took in at a glance what she had to offer, and then slid briefly to Hank Lowery before dismissing him. Odell sat at an empty table where he could keep an eye on Kate and ordered coffee.

Kate leaned across the table and whispered, "That's—"

"I know who he is." Lowery answered the question on Kate's face. "In a saloon up on the Red River I saw him take on two named pistoleros and kill them both. Draws from a shoulder holster and he's fast, mighty fast."

Kate looked for fear in Lowery's face but saw none. "Do you think he recognized you?"

"I'm sitting with you, Mrs. Kerrigan, so I'm sure he's got a pretty good notion of who I am. But he won't remember me from back then. I was working as a waiter in that Fleetwood Saloon, and men like Drugo Odell don't remember waiters."

Kate said, "I'll pay our score and get out of here."

"You don't have to leave on my account, Mrs. Kerrigan."

"I know that, Hank, but I still think we should leave."

On the way out of the saloon, Odell smirked and said something under his breath. Lowery heard it clearly, but Kate didn't.

When they were outside in the street, she laid her hand on Lowery's arm. "What did that man say to me?"

"Nothing you need to hear, Mrs. Kerrigan." Lowery stared straight ahead. "Not now. Not ever."

CHAPTER TWENTY-NINE

"Do you know what you're doing?" Sheriff George Hinkle said.

"I've got my mind set on it," Hank Lowery said.

"He'll kill you, and there's nothing I'll be able to do about it. You kill an armed man and it's self-defense. Understand me? There's no argument, no shades of gray. Drugo Odell blows the smoke off his gun and rides the train."

"I'm aware of that."

"You can't shade him. He's too fast. He killed Morgan Braddock."

"I'll take my chances."

"Go get Frank Cobb. He's good with a gun."

"I'll do this on my own. I don't want Cobb to know . . . or Mrs. Kerrigan, either. This is between us, Hinkle."

"Where's your own revolver?"

"In the chuck wagon. Halfway to Texas by now."

Hinkle drew his Colt. "At noon today I won't be in town. Gonna find me a bucket of water out in the flat country somewhere and go fishing. I won't be here to help you, Lowery."

"I don't need your help. I can handle Drugo Odell. I saw him shoot one time."

After a few moments of silence, Hinkle said, "And?"

"And I'm faster." Lowery took the sheriff's Colt and looked it over. "You ever clean and oil this thing?"

"No."

"You got cleaning stuff and gun oil?"

"Sure. In my desk, right-hand drawer. Got an un-opened box of shells in there as well. Coffee's on the bile."

Lowery smiled. "Coffee? Feeling guilty about yesterday, huh?"

"You could say that." Hinkle crossed to the stove and poured coffee into a couple tin cups. He laid one on the desk in front of Lowery. "Clean that pistol real good and after your business is done, return it here. I'll be gone, but just lay it on the gun rack. And then—"

"And then what?"

"And then you and Mrs. Kerrigan get the hell out of my town."

Lowery smiled as he removed the rusty cylinder from the Colt. "Count on it."

"You want to tell me about the Longdale Massacre, Lowery? I never did hear the right of it."

"Some other time, Sheriff."

"There won't be another time," Hinkle said.

"Then when you tell your grandchildren about the time you had the man who pulled off the Longdale massacre in your jail, make up whatever pleases you."

"Maybe you won't like it."

Lowery smiled. "I never do."

"That's all Mr. Lowery said? That he was going to the bath house and then for a haircut and shave?" Kate said.

Trace nodded. "That was all, Ma. It was really early and we didn't speak much."

"Why were you up so early, Trace? You know I forbid you to not get enough sleep."

"I was headed for the outhouse, Ma. All that coffee I drank last—"

Kate said, "We will forgo the details, but I do think Mr. Lowery could have joined us for breakfast on this our last day in Dodge City."

"Man needs to get rid of the jailhouse stink, Kate," Frank said.

"Again, that is too much detail." She glanced around the crowded hotel dining room. "Not a cattleman in sight. It really is high time we were back in Texas."

"I'm all for that," Frank said. "I wonder how your pirate and his scurvy crew are doing with your new house?"

"Frank, I agree that Barrie Delaney is a pirate and a rogue, but I doubt his men have scurvy. As for my house, we'll soon see for ourselves, won't we? Please pass the butter. And the jam." Kate said, "No, Frank, the strawberry. I don't much care for blueberry."

Although she appeared calm, Kate's instinct for danger was sending out alarms and she said a silent

prayer that Hank Lowery would not run into Drugo
Odell. The gunman might shoot him out of spite.

The clock on the sheriff's office wall said eleven-
thirty as Hank Lowery shoved George Hinkle's Colt
into his waistband and stepped into Front Street. The
boardwalks were busy as matrons in cotton afternoon
dresses with demure collars and cuffs did their gro-
cery shopping. Of the sporting crowd there was no
sign and the fashionable Dodge City belles in their
bustled gowns were not yet taking the air. The day
was already stifling hot and the recent rains had left
puddles of mud everywhere.

Lowery walked past the cattle pens, empty now that
the season was over, his eyes fixed on the train depot
ahead of him. The place seemed deserted, but he
knew Drugo Odell was there. He could sense his presence. The man's malevolent evil reached out for
Lowery's throat like a grasping hand and all at once
the gambler found it hard to breathe. He stopped,
wiped the palm of his sweaty gun hand on his pants,
and continued walking.

A single set of stairs led to the platform, ticket
office, and the waiting rooms, one with a sign hanging above the door. LADIES ONLY. A tall, thin black
man wearing a shabby black coat to his ankles and a
collarless white shirt sat outside on a bench that
looked like a church pew and stared listlessly at the
rails. He seemed to be in his early fifties, but he could
have been younger. Either way, he ignored whatever
was happening around him and posed no threat.

Hank Lowery couldn't see Drugo Odell, but figured

he was inside the waiting room out of the sun and the growing heat of the day. There was no future in opening the waiting room door, stepping from bright sunlight into shade, and expecting Odell to wait politely before drawing down on him while his eyes adjusted to the gloom.

Lowery stayed where he was. He'd wait until Odell came out onto the platform and then call him out. The black man was minding his own business, still moodily staring at the rails, and wouldn't interfere. Besides, around these parts a black man didn't count for much.

Dressed in a broad-brimmed hat, boots, canvas pants, worn gray shirt, and red bandana, to the casual observer Lowery looked like any other puncher up from Texas with the herds, even if he was older than most. The Colt stuck into his waistband might give pause, but armed men were not rare in Dodge.

Long minutes passed. Fat blue flies from the stockyards buzzed in the corners of every windowpane and the black man, staring straight ahead, constantly brushed them away from his face. From the distance came the three-note whistle of an approaching train. The hands of the railroad clock in the ticket office were joined at noon.

The door of the waiting room opened and Drugo Odell, carrying a carpetbag in his left hand, stepped onto the platform. His eyes went to the black man who'd stood up, dismissed him, and settled on Lowery. Odell grinned and dropped the carpetbag, knowing why Hank Lowery was there. "Payback time, huh?" His hand blurred as it went for his gun.

Lowery drew. Even as his fingers closed on the

Colt's handle he realized he was a full second too slow. Odell's gun came up, the man still grinning, but then the morning exploded. Odell's back arched like a drawn bow as two barrels of buckshot slammed into him. Hit hard, he turned, his face shocked.

The black man held a smoking Greener in his hands. "That's for my sister. It's for Alva."

The Colt dropped from Odell's hand. He staggered a few steps, stunned and horrified at the time and manner of his death, and then crashed onto his back. His bowler hat fell from his head and rolled away on its rim before it stopped, spun a few times on its crown, and then lay still.

The locomotive, hissing steam, its bell ringing, drew to a clanking halt and the guard stepped onto the platform. The man peered at Drugo Odell, at the black blood pooling around his body, and then to Lowery.

"Wasn't me. I didn't shoot the bastard."

The guard had seen enough and he yelled, "All aboard!"

The black man, his shotgun again covered by his coat, stared at Lowery.

Lowery shoved the Colt back into his pants. "You'll miss your train."

The black man nodded. "Name's Eustace. Eustace Cranley."

"Good luck, Eustace."

"You, too, cowboy. Good luck." Cranley stepped into the train's only passenger car. The guard, in a hurry after one last glance at Odell's body, waved his flag and the locomotive lurched into motion.

Lowery watched the train until it was out of sight, only its column of dirty gray smoke still visible. Only then did he answer the horrified station agent's question. "I don't know who shot him."

"Somebody cut loose with a scattergun," the agent said.

Lowery nodded. "Seems like."

"I'd better go get the sheriff."

"As far as I know, he's gone fishing."

CHAPTER THIRTY

"Drugo Odell is dead." Hank Lowery toyed with the pork chop on his plate and didn't look up. "As dead as two barrels of double-aught buck can make him."

Kate was surprised. "Who shot him?"

"Black man by the name of Eustace Cranley." Lowery lifted his eyes to Kate's. "Alva Cranley's brother. I have a feeling he lived in this town, but he's gone now."

"Where did this happen, Hank?"

"The railroad depot. Odell came out of the waiting room to catch the noon train and Cranley cut him in half. Bang! Both barrels."

"Did you see the killing?" Frank said.

"Sure did. I was there to kill Odell, but the black man beat me to it."

Kate's face took on a horrified expression. "Hank, Odell could have killed you."

"He almost did. He was a sight faster on the draw than me." Lowery smiled. "Then Eustace cut loose and evened the odds."

"Where is Eustace now?" Kate asked.

"He left on the noon train . . . northbound."

"And Sheriff Hinkle?"

"George went fishing. He knew I intended to brace Drugo and he said he was going to fish in a bucket out on the grass. When he comes back he'll know I didn't kill Odell . . . that somebody else did."

Trace said, "Hank, will you tell him about the black man?"

"Nope. I didn't see a thing. The morning sun was in my eyes and the station was deserted. Somebody cut loose with a scattergun and blew out Odell's backbone. That's all I can tell him."

"Well, God forgive me for saying this, but I'm glad Odell is dead. And I'm glad you're alive, Hank." She let a frown gather between her eyebrows. "You will return to Texas with us, won't you?"

Lowery smiled. "Of course. I want to see your new house."

"Don't get your hopes up. But I tell you this. If Delaney has messed it up again I'll hang him myself."

Frank's eyes were hard, his mouth a tight line. "Lowery, you're not going back to Texas with us until you tell me what happened in Longdale."

"What is there to explain?"

"You can start by telling me how Levi Fry died."

Kate said, "Frank, we're leaving for home in an hour. Can't this wait?"

"No, it can't. I liked the old man and I want to know why Lowery killed him."

"Because he asked me to kill him." Lowery glanced at the faces of those sitting with him at the lunch table.

Kate looked puzzled and Frank appeared openly hostile. Trace, leaning forward in his seat, seemed greatly interested.

"I was twenty years old when I walked into the hotel

to avenge my brother's death. It was high time for a reckoning," Lowery said. "When I opened fire the shooting quickly became general. When it was over and men were dead or dying on the ground, Levi Fry was on his hands and knees, coughing up black blood. He'd been gut-shot, by me or one of his own men I don't know." Lowery looked Frank in the eye. "You ever see a gut-shot man die? No, that's not the question. This is. You ever *hear* a gut-shot man die in a place where there's no doctor and no morphine?"

"Yeah, I've heard it," Frank said, his face stiff, remembering.

"Levi Fry hadn't started to scream," Lowery said. "Not yet he hadn't, but it was only a matter of time. He asked me to kill him, end it. Both my guns were empty and I wore no cartridge belt. The old man didn't want to wait while I took a gun from one of the dead men. He reached into his pants pocket, handed me the .32, and said, 'Do it now. Back of the head. Quick.'" The shock had worn off and he was beginning to suffer."

"And you shot him," Frank said.

"Not right away. It didn't seem right to kill a man like that. Then he called down a terrible God's curse on me and screamed at me to shoot him. I was young and I got scared. The curse scared me. I panicked, put the muzzle of the Smith and Wesson to the back of his head, and pulled the trigger." Lowery dropped his fork onto his plate and it made a loud clang that startled Kate. "Levi Fry's curse has followed me to this day . . . and it will until the day I die a violent death."

"Our merciful God does not curse people, Hank," Kate said. "I will say a novena for divine mercy that your poor tormented soul may find peace."

Lowery smiled. "I think Frank would rather shoot me."

Frank was silent for a while and then spoke. "For a spell I'll study on what you said. Right now I can't figure the right or the wrong of it."

"Plenty of time for all that studying when we get back to Texas," Kate said. "It's time to shake off the dust of Kansas and head for home . . . and that includes you, Hank Lowery."

BOOK TWO
Gunfight at Eagle Pass

CHAPTER THIRTY-ONE

Kate Kerrigan returned home to trouble.

Her son Quinn said, "A rancher by the name of Hood Crane—"

"I believe he has a spread about sixty miles to the east of us," Kate said.

Quinn nodded. "Yes, he does, and it's a fair piece away, thank God."

"What was in the message he sent?" Frank said.

Quinn swallowed hard, his young face troubled. "There are cholera wagons headed our way. People are dying . . ." The sixteen-year-old took a paper from his shirt pocket. "Here, Ma, read the note for yourself."

Kate unfolded the paper and read.

CHOLERA WAGON TRAIN COMIN YOUR WAY. FOURTEEN WAGONS. FOLKS DYING EVERY DAY. SICKNESS AT THE ROCKING C. THREE HANDS DEAD. MY WIFE DYING. ME MIGHTY SICK. SAVE YOURSELFS AND GOD HELP YOU.

It was signed *H. Crane, Esq.*

Kate read it again and when she looked up her beautiful face was pale. "We have to stop them. Where is the rider who brought the note? Is he sick?"

"I don't think so," Quinn said. "At least not yet he isn't. He's up there on the rise."

"At the cemetery?" Kate said.

"It was the only place I could put him until I was sure he's not sick. He doesn't want to go back to the Rocking C. He says everybody there is already dead by this time."

"How long has he been up on the rise?" Kate said.

"Only since yesterday. I laid coffee and grub up there this morning and told him to come get it."

"I'll go talk with him. What's his name?"

"Verne Bohlen. He's a young feller, no more than eighteen at a guess."

"*Feller?* Quinn, do you mean fellow?"

"Yes, Ma. I meant to say *fellow.*"

"I sincerely hope you did. Frank, you come with me. Trace, you and Hank Lowery saddle up and scout for that wagon train, but keep your distance. Take some supplies, because you'll probably need to sleep out tonight. And don't forget your mackinaws. There's a fall chill in the air after sundown."

"Ma, should I go with Trace and Hank?" Quinn asked.

"No. I want you and Moses out on the range. Make sure that the men you hired are cutting and stacking hay and not loafing." Kate drained her coffee cup. "Frank, are you ready?"

He nodded and laid his napkin on the table. "That young feller . . . fellow . . . gets too close I'll shoot him."

"Is cholera so easily spread, Frank?"

"I don't know, Kate, but I sure as hell don't aim to find out."

"If the wagons keep coming this way we could be in serious trouble, couldn't we?" She addressed the question to Frank, but Moses, his mahogany face lined and serious, answered.

"Miz Kerrigan, if them wagons pass across your land, we could all get sick and most of us will die. I seen the cholera afore, back in the time when I was a slave, and I saw a fine plantation, slaves, overseers, Massa, Mistress, and their seven children, wiped out. The Massa bought a dozen new slaves that already had the cholera and that's all it took. Miz Kerrigan, the answer to your question is, yeah, we're in serious trouble. It's a time for prayin' and maybe for runnin'."

"I will not run," Kate said. "Be assured of that. I'll wait for Trace's report before I decide what to do."

Moses's dark face split into a lopsided grin. "Miz Kerrigan, with all respect, what this ain't is a time for waiting."

Kate said nothing, but his words deeply troubled her. Just how much time did they have? She was sure Trace would answer that question very soon. He had to.

When Kate and Frank Cobb stepped out of the cabin, Black Barrie Delaney approached them, swept off his hat, and made an elaborate bow. "I didn't hear you ride in last night, Kate me darlin'. It must have been uncommon late."

"Barrie Delaney, you didn't hear because you and your pirate rogues were probably sleeping off a drunk," Kate said.

"Ah, but isn't that the truth of it. It was Fighting

Tom Flanagan's fortieth birthday yesterday, and we made a day of it." Delaney's face was crafty as he waved a hand toward the partly constructed house. "Do you wish to inspect your prairie mansion now, Kate? See, the siding is up and the roof is shingled and when this fine dwelling is finished, why, you'll be so proud you wouldn't call a king your cousin."

Kate's eyes wandered over the two-story structure without noticeable enthusiasm. "I'll inspect it an hour, Captain Delaney. I'll have more time to hang you then."

Delaney grinned. "A hanging is it? And me with a beautiful surprise that will make your young heart sing."

"And what might that be? I thought you were done with piracy."

In his blue coat with its brass buttons, a cutlass and two revolvers thrust into a red sash, Delaney did look more sea wolf than builder. "No, not emeralds grabbed from the throat of a Spanish contessa, though surely such gems could only enhance your beauty, Kate. No, I'm talking bricks and plaster, aye, and the man who'll shape them into a pair of columns to grace the front of your plantation house."

"Ranch house," Kate said.

"Whatever it may be," Delaney said.

"Where is this man and who is he?"

"As to where"—Delaney waved—"he sits under yonder oak. As to who, his name Hargate Webbe, and a fine craftsman he is."

"He's tied to the tree," Kate said. "What villainy is this, Barrie Delaney?"

"And so he is tied to a tree," Delaney said. "Isn't it

said in the old country that the Kerrigans have the eyes of hawks?"

"You kidnapped him," Kate said.

"In a manner of speaking, yes."

"Then you will release him." She hesitated a moment and then fluttered her eyelashes at Delaney. "After he builds the columns, of course."

CHAPTER THIRTY-TWO

Verne Bohlen was a short, stocky young man with a round, pleasant face and deep-set hazel eyes. He wore dusty range clothes and had a Colt belted around his middle. He proved right from the git-go that he was no blushing violet.

"What the hell am I doing up here?" he said, his face red with anger. "I don't have the goddamned cholera."

"Mr. Bohlen, I presume," Kate said, smiling.

"Damn right. Texas born and bred and proud of it."

"I'm glad to see you looking so well, Mr. Bohlen. Doesn't he look well, Frank?"

Frank Cobb had already dismissed the youngster as just another eighteen-year-old trying to prove he was tough. "As well as can be expected, I guess."

"I ain't spending another night in this boneyard, I can tell you that." With the typical cowboy's dread of haunted places, Bohlen added, "Too many dead folk buried here. I've heard tell a man's hair can turn white overnight if he's around ha'nts an' boogeymen an' sich."

Frank glanced at Bohlen's carroty mop. "Not much chance of that happening to you."

"Well, as I said, you look healthy enough to me, Mr. Bohlen," Kate said. "Now tell me what happened at the Rocking-C."

"And then you'll give me back my hoss?"

"Yes, I will."

Bohlen's young face settled into a frown as he collected his thoughts, then he said, "The cholera wagons were already on Rocking-C range when a man rode up to the ranch house just after breakfast and said his wife and children were almighty sick and needed help. Mr. Crane and his wife, her name is Ellie, are good Christian folks, and they rode out with three of the hands to see what they could do to help. I reckon they're both dead by now. See, the cholera was already on the ground."

"Where were you?" Frank said.

"I was out on the range stacking hay. When I got back to the Rocking-C Mr. and Mrs. Crane had been among the wagons for two days. None of us had ever seen the cholera before, didn't know what it was, and that's how come Charlie York, Dave Brown, and Sam Nolan sickened and died." The young cowboy was distracted by a hawk in flight, his eyes on the sky for a few moments. "Mr. Crane brought his wife home. He stood off a ways, fired his rifle into the air, and when that got our attention, he yelled at everybody to clear out, that he was bringing death with him. Then he helped Mrs. Crane onto the ground and he wrote out a note on a page torn from his tally book, wrapped it around a rock, and chucked it in my direction. Mr. Crane told me to deliver it to the next ranch west of the Rocking-C. I was afraid to pick up the paper because it might have the sickness on it, but old man Crane and his wife had been good to me, so after a while I scooped up the note and brung it here."

Kate asked if he had any idea where the wagons were headed. "West I know, but going where?"

Bohlen said he didn't know, but then he said, "Mr. Crane drug a piece of board behind him, about the size of a door. He let it go before him and his wife went into the house. I rode past that board at a gallop and there was a word painted on it that I'd never seen before. It said *nirvana*. Any idea what that means?"

"Some woman's name, maybe?" Frank said.

Bohlen shrugged. "Beats me."

Kate said, "I don't know, either, but I'll ask Barrie Delaney. He's a scoundrel and a robber, but he's sailed all seven seas several times, and it's remarkable what he's learned."

"I can imagine." Frank nodded to Bohlen. "You can come get your horse and then ride."

"Damn right I'll ride," the young puncher said. "I want a heap of git between me and them plague wagons."

"When will they reach my range?" Kate said.

"Ma'am, I can't tell you that because I don't know," Bohlen said. "But I reckon it will be a lot sooner than you think or want."

CHAPTER THIRTY-THREE

Captain Barrie Delaney stroked his beard and turned to Kate, his eyes as black and bright as a sparrow's. "It is a thing you are asking, Kate, that has puzzled many a man and has sent a multitude of others on a quest to find it. Nirvana, is it? There's a word for a man to rassle with, and I'll grab it by the throat soon enough, lay to that." Black Barrie beamed, grinning from ear to ear. "Now look around you, Kate me darlin', as you can tell this house now stands steady enough to brave the fiercest tempest. There's no mighty wind or rain that will stove in her timbers, and you can lay to that." He waited, expecting Kate to say something, but she only stared at him, a slightly irritated glint in her eye. "So, says you, how did this miracle happen? Because, says I, I had that Chinese blacksmith of yours brace the frame with iron—"

"Marco Salas is Mexican," Kate said.

"Is that right? Well, I took him fer some kind of foreigner. Kate, we scoured the countryside around for iron and used it to support every stud and joist. And there she stands, a dwelling that will soon be fit for a queen . . . or a Kerrigan."

Kate stood in what would be the hallway of the house and looked around her. "It seems you've finally started to do a good job and earn your wages, Captain Delaney. And that's good, because I dislike hanging rogues on a Monday. Now, what about that word *Nirvana*?"

"Ah, well, here's the explanation of it, as best as I can describe," Delaney said. "In the Orient, in heathen Cathay and such places, the natives have a name for Heaven and they calls it Nirvana. It's a place where all suffering and carnal desire ceases and souls live in a constant state of bliss. Now that's not for a man of my ilk. Black Barrie wants a heaven where he can sail the old *Octopus* along o' the likes of Captain Kidd and Edward Teach, the one they called Blackbeard. A willing wench and a bottle of rum is nirvana enough for any lively sailorman, I'll be bound."

"You won't be lively, Barrie Delaney, not when you're dead," Kate said. "And by the way, that's not raindrops you feel. It's the Holy Virgin shedding tears over your sacrilege. Willing wenches and rum in heaven, indeed. I have never heard the like. Well, I won't talk of this again until later. Now, show me my columns and introduce me to the man who'll build them."

Delaney bowed. "Step this way, milady, and meet the finest worker in stone the world has ever seen."

"I'll be the judge of that." Then to Frank Cobb, "Could the KK Ranch be Nirvana to those people on the wagons?"

"Kate, I think anyplace they can escape the cholera will be their heaven."

"I'm worried, Frank."

"Sooner rather than later we need to make a decision, Kate, but let's wait to hear what Trace has to say. Maybe the wagons have stopped or turned."

"Is that likely?"

"No. I can't say that it is."

"It will be a terrible thing if we have to go to the gun," Kate said. "I don't even want to think about it. Women . . . children . . ."

Delaney said, "Beggin' your pardon, Kate, but me and my lads haven't built this fine house to see it destroyed by others. Aye, we know about the cholera. How many times have I seen it shipboard? Too many if the truth be told. But if it comes to slaughter you can depend on me and my brave lads to do our share and there's my hand on it."

Kate's hand disappeared inside Delaney's massive paw as she said, "I'll hope and pray that we will find another way."

"Aye, that's the ticket. While you sharpen your cutlass pray to the good Lord, Kate. That's always worked for Barrie Delaney. A divine hand has oft times guided my steel."

"You're a bloodthirsty rascal, Captain Delaney, and I doubt that the fear of the Lord is in you. I will say a prayer for you at my devotions tonight."

"And a sweet mercy it will be, Kate, for there's no worse sinner in all the world than the poor, frail wretch that stands before you," Delaney said. "And while you're at it, say a prayer for me poor auld father, hung as a pirate off Tortuga by the Portuguese on this very day twenty years ago."

"You're about as frail as a grizzly bear," Kate said,

"but I'll pray for your father's soul. And now I'll see your brick mason."

Delaney led the way to a ratty tent city he'd set up for his crew. Where he'd gotten the tents, most of them bearing US ARMY on their canvas, Kate did not dare guess. He stopped at one of the smaller tents guarded by a scar-faced ruffian with a Henry rifle.

"Kate me darlin', the name of the gentleman inside is Mr. Hargate Webbe, from Boston town, and he's an excitable cove, much given to hollering at the top of his voice." Delaney tapped the side of his nose. "But here's a lark. I can have my man Mad Fern Reed here cut out his tongue and shut his yap permanent, like."

"That will be quite unnecessary. Now raise the tent flap, Captain Delaney, if you please."

"I'll come with you, Kate," Frank said.

"No, I'll interview Mr. Webbe myself. The poor man needs compassion, not more threats," she said as she stepped into the tent.

"I have no wish to hang you, Mr. Webbe. Not over a trivial matter like a pair of columns."

Hargate Webbe was so outraged he spluttered, saliva flying from his mouth like water from a ruptured drainpipe. "That, madam, is unheard of. A threat against my person while a captive in your custody. The law shall hear of this."

"Oh, I know how menacing I must sound, dear Mr. Webbe, but in this neck of the woods I am the law."

"But—but I was kidnapped by thugs and dragged here against my will," the little man said. He wore a long leather coat and a top hat with goggles above the brim. A large pair of canvas gloves were thrust into his pocket. Tiny scars pockmarked his narrow face, the result, Kate guessed, of chips of stone flying from his chisel.

"You must forgive Captain Delaney," Kate said. "He's trying to make a life ashore for himself and he can be quite impulsive. I gave him the job of building my new home out of sympathy for his plight. His brig, the *Octopus,* lies anchored in Corpus Christi Bay, and I fear he vows to never walk her deck again."

"Black Barrie Delaney vows never to walk her deck again because he knows half the world's navies want to hang him," Webbe said. "For a full week the Boston newspapers were full of his exploits after he captured the clipper ship *Southern Cross* and stole her cargo of Chinese tea and porcelain. Many a God-fearing mariner went to the bottom that day and Black Barrie was the one who sent them there."

"Very distressing indeed, Mr. Webbe, but we can't believe everything we read in the papers, now can we?"

"Kate, do you need me?" Frank's voice came from outside.

"No, I'm just fine, thank you. I'm just setting dear Mr. Webbe to rights."

"Then let me put you to rights, Mrs. Kerrigan—"

"Ah, you know my name."

"Delaney didn't keep it a secret," Webbe said. "He told me you were beautiful, which you are, but he didn't tell me you hang folks."

Kate smiled. "Ah, the captain sees only the good in people, bless him."

"It wasn't him who kidnapped me from the building site. It was another set of villains, led by a blackguard his men called Coot Lawson. This Lawson rogue sold me to Delaney for fifty dollars and two jugs of Jamaica rum."

"That is doubly distressing," Kate said. "Selling a white man like a slave at auction is beyond barbaric. How much did Lawson charge for the columns?"

"Nothing. As far as I know. Lawson and Delaney are friends, sailed together before the mast on some pirate scow back before the war."

Kate decided to tread carefully, half-fearing what Webbe might have to say. She asked the question anyway. "Where were you building the house and for whom?"

"Where? Southeast of here on the Trinity. For whom? A gentlemen by the name of Lester Moorhead. He plans to use the house as a winter retreat away from the ice and snow of Vermont."

Kate smiled. "Ah, so he's a carpetbagger."

"What you Texans would call a Yankee, I suppose."

"No, Mr. Webbe, we never use the word *Yankee* to describe a northerner," Kate said. "We always put the word *damned* in front of it." She moved to the tent flap. "I'm so relieved it wasn't Texans building the house. Of course, I'll reimburse the owner for the columns. You'll enjoy working here, Mr. Webbe and I'll pay top wages once the columns are erected to my satisfaction on either side of my front door."

"Mrs. Kerrigan, I have no intention of working for you," Webbe said. "And I insist that you and your pirates release me instanter."

"That's not a very helpful attitude," Kate said, frowning.

"I'm not trying to be helpful."

Kate opened the tent flap. "Frank, could you step inside for a moment and shoot Mr. Webbe through the heart?"

"Here, that won't do." Webbe looked at Kate like a man with a toothache eyes a demented dentist. "You wouldn't dare."

Kate smiled. "Please forgive our little Texas ways. We do tend to shoot stubborn stonemasons out of hand." She placed her forefinger in the center of Webbe's chest. "Right there, I think, Frank. Do you wish me to take my finger away?"

"No, Kate, I can shoot around it." Frank raised his Colt.

"No! No! Stop!" Webbe said. "You're all mad. I'll build the columns."

"Are you sure, Mr. Webbe?" Kate said. "I don't wish to cause you any inconvenience."

"It's no inconvenience." To underscore the point, "No inconvenience at all."

"You're such a dear," Kate said. "Now go talk with Captain Delaney and he'll put you to work. Frank, you may put your revolver away. You've made poor Mr. Webbe come over all pale."

CHAPTER THIRTY-FOUR

Trace Kerrigan and Hank Lowery rode into the KK Ranch under a Comanche moon that bathed everything in mother-of-pearl light and deepened the shadows to an intense, cobalt blue.

Usually Trace was one of those bolt-upright riders who look as though they've an iron poker for a backbone, but that night he was bent over in the saddle supporting the slumped Lowery, and his hands were covered in blood.

"He's hurt bad," Trace said to Moses Rice, who a moment earlier had been one with the darkness.

"What happened?" Moses said.

"He got shot. Rifle shot."

"We'll get him into the cabin."

"Moses, what's going on?" Kate emerged from the gloom, dressing gown hurriedly tied around her waist. She carried a short-barreled Colt and the question on her face.

"Mr. Lowery got shot, Miz Kerrigan."

Frank appeared from the bunkhouse, pulling his suspenders over his vest, and asked the immediate question of a man schooled in the ways of gun wars. "Trace, who did it?"

"A fellow named Dobbs," the young man said. He and Moses helped the unconscious man out of the saddle. "Hank was shot after he tried to save an Indian woman."

"Gently now, inside with him," Kate said.

"The bunkhouse?" Frank said.

"You'll do no such thing. Bring him into the cabin."

Kate's daughters Ivy and Shannon, pale in the moonlight, moved aside from their position at the doorway as Lowery was carried inside.

Quinn had left the bunkhouse and said to Frank, "What happened?"

"Lowery got himself shot. That's all I know."

"Is he badly hurt?"

"You're standing on his blood. What does that tell you?"

Quinn leaped aside. "Damn!"

"Man bleeds like that, he's been hit hard."

"The bullet went right through him," Kate said.

Jazmin Salas stood with her. "Is that a good thing?"

"Good and bad. It means I don't have to dig for the bullet, but it means he's got two wounds instead of one." Kate looked up as Frank and Quinn stepped inside. "Frank, the bullet entered Hank's back just under his left shoulder blade and came out through his shirt pocket."

"He can't survive such a wound, Kate," Frank said. "All you can do is make him comfortable. He'll die soon."

"No. That is unthinkable," Kate said. "Hank will not

die because I won't allow him to die. Quick, help me get his shirt off. We have work to do."

"Ma, do you want to know what happened?" Trace said.

"Once I save Hank's life you can tell me. Now move the lamp closer. Jazmin, tear up my most worn tablecloth for rags and then wash them well with carbolic soap. And before you do that I'll need my sewing scissors. Trace, Quinn, you and the girls find a quiet place and say a rosary to Saint Fiacre of Breuil that he may ask the Blessed Virgin to assist my healing endeavors. Saint Fiacre was an Irishman born in County Kilkenny, so he will not turn a deaf ear to our prayers."

To Frank's considerable distress, Kate ordered Moses to bring the jug of the best Irish whiskey and then help Frank raise Lowery's upper body. Using a US Navy pocket surgical kit supplied by a concerned Barrie Delaney, whose massive presence, even wearing his blue coat over his nightgown, seemed to fill the entire cabin, Kate snipped away damaged tissue from the entry and exit wounds and then probed for and removed any foreign material, such as bone fragments, pieces of clothing, or dirt. By its very nature, this operation had to be thorough, and it took all of thirty minutes before she was satisfied that there was no more debris in the wounds. Lowery had groaned a few times as the pain of the probe lanced into his comatose brain, but he was now silent, his head lolling on his shoulders as Frank and Moses held him upright.

Kate picked up the whiskey jug. On its side, written around its entire circumference, were the words, *Jas. Connell & Sons Irish Whisky ~ The Best in Ireland By Far.*

Black Barrie Delaney cast an anxious eye on the jug. "And what will you do with that fine grog, Kate me darlin'?"

"I'll pour it on Hank's wounds to stop any possible infection." Her forehead was beaded with sweat, the strain and the heat of the cabin taking its toll.

"Ah, then maybe just a little will do it," Delaney said. "Is that not so, Mr. Cobb?"

Frank nodded. "I would guess so, Captain."

Kate ignored them both and poured the amber liquid liberally into Lowery's wounds. The jug made a *glug-glug-glug* sound as its contents rapidly diminished. "Now, Jazmin, bring the bandages, both the washed ones and some dry."

Kate passed the jug to Delaney, who quickly gauged the lack of liquid within and looked crestfallen. He tilted his head back and held the neck of the jug above his mouth. A single fat drop teetered on the rim for a few seconds and then fell. A miss. Sadly, Delaney wiped the bead of whiskey off his mustache.

After Kate bandaged Lowery, she said, "Now we'd better get him in bed."

"Trace and me will carry him to the bunkhouse," Frank said.

"You'll do no such thing," Kate said. "This man was at death's door until I saved him. Hank will rest in my bed."

Delaney winked at Frank. "Hey, Cobb, want to shoot me where it don't hurt too much?"

"And I will sleep with the girls," Kate said, slowly and with great emphasis. "Captain Delaney, if you knew that every time a Catholic has an impure thought

Our Lady hides her face for shame, would you be as quick to say what you just did?"

"Ah, no, Kate, I wouldn't. It is a poor sinner that I am, and the Blessed Virgin has shed many a salt tear over me."

"Of that I have no doubt," Kate said. "Now you men help me get Hank into my bed. And Barrie Delaney, don't you say another word."

CHAPTER THIRTY-FIVE

"The hour is late, but Trace must now tell us what happened and why Hank was shot. Captain Delaney, it's so kind of you to stay."

"My villainy has few limits, Kate, but when it comes to you I'll fight at your side, aye, even unto death," Delaney said.

With a teenager's forthrightness, Quinn said, "Why, Captain? You hardly know us."

"Hardly know, yes, that is right. But heard? Ah, I've heard much. Talk of a beautiful, flame-haired Irish lass who's building a cattle empire out of a wilderness and whose dear husband was killed in battle at Shiloh, leaving her young children orphans. That's why me and my lads came to this place, to see this lovely wonder of womanhood for ourselves . . . and to offer my hand in marriage."

"To who?" Quinn said.

"To whom?" Kate corrected.

"To you, dear Kate," Delaney said. "It is to you and to no other that I wish to pledge my troth."

Kate was flustered and Frank hid a grin behind his coffee cup.

"Captain Delaney, now is not the time to talk of such things," she said finally. "Trace, please relate the happenings of yesterday and let us know the where-abouts of the cholera wagons."

"What does 'pledge my troth' mean, Ma?" Shannon said. Her seven-year-old eyes round as coins were fixed on Delaney.

"I'll tell you later," Kate said. "We have much more urgent matters to discuss. Trace, you have the floor."

"The wagons are a day's ride to the west of us. Hank and me drew rein a fair piece away and I studied them through the brass telescope that Captain Delaney was kind enough to loan me."

"Did you hear that, Kate? Kind. Aye, Barrie Delaney is as kind as ever was and he'll be a kind and consid-erate husband, lay to that."

"Please, Captain Delaney, let Trace speak. You studied the wagons though a telescope and what did you discover?"

"I counted thirteen wagons drawn into a circle. They had fires going, so there are folks still alive. But one wagon was drawn off a ways by itself, maybe a quarter mile, and a man stood guard with a rifle while another sat by the fire and drank coffee."

"Did anyone see you?" Frank said. "Somebody that considered you a threat?"

"I don't think so, at least not then," Trace said. "It's rocky, broken country out that way, pretty flat, but we were hidden by some scrub oak. At least I thought we were. Then we saw the murder and that's the reason Hank got shot."

"You witnessed a murder?" Kate said.

"Yes, Ma, it was a murder all right, and I saw it happen . . ."

"Hey, Jesse, man leaving the wagons, headed this way." With a grin peppering his voice, Zebulon Magan said, "He's got hisself a gun and grown a pair of cojones."

"Is it Scanlon? Is it Newt Scanlon?" Jesse Dobbs asked.

"I can't tell yet. Looks like him. Hell yeah, it's him and his Pima woman is running after him, grabbing him by the coattails."

"Hell, the man is a pest," Dobbs said, rising to his feet. He smoothed his black, spade-shaped beard and adjusted the lie of his Remington. "I'll go talk to him. Give me your Winchester. I got to keep that bird at a distance."

Dobbs walked away from his wagon until he and Scanlon were separated by a hundred yards of rock, sand, and sun glare. "Stop right where you're at, Scanlon, and state your business."

"Damn you, Dobbs, you're my business. I've got people dying from the cholera and now what's left of the others are starving."

"What's that to me?"

"Dobbs, when you cleared out you took all the grub and clean water." Scanlon was tall, gaunt, and bearded and carried the death stench of the wagons on him.

"Scanlon, I'll say this to you for the last time so listen up. There are plenty of ranches west of here where you can get grub and help for your sick," Dobbs said. "I ain't your damn nursemaid."

Scanlon's wife, a tall, elegant woman with coal-black hair to her waist, pleaded with her husband to return to the *wagons. She spoke the complex Pima tongue, a language Dobbs did not understand, but he took advantage of the woman's tirade.*

"Listen to your wife, Scanlon. Go back to your wagon and then head west."

"West is where Nirvana lies, but we already brought death to one ranch. We will not do it to another," Scanlon said. "We have talked about this and will stay where we are until the cholera has run its course."

Dobbs shrugged. "Suit yourself."

"Brother Nathanial Miller found a spring with good water, but we need food to sustain us while we clean and refill our barrels."

"Turn around, Scanlon, go back to Jonesboro where you belong. Plenty of grub there."

"In Jonesboro you promised to lead us to Nirvana. You lied to us."

"Hell, I didn't know you were all gonna get sick," Dobbs said. "Besides, there is no Nirvana. There's nothing across the Mexican border but sand . . . hundreds of miles of sand, thornbush, and buzzards."

"You told us that with your own eyes you'd seen a land of milk and honey just twenty miles south of the Rio Grande," Scanlon said.

Dobbs grinned. "Yeah, well I lied, didn't I? That country down there ain't Nirvana. It's Hell." He lowered his rifle. "Well, been good talking with you, Scanlon, but me and Zeb Magan got to be moving on, headed for the New Mexico Territory."

Scanlon's face purpled with anger. "Damn you, Dobbs!" he roared. "You're going nowhere unless you leave behind the grub and whatever medicines you have."

Newt Scanlon made bad mistakes one after another.

His first was that he underestimated just how vicious and uncaring a career criminal could be. The second was not to heed his wife, who begged him in tears to return to the wagons. His third and fatal blunder was to try to run a bluff with a rusty .32 revolver he'd never fired before.

The three bullets that Jesse Dobbs slammed into Scanlon's chest could have been covered by a playing card and summed up the man's mistakes nicely, dropping him stone dead on the ground.

The Pima woman screamed and lunged for her husband's gun. Dobbs raised his rifle and an instant later yelled, "What the hell?" as bullets kicked up exclamation marks of dirt around his feet. His head swiveled around on his shoulders. Who was taking pots at him?

Kate said, "Hank grabbed your rifle from the boot under your knee? Trace, you couldn't stop him?"

"No, Ma, it happened too fast. He rode forward onto the rock ledge in front of the wild oaks and cut loose at the man called Dobbs. I guess the range was maybe fifty yards, but Hank wasn't trying to kill him. He was trying to stop him from shooting the Indian woman."

"Damn stupid thing to do," Frank said. "Why didn't Lowery just put a bullet into him, for God's sake?"

"Because he's made some kind of vow not to take another human life and I guess he's determined to stand by it," Trace said.

"Holy Joe. That ain't much good in West Texas," Frank said.

"That will do, Frank," Kate said. "Hank Lowery has

become a man of peace and we must respect him for that."

"And look where that got him," Frank said. "Men of peace don't last long in West Texas."

"No sir," Moses said, grinning. Then, as Kate glared at him, he wished he hadn't said it.

"How was Hank wounded?" Kate said after one last glare at Moses.

"Dobbs spotted him and fired. Hank slumped in the saddle and I dismounted to help him. He dropped my rifle after he was hit and I used it to drive Dobbs and the other man into the cover of their wagon, but they were still shooting. After I saw the woman dragged back into the wagon circle I knew I had to get Hank out of there. I led his horse into the oaks and then we lit a shuck for the KK."

Kate glanced at the front window, still a rectangle of darkness. She lifted the coffeepot and held it up. "Anyone?" She refilled Frank's cup and then her own. "We ride out at first light. I will hang this Dobbs person for murder and if, despite my ministrations, Hank should die, I'll cut him down and hang him twice."

Frank smiled. "Not one to hold a grudge, are you, Kate?"

"I will see justice done, Frank. In this part of Texas I'm the only law." The little calico kitten she had rescued in Dodge sprang onto her lap, opened her pink mouth in a yawn, curled up in a ball, and promptly fell asleep.

Frank glanced around the table. "Anyone else put away their guns and become a man of peace? How about you, Captain Delaney?"

"You won't live long enough to see that day, Mr. Cobb." Delaney slapped the revolvers thrust into his sash. "These cannons have loosed many a broadside and are minded to loose a few more should the need arise."

"It will arise, Captain," Frank said. "You can depend on it."

"Then, says I, Black Barrie Delaney stands ready to run out his guns."

CHAPTER THIRTY-SIX

The dawn threw wide the curtains of the night and welcomed the morning sun as Kate led her small posse into the badlands.

Behind her rode Frank, Trace, and Delaney. Quinn had been left behind to help Moses with hay cutting while Jazmin and the girls did chores and cared for Hank Lowery. Kate, never an enthusiastic housekeeper, relied on Ivy and Shannon to keep the cabin swept and clean, the beds made, and the pots, pans, and dishes washed and put away. Those tasks and others like ironing and cooking were totally alien to Kate and she made no secret of that fact. She could handle a Colt and a Winchester as well as, if not better than, most men, but she threw up her hands in despair at the prospect of boiling an egg. When she set her mind to it, she could bake a tasty sponge cake, and most folks agreed that was to her credit.

Kate drew rein. "The rifleman's wagon should be here. Where is it?"

Frank stepped out of the saddle, got down on one knee, and studied the rocky ground. After a while he rose and scouted the area and then stepped back to Kate and the others. "My guess is that they pulled out during the night and are headed due south. A team of big horses is pulling that wagon, Kate, and the wheels dig in mighty deep."

Kate was only half-listening. Her gaze stretched out across a wilderness of sand, scrub, cactus, and scrawny wild oak to the circled cholera wagons, smoke from several fires rising into the air like sooty thumbprints against the blue sky. Finally she said, "Frank, is there anything we can do for those people?"

"No, there's nothing, but if they don't come any farther west they present no danger."

"I can smell those wagons from here, same as I've smelled plague ships from half a league away," Delaney said.

"It smells like rotten fish," Trace said.

"Aye, lad, that's the stench of the Asiatic cholera that comes to our shores from foreign lands," Delaney said. "I've seen it kill a ship's crew in a single day and I saw that same ship run herself aground on a lee shore with a dead man at the wheel and corpses hanging in the rigging like rotten fruit."

Kate said softly, "Frank . . ."

"I see him." Frank drew his gun. "If he tries to get any closer I'll kill him."

But the man had stopped when he was still a fair ways off. He cupped hands to his mouth and yelled, "Last night, two dead out of the same family, a young girl and a six-year-old boy. This morning before sunup sister Edith Chigwell died of the cholera and brother Elisha Hardy is mighty sick. We have no grub. The fires are burning to keep the flies and the carrion crows away from the hurting dead."

Kate put a hand to her mouth and yelled, "We will bring—" She realized her voice was not equal to the task. "Frank, tell the man we will bring him food."

Frank hollered that promise and the man waved.

He called out, "We may all be dead soon but I appreciate your concern."

Then from Trace came, "Rider coming."

"Where away?" Delaney said. "Scrub around that. I see him."

Fall was cracking down but stubborn summer heat still seared the badlands. To the west the rider came on at a walk through a rippling haze that elongated both horse and man like a skinny frontier Don Quixote astride Rocinante.

"He's headed straight for the wagons," Kate said. "Trace, go warn him away."

"Right, Ma." Trace kicked his mount into motion and galloped in the oncoming rider's direction.

"I hope that ranny is a right trusting feller," Frank said.

He wasn't.

The rider drew rein and slid a rifle out from under his knee. He placed the butt on his right thigh, held the Winchester upright, and waited . . .

Trace was young, but he was danger savvy and he reined in his horse to a walk.

"That's far enough," the rider said when Trace got within twenty-five yards. "I'm not a trusting man, and this here Winchester gun is wife and child to me. You don't want to hear it speak."

Trace bit back the sharp retort that was on the tip of his tongue and said, "Cholera in the wagons."

The rider lost a little of his composure. He was a tall, gloomy-faced man with a big Texas mustache that drooped under his nose like something dead. He turned his head and glanced at the wagon circle. "The hell you say?"

"Yeah, that's what I say. And hell is right over there."

"You don't scare worth a damn, do you, kid?" the rider said.

"Nope."

"That your kin on the ridge?"

"My ma, Kate Kerrigan, owner of the KK ranch. Got Frank Cobb, her *segundo,* with her and Captain Barrie Delaney."

"A soldier or a sailorman?"

"Sailorman. He's building a house for my ma."

"Is that a fact? I never afore cottoned to the fact that sailormen build houses."

"That one does . . . after a fashion."

The rider fell into silence for a few moments, then said, "My name is JC Brewster. I'm a Texas Ranger, and why they call me JC is because my folks couldn't come up with anything better. And you?"

"Trace."

"Your folks couldn't come up with anything better, either, huh? Here's your ma and she looks like she's mad at somebody." JC seemed even gloomier. "Probably me."

"Who are you and what is your business here and why are you threatening my son?" Kate was flanked by Frank and Delaney.

"Ma, this gentleman's name is JC Brewster and he's a Texas Ranger. He didn't threaten me . . . much."

"I'm in pursuit of a couple outlaws who robbed a Fort Stockton army payroll and murdered the paymasters and the two guards." Brewster slid his rifle back into the boot. "They go by the names of Zebulon Magan and Jesse Dobbs. Magan is a killer, but he isn't a patch on Dobbs. Don't you worry your pretty little head, ma'am. They won't come back this way. They know I'm tracking them."

"Ranger, my name is Kate Kerrigan and I can take care of myself. Yesterday, my son exchanged shots with the criminals you describe after they shot one of my hands."

"Is he dead?" Brewster said.

"No, he is not. He's severely wounded, but I will nurse him back to health."

"Frank, that's why the wagon wheel ruts are so deep," Trace said.

"You're right about that, son." Brewster looked to be in his early forties, but he could have been years younger or older. "Thirty thousand in gold, silver, and scrip weighs a considerable piece."

Kate told Trace to describe the events of the previous day, including the murder of Newt Scanlon and Dobbs's attempt on the life of the Pima woman.

Brewster listened attentively. When Trace finished speaking, he said, "Then Dobbs will hang for murder."

"Tracks head south, Ranger," Trace said.

"I know, but then they swung west." Brewster saw the questions on the faces around him. "I already scouted the country south of here. I found the wagon, but the money and the horses were gone. I figure Jesse decided the wagon was slowing him down and he and Zeb loaded the money sacks onto the team."

The Ranger's eyes moved to the wagons. "I heard Jesse had hooked up with a bunch of folks looking for serenity and salvation, but I never paid it much mind until now."

"All they found was cholera," Kate said. "And now they're starving. I plan to feed them."

"It's a good Christian's duty to feed the hungry and nurse the sick, Mrs. Kerrigan, but when it comes to cholera, those rules don't apply." The Ranger rubbed the stubble on his throat. "There's a complication here."

"And what's that?" Kate said.

"I got a telegram in San Angelo that Jesse plans to meet up with his brother Seth and a pair of lowlifes by the names of Ben Lucas and Bob Corcoran who just broke out of Huntsville. The five plan to cross into Old Mexico at Eagle Pass, but I don't think they've got together yet. Young feller, you said you saw only one man with Jesse, right?"

"There were only two of them," Trace said.

"Then I got to stop them from joining forces," Brewster said.

"Seems like you need help," Frank said. "Are there other Rangers to back your play?"

Brewster shook his head. "Hell no. I don't need help. One Ranger is a handful, two is an army, and I don't need an army." He glanced at the sky and then said, almost bashfully, to Kate, "Ma'am, I've been doing some long riding and for the past three days all I've eaten is a piece of jerky and my own dust. If your ranch is close, I'd surely like to belly up to a mess of bacon and beans."

"My ranch is close and I'm sure we can do better than bacon and beans," Kate said. "Ranger Brewster, you're welcome to join us for supper."

Brewster touched his hat. "Much obliged, ma'am. I took ye fer a fine lady the first time I set eyes on you and I wasn't disappointed."

Frank said, "Ranger, I don't want to stand between a man and his grub, but—"

"Why am I not following them wagon tracks?"

"That was my general way of thinking."

"A couple of reasons, Mr. Cobb. For one, when Jesse and his boys meet up, the payroll money will be burning a hole in their pockets. There's whiskey and women in Eagle Pass, just what Seth and them need after three years in Huntsville. Jesse figures he shook me off his trail a while back and he'll linger in town for a spell before he crosses the Rio Grande into Old Mexico."

"Then it's time we got back to the KK," Kate said. "Jazmin and I still have enough daylight left to load up supplies for the people in the wagons."

"Mrs. Kerrigan," Brewster said, his long face as gloomy as a bloodhound with a bellyache, "them folks are already dead. I was scouting for the army when the cholera struck Ellsworth and folks died in the hundreds. There's nothing we can do for them pilgrims. We can't even bury them."

"Perhaps, but I intend to do what I can," Kate said. "With God's help, of course."

Chapter Thirty-seven

When Kate Kerrigan returned to the ranch, Hank Lowery's condition had not improved, but he was no worse and she took that as a positive sign.

Despite Frank's protests she refused to take him along to the wagons as a guard. He and Trace were needed on the range. With winter so close, cutting hay, a tedious, laborious task, was not a job that could wait.

"Jazmin and I will drop the supplies and come right back," Kate said.

"Take Captain Delaney or one of his crewmen along," Frank said.

"No, Frank. I want Barrie and his men working on my house before the colder weather hits." She smiled. "We'll be quite safe, you know. You heard what the Ranger said. The outlaws are headed for Eagle Pass, miles from here."

"Kate, I have a bad feeling about this."

"Frank, you have bad feelings about everything and nothing ever comes of them."

"Can you say that about Drugo Odell, Kate?"

"I think we all had bad feelings about him." She climbed into the seat of the ranch buckboard beside Jazmin. "Don't worry about us, Frank. We'll be home well before dark to make sure Ranger Brewster gets his supper." She passed her Winchester to Jazmin and slapped the team into motion.

"Marco made this for the sick people." Jazmin picked up a large cross of forged iron. "He says it might comfort them."

"Your husband is a thoughtful man and a fine blacksmith," Kate said. "I feel so lucky to have him."

"I think he's worried," Jazmin said.

"He's been listening to Frank, I think."

"Marco says that Santa Muerte, the Angel of Death, will hover near the plague wagons. If we meet her we must bow our heads because she is a very powerful goddess and must be treated with great respect."

"And I will say a prayer to the Blessed Virgin and ask her protection," Kate said.

Jazmin nodded. "That is good, because the Blessed Virgin is also a mighty goddess."

Kate did not think it the place and time to set Jazmin right on the status of the Holy Mother, but she made a mental note to instruct her at the earliest possible moment.

Something was wrong. A jagged crack in the day. The quietness of the insects, the lack of birds, and the air of menace that Kate inhaled like a bad odor sounded an alarm inside her.

Jazmin felt it, too. "Santa Muerte is close," she whispered.

"Something is close." Kate grabbed the Winchester and levered a round into the chamber. The wagon seat was not a good fighting platform and she dropped to the ground and motioned to Jazmin to do the same. Something was out there, close. Kate couldn't see anything but rock, cactus, and a land dry as dust. In the old days, she would have suspected Apaches in hiding, but like the Comanche, they were long gone and all the dangers they'd brought to Texas had gone with them. Who . . . or what . . . was stalking her?

Kate stepped to the back of the wagon and again studied the terrain. There was no sound and nothing moved. She waited. The feeling that she was being watched was a palpable thing that made her skin crawl. It was as though the exploring, blue-veined hand of an aged lover was violating her body.

A step. Behind her!

Kate swung around, the Winchester ready in her hands. A bearded man came at her. His grin was fixed, amused, nasty, and he held a knife in his right hand. Kate had only a split second to react, no time to think it through. She triggered the rifle and slammed a shot into the center of the man's buckskinned chest. He stopped, stared stupidly at what he knew was a death wound, then staggered toward Kate, knife upraised, his face savage. Kate levered the Winchester. She heard Jazmin scream as though from the end of a long tunnel. She fired again. The belly shot sent the man to his knees. He had time to meet Kate's eyes for just a split second. His own were clouded in disbelief at the nearness of his death and then he pitched forward on his face and the darkness took him.

Kate turned in time to see a man drag Jazmin from the back of the buckboard. She worked the Winchester, but then strong arms grabbed her from behind and wrenched the rifle from her hands. Kate fought like a tigress, but the man was big, huge in the chest and shoulders. He held her at arm's length with his left fist and backhanded her across the face with a wicked right. She fell and rolled away from the man's swinging boot. Dust rising around, her head ringing, she staggered to her feet, her eyes blazing. Her hand almost dropped for the Remington derringer in the pocket of her plain cotton dress, but she hesitated. Her assailant had a Colt, hammer back in his hand, and she realized she was up against a stacked deck.

"You've lived too long, lady," the man said, a surly, scar-faced brute with black eyes of a creature that eats the dead. He raised his revolver.

"No, Ben!" the other man yelled. He had an arm around Jazmin's waist. "You know how much that red-headed witch will bring in Chihuahua?"

The man called Ben's gun was still pointed at Kate's head. Without turning he said, "How much?"

"A small fortune. Too much to throw away."

"She killed Seth," Ben Lucas said.

"Yeah, well, the woman is worth a sight more than Seth and now there's one less to share the army payroll."

Lucas thumbed down the hammer and slid the Colt into his holster. He jutted his chin in the direction of Kate. "You want a taste, Bob?"

Bob Corcoran said, "Hell, sure I do, Ben, but let's keep her for Jesse. He'll like that."

"Like that? She gunned his brother," Lucas said.

"Yeah, but even at the best of times he was never too fond of Seth. You know he wasn't."

"How much will Jesse give us for her?" Lucas said.

"An even thousand."

"No woman is worth that."

"This one is, and more." Corcoran pulled Jazmin closer. "Besides, we got this Mexican mare all to ourselves."

"Harm her and I swear to God I'll see both of you hang," Kate said.

Corcoran changed tactics. "What's in the wagon?"

"Supplies for a stranded wagon train," Kate said. "The people are sick and they need food."

"Heard about that. They got the cholera. Ain't that right?"

Kate said, "That is correct. I'm sorry about your friend, but we must be on our way or my men will come looking for us."

"Men? What men?" Ben Lucas grinned. His teeth under his mustache looked like yellowed piano keys. "You got a bunch of husbands, pretty lady?"

Kate again thought about the derringer. Only two shots from a pistol that was both inaccurate at distance and awkward to shoot. Against gunmen like these two, she wouldn't stand a chance. She put the idea out of her head and said, "My name is Kate Kerrigan and my ranch is nearby. Perhaps you've heard of Frank Cobb, my *segundo*. Behind him he'll have a dozen riders, all well-armed and determined men."

Corcoran was taken aback. "Big ranch?"

"The KK is big enough."

"You go up the trail to Dodge last summer?"

"Yes, I did, with three thousand head."

"Get a good price for the herd?"

"It was sufficient."

Corcoran looked at Lucas. "Ben, are you thinking what I'm thinking?"

"I'm way ahead of you." Lucas stepped to Kate, grabbed her by the upper arm, and ducked the looping left she swung at his chin with her free hand. "Help me tie up this hellcat, Bob, and then we got some serious talking to do."

Kate collected some bruises and so did Lucas and Corcoran before she was bound, gagged, and tied to one of the buckboard's wheels.

Jazmin kneeled beside her and used a small handkerchief to dab a trickle of blood from her mouth. "Mr. Cobb and Trace will come looking for us soon, Miss Kate. And then you'll be free."

Kate nodded and smiled under the bandana that tightly covered her mouth, but she knew it could be a couple hours before Frank felt sufficiently alarmed to come searching for her. And by that time . . . well, she had no idea. Whatever was to come would not be pleasant.

Lucas and Corcoran had retrieved their horses from the dry wash where they'd been hidden and had tethered them to the wagon. They stood on the other side, away from the women.

"I asked you once, and I'll ask you again," Lucas said. "Can you shade Jesse Dobbs on the draw?"

Corcoran sighed. "And I'll tell you what I told you before . . . I don't know."

Lucas threw up his hands, "Man, this is impossible. I need an answer."

"Can you shade him?" Corcoran said.

"No. There, I said it plain. No, I can't."

Corcoran said, "Then I'll bide my time, shove my gun into his face, and pull the trigger. *Bam!* His damn skull explodes."

"That will do . . . if you can get close."

"Man's got to let his guard down sometime. Hell, Jesse James was straightening a picture on the wall when Bob Ford got close and scattered his brains. It can be done. Once we get to Eagle Pass I can get near to Dobbs."

"What about Zeb Magan?" Lucas said.

"What about him?"

"Should he worry me?"

"He's a two-bit chicken thief," Corcoran said. "I can take care of him."

"All right, then here's how I see it, Bob. Here's the play. We do for Jesse and the other feller and the payroll becomes a two-way split. A straight fifty-fifty, no ifs, buts, or maybes."

Corcoran extended his hand. "Amigos, in prison and out."

Lucas took the other's hand and said, "We trust each other, Bob, and that goes a long way."

"Damn right it does," Corcoran said. "We're good pals, me and you."

"Then to sweeten the pot, we let the Mex gal go and give her a hoss and a ransom note. This ransom note." Lucas held out a scrap of paper.

Corcoran took it and read, his lips moving.

BRING TEN THOUSAND DOLLARS
TO EAGLE PASS OR KATE KERAGAN DIES.
NO LAW OR ELSE.
FROM TWO GOOD PALS.

"But how are them boys gonna know how to con-
tact us with the money?" Corcoran asked.

"That's their problem. If they ever want to see
their woman boss alive again, they'd better figure a
way. If they don't, we'll take her to Mexico with us as
merchandise. Either way, we win."

CHAPTER THIRTY-EIGHT

"I'll ram my cutlass into their guts and spit in their eyes as they writhe like speared fish on my blade," Captain Black Barrie Delaney said after he'd read the ransom note. "I'll use their guts for me garters, damn them. Strike me down dead this very minute if I don't."

Only half-listening to Delaney's bloodthirsty rant, Trace said, "Frank, when do we ride? I'll bring Quinn off the range."

"Quinn stays where he is, Trace, and so do you," Frank said. "Captain Delaney, you and your cutlass remain as well. Get Kate's house finished."

"And what about you?" Delaney said.

"I'm going alone. Well, with Ranger Brewster, I guess."

"You can count me in," Brewster said.

Anger flared in Trace's face. "Why can't I go? She's my mother."

"And that's why you're staying here at the ranch," Frank said. "I don't need a reckless kid going off half-cocked and announcing to everybody who'll listen that you're in Eagle Pass to rescue your ma."

"I wouldn't do that," Trace said.

"You don't know what you'd do," Frank said. "I don't want you scaring the kidnappers. Abducting a woman is a hanging offense in Texas, and if they panic and want to get rid of the evidence, Kate's life will be in danger. Working by ourselves, Brewster and me can find her without rousing suspicion."

"Frank is right, youngster." Brewster held a huge wedge of apple pie in his hand. "I reckon one of the pals is Jesse Dobbs's brother Seth and the other is either Ben Lucas or Bob Corcoran. If they suspect a trap, they'll kill Mrs. Kerrigan or take her across the Rio Grande and sell her in Mexico."

"Sell my mother?" Trace said.

"There are rich men across the border who'll buy a pretty woman," Brewster said.

"As a slave?"

"Yeah, a special kind of slave." He saw the shock in Trace's face and said, "Don't worry, son. We'll bring your ma back safe and sound."

Frank said. "I just had a thought. Do you think the presence of a ranger in Eagle Pass will tell Seth Dobbs that there's something wrong?"

"Hell, Seth has never seen me and neither has Jesse," Brewster said. "And another thing, do I look like a ranger to you?"

Frank smiled, giving Brewster the once-over from the battered crown of his hat to his scuffed, down-at-the-heel boots. The man wore his holstered Colt as though it was an afterthought and his sad brown eyes held no aggression. He looked about as danger-ous as a circuit preacher.

"JC, you're right. You don't look like a ranger. You don't look like any kind of lawman."

Brewster smiled. "Gives me an edge when I come up against draw fighters like you, Frank."

"You pegged me, huh?"

"Not too difficult," Brewster said. "You got the gunman look. Something in your eyes draws folks' attention."

"I don't mind looking look like a gunman in Eagle Pass. Plenty of them around that town from both sides of the border. I'll be a face in the crowd is all."

Trace's protests and Delaney's claim that Kate pretty near agreed to be his betrothed and was thus as near to being his bride, "dammit," had no effect. Frank and JC Brewster rode out together the next day at first light.

There was no real hurry.

The terrain between the KK Ranch and Eagle Pass was flat, rocky country where their dust would be seen for miles and warn Seth Dobbs that riders were on his back trail. Frank's bid to free Kate must happen in Eagle Pass, not in an open landscape where a man with good eyes could see forever.

They carried no money. Kate would never agree to pay a ransom . . . even for herself. What had to be done must be accomplished by the gun and there was no way around that.

CHAPTER THIRTY-NINE

Apart from a sack of coffee and some sugar, Ben Lucas and Bob Corcoran had dumped the supplies for the cholera wagons and had taken great delight in ruining what they didn't want. Flour lay scattered over the ground as though there had been a snowfall.

Bound hand and foot, Kate had been thrown into the empty buckboard and driven away

Across the broken country north of Eagle Pass, the buckboard bounced. Around Kate lay a wasteland of scattered mesquite, a few live oak, cat's claw, *huajilla, cenizo*, and prickly pear, all of it struggling to survive on limestone bedrock. Of people or animals there was no sign. She knew that Frank would not follow closely, but that realization only increased her feeling of isolation and vulnerability. Thank God the derringer had not fallen out of her pocket during her struggles with her two captors. The weight of the little pistol in her pocket brought her comfort, slight as it was.

Kate had long since ceased to struggle against the

ropes that bound her so tightly, and she lay on her back and watched the light change as the day shaded into night and a horned moon rose and gored aside the first stars. The desert smelled of dust and rock. She was thirsty, but would not ask her captors for water. She imagined that in all the vast expanse of barren wilderness somewhere lime green frogs dived into a blue, ice-cold pool, each one making a soft *plop!* under the overhanging ferns.

Despite her discomfort, Kate dozed. She was aware that the two men made a stop and cigar smoke drifted over her as they passed a bottle back and forth between them. Half an hour later the team once again lurched into motion.

At first light, she woke to the smell of boiling coffee. Ben Corcoran brought her a cup that she didn't refuse. What was it her grandmother used to say? Ah yes. *Don't cut off your nose to spite your face.* The coffee was strong, bitter, and black as mortal sin but it tasted heavenly.

The sun was just over the eastern horizon when Corcoran climbed into the buckboard's seat and **Ben** Lucas mounted and took up his station a few yards to the rear where he could keep his eyes on Kate and his back trail.

Turning his head, Corcoran said, "You'll be the guest of Tilly Madison until we get the ransom money. She has a cabin a mile outside of town."

"Who is she, may I ask?" Kate said.

Corcoran grinned. "Sure you can ask. She's a hunchback who done for seven husbands, maybe more. Before she gives you anything to eat or drink make sure she tastes it first." Corcoran thought that last very amusing and launched into a roar of laughter. After he regained his composure and wiped a tear from his eyes, he said, "Some say Tilly is a witch and she probably is."

"Did you say *witch* or . . . something else?" Kate asked.

"She's both." He laughed again and slapped his thigh.

The Madison cabin lay close to a narrow creek that was dry for nine months of the year. Nearby a single cottonwood struggled for life and cast thin shade onto the cabin's tarpaper roof. When the buckboard rattled to a halt, the door opened and a small, bent old crone with an incredibly wrinkled face stepped outside.

Kate thought Tilly Madison looked like a wicked witch in a child's picture book . . . but instead of a broom she held a .44-40 Winchester in her hands.

Her voice sounded like a rusty gate. "Hell, I heard you two had been hung fer outlaws in Huntsville. I see I was told wrong."

"Yeah, Tilly, we're still kicking," Corcoran said. "Jesse Dobbs pass this way?"

"I ain't seen him. Who's that in the wagon?"

"A guest. We want you to take good care of her."

"She looks hoity-toity."

"She is," Corcoran said. "Her name's Kate Kerrigan and she owns a ranch northwest of here. She's worth a pile of money to us."

"Her kind doesn't come cheap," Tilly said. "Not

when it's crowned with red hair. You, Ben Lucas, get her down from there and let me take a look at her."

When Lucas pulled Kate out of the buckboard and she stood in front of Tilly, the old woman said, "Look at those bold, insolent eyes. No mistake what she is."

"I'm a respectable, widowed woman and I'll ask you to keep a civil tongue in your head, missy," Kate said. "If you don't, I'll slap your face."

"And I'll ask you to get off my property"—Tilly leveled the rifle—"if you know what's good for you."

"Tilly, the woman is worth thousands of dollars to us," Corcoran said. "Harm her in any way and you'll deal with Jesse."

The old woman's face changed, showing fear. "He's a rum one, is Jesse. Got a demon in him. One time I heard it. Said to me that its name was Malphas, a great prince of hell."

Corcoran said, "So now you know. Best you do what we told you."

"Bring her inside," Tilly said. "I'll keep watch on her."

To Kate's surprise the cabin was clean, the wood polished, and the stove blackened and shiny. A red rug lay on the floor in front of the fireplace and something cooked in a pot. Peppers hung from the rafters like bunches of bloodred grapes and to Kate's surprise, above the mantel, looking unamused and imperial, hung a portrait of Queen Victoria. Bonded by sponge cake, any friend of old queen Vic was a friend of Kate's. But it seemed that Tilly Madison did not share that opinion.

"I don't sleep, ever, so don't think about making a

fancy move," she said. "I see you trying to escape, I'll kill you."

Tilly kept the Winchester close, and within the confines of the small cabin that was very close. The derringer hung heavy in Kate's dress pocket, but she would have to choose her time carefully to make a play. Everybody must sleep. Eventually the old woman must close her eyes and rest.

CHAPTER FORTY

"So Seth is dead," Jesse Dobbs said. "I can't believe a woman killed him. Wait, yeah, I can believe it. He was always a skirt chaser."

"A woman done fer him all right," Bob Corcoran said. "And then me and Ben done fer her."

Dobbs laid his whiskey glass on the bar. "Fill it." To Corcoran and Lucas, he said, "Seth wasn't much, but he was kin. Did you bury him decent?"

"Sure did, Jesse," Corcoran said. "Piled rocks on him, made his last resting place look nice."

Dobbs smile was twisted, contemptuous. "Seth ain't resting. He's roasting in hell with our pa." He shook his head. "Pa wasn't much, either."

Zebulon Magan said, "He was good with a gun, was Seth. Mighty sudden."

Jesse nodded. "He was that. Killed three, four white men in his time."

The bartender coughed to draw attention to himself and then, still polishing a glass, leaned toward Dobbs and whispered, "A word to the wise, mister. You got three men watching you. I think they're Pinks."

Dobbs gave a short nod. "Seen them right off."

"You on the scout? Just askin'."

"Yeah, headed over the border after I have me a woman or two," Dobbs said.

"They're Pinks for sure," the bartender said.

"Thanks."

"We don't cotton to lawmen in Eagle Pass." The bartender's black hair was parted in the middle, slicked down on each side of his head, and it gleamed like patent leather. "The Pinks are the worst. Bounty hunters is what they are. Hired killers, all of them.

Dobbs glanced in the mirror. Three men in high-button dark gray suits and bowler hats sat at a table in a corner to the left of the door. They had a bottle and glasses on the table but weren't doing much drinking. Another dozen or so patrons sat at other tables—the typical flotsam and jetsam of the border—gamblers, gunmen, and young men on the make.

Corcoran gave Lucas a sidelong glance before he said, "How you want to play this, Jesse? And where is the payroll stashed?"

"You never mind where the payroll is stashed, Bob," Dobbs said. "It's in a safe place. What did you do with the woman's body?"

"It's out there, Jesse," Lucas said. "I'm sure the coyotes got to it by this time."

"Bad thing not to bury a person," Dobbs said. "His soul doesn't rest and comes back to haunt them who left his body to the wolves."

Lucas smiled. "Maybe that don't apply to women."

"It applies to everybody. Step over to the Pinks, Ben, and tell them I want to buy them a drink. See if you can get them to state their business."

Again Lucas and Corcoran exchanged a glance, but Lucas nodded. "Sure thing, Jesse." Smiling, he stepped to the table and in the mirror Dobbs watched him talk to the Pinkertons then point in his direction.

What he didn't hear were the words whispered from Lucas's smiling mouth. "He's got you pegged. Take care."

Lucas walked back to the bar. "The gents said they buy their own drinks, Jesse. And they refused to tell me why they're in Eagle Pass."

"Too bad," Dobbs said. "It's a thing I'd like to know."

Corcoran, smarter than Lucas by far, was worried, sure that the Pinks were on Jesse's trail. He swallowed hard, well aware how fast Dobbs was on the draw and shoot. He had to take a risk. He had to know about the payroll and know now. "Jesse, you got to tell us where you stashed the money. I mean if, God forbid, something happens to you . . ."

"Nothing is going to happen to me, Bob," Dobbs said, his voice low, seemingly friendly, but ominous. "When the time is right, we'll go for the payroll together."

"Well . . . I mean . . . what if we get separated?"

"We won't get separated, Bob. Why would we?"

"I don't know, Jesse. If them boys are Pinkertons . . ."

"Oh but they are, Bob," Dobbs said. "I've seen their kind before, but they won't make a move against me until they know where I've hidden the money. Then they'll kill me." He smiled. "Just like you and Ben aim to do." He slapped Corcoran on the shoulder and grinned. "Ain't that right, Bobby boy?"

CHAPTER FORTY-ONE

Frank Cobb and JC Brewster made a cold camp at the base of a low, rocky ridge not twenty feet from the yellowed bones of a long-dead mule deer. Their discomfort was alleviated to some extent by a bottle of wine, bread, and slices of ham that Jazmin had hurriedly packed for them. A crescent moon hung in the sky and the night was as peaceful as a country graveyard, but an insistent west wind gusted from the direction of the Sierra Madres and lifted veils of sand that rustled against the legs of the two men.

Brewster didn't like it and he made his feelings known. "Wind's picking up, Frank. If it gets any stronger, we've bought into a heap of trouble."

Frank smiled, his mouth a thin line under his mustache. "Sandstorm. I had that same thought. We can't ride it out here."

Brewster, small but lean as a lobo wolf and as enduring, was used to the ways of the desert. "We'll ride. Look for somewhere to hole up. Hey, don't throw that out." He grabbed the wine bottle from Frank, put it to his mouth, and drained what was left. "Waste not, want not, my friend."

"Slice of ham left. You want that?"

"Sure I do. A Ranger learns to eat and drink when he can. It could be days or maybe weeks before he happens on anything else."

Both men donned slickers to keep the blowing sand from finding its way under their clothes and saddled up. They headed south in the direction of Eagle Pass, neither of them real confident that they'd ever reach it.

The wind was up, the sand drove against them and growled like a cougar, and the moon was lost so that earth and sky became one, a cartwheeling maelstrom of sepia and shadow painted by Mother Nature, the maddest of all mad artists.

Kate stood at the rattling window of the cabin and looked outside but saw only darkness and an occasional glimpse of slanting, windblown sand.

"What you expect to see out there?" Tilly Madison sat in a chair by the fire, the Winchester across her lap.

Without turning, Kate said, "The Seventh Cavalry."

"Well, they ain't comin', lady." A mean glint filled Tilly's firelit eyes, "Only feller coming for you is Jesse Dobbs, and God help you when he does."

Kate turned. "What makes you the way you are, Tilly? What makes you such a mean, nasty old woman?"

"You'd like to know," the old crone said.

"Yes, I would."

"Why the interest?"

"So I don't do the things you've done and end up like you," Kate said.

Tilly slammed the rifle up and down on the arms of her chair as though to emphasize what she was going to say next. "Maybe you think it's all them husbands I poisoned made me the way I am? Well, that's bull crap. All seven of them got what they deserved. A bunch of lazy, no-good loafers . . . every damn one of them."

"Then why did you marry them?"

"So I could kill them later." Tilly's face became crafty. "Maybe the crooked carcass I was born with made me cruel, huh? Maybe all the abuse and the fun made of me as a hunchback I endured after my ma died made me nasty? Know how many foster parents and their offspring I poisoned? Nah, you don't know. And you don't know what rat poison does to folks, either. Kills them bit-by-bit it does, and nobody any the wiser. When it was done, some relative of the departed would say, 'Poor Tilly, poor little hunchback, alone again. But now you can come live with us.' And then I'd begin all over again with the poison." The old woman cackled. "Rats! Rats! I killed lots of rats, whole families of rats. And maybe I'll kill you because you're pretty and I'm not. You're a rat!"

Kate was horrified. "What kind of hellish creature are you?"

"The worst kind that you'll ever meet, dearie. I've seen hell. Seen the fire and heard the screams of the suffering damned. Satan himself told me there's a place reserved for me among the princes and princesses of the abyss. Now lie down on the floor and go to sleep."

"I won't sleep in your house or eat or drink here," Kate said.

"Then stay awake and starve to death for all I care," Tilly said. "But remember, I'll shoot you if I have to and do it gladly."

"You're a horrible woman and you'll have to sleep sometime."

"No sleep!" Tilly said. "There will be time enough to sleep in Hades. I'll be overworked tormenting the damned, see? How could the devil find a more vicious, heartless demon than me?" The old woman convulsed with glee. She bent over and her frail body shook with laughter, bellow after bellow of mad mirth.

In that moment, Kate knew that Tilly was insane. It made her unpredictable and dangerous. Kate slipped her hand into her pocket and stepped slowly toward the madwoman, but Tilly was alert. The laughter stopped like the turning off of a faucet and the muzzle of the Winchester pointed at Kate's chest.

"One more step, dearie," the old woman said. And then, harshly, "What do you got in your pocket? A knife? Out with it, real slow."

Kate hesitated. She'd draw and shoot and be too slow. She knew that, but Tilly would kill her anyway. It was time—

"Hello . . . cab. . . ." A man's voice came from outside, his words shredding away in the hurtling wind of the violent sandstorm.

Long moments passed. Tilly stood, the Winchester up and ready in her hands. She was set, ready to kill.

The door burst open and a man stumbled inside. "Sorry I—"

"Frank! Look out!" Kate yelled.

The Winchester roared just as he dived for the floor.

Tilly levered the rifle and fired when JC Brewster filled the doorway. The Ranger cried out and staggered backwards into darkness.

"Drop it!" Kate yelled, her derringer hammer-back at eye level.

Tilly Madison snarled like an animal, levered the rifle, and turned.

Kate fired and thumbed back the hammer again . . . but a second shot wasn't necessary. The old woman shrieked when the .41 crashed into the middle of her forehead. For a moment, she stood still, her ashen eyes wide and round as moons. The Winchester clattered onto the floor and Tilly followed it.

Frank was on his feet, Colt in hand. "Kate, are you hit?" he said, talking through a drift of gun smoke.

"No, I'm not hit." She slipped the derringer back into her pocket.

Frank stepped to Tilly's body and turned it over with the toe of his boot.

Kate said, "Is she . . . ?"

"Yeah, she's on a stony lonesome. Who the hell was she?"

"A horrible, hellish creature. The world is better off without her shadow falling on it." As though waking from a bad dream, Kate said, "Frank! JC Brewster was shot."

Frank holstered his revolver and ran out of the cabin into the storm. He stumbled back inside a few moments later, his arm around Brewster's chest. The Ranger's toes dragged behind him and the front of his shirt was scarlet with blood.

"On the table," Kate said. "Gently now, Frank."

"I think he's hit hard," Frank said.

"Unbuckle his gun belt and help me get his shirt off."

Frank stared into Brewster's gray face. "Is he still alive?"

The Ranger opened his eyes. "No, I'm dead. Now let Kate undress me and don't interrupt."

Kate smiled. "It seems there's life in you yet, JC. Frank, there's a well outside. I need water."

There was no letup in the wind. It shook the frail fabric of the cabin and violently hurled sand against the windowpanes like birdshot. Brewster pretended to be in no pain, but his strained face and tortuous breathing gave lie to that. The rifle bullet had entered his left shoulder, smashing bone, and was still in there, too deep for Kate to dig it out.

Frank dragged the old woman's body outside.

When he returned. Kate said, "We need to get JC to a doctor. The bullet is where I can't reach it."

"I reckon the nearest doctor will be in Eagle Pass"—Frank's face was clouded by doubt—"if we can risk it."

"Of course we'll risk it," Kate said. "Besides, I have scores to settle. I will not be abused and manhandled and discussed as though I was a head of cattle to be bought and sold."

"Tell me what happened, Kate. Why did Seth Dobbs bring you here?"

"Seth Dobbs is dead. I killed him." She saw the shock in Frank's eyes and added, "I had no choice." While she did what she could to clean Brewster's wound she told him about the kidnap and Bob Corcoran and Ben Lucas's plan to sell her in Mexico. "They brought me here and went on to Eagle Pass."

"Then thank God for a sandstorm, huh?"

"Indeed and to His Blessed Mother who heard

my prayers." Kate bent over Brewster. "How do you feel, JC?"

The Ranger looked up at Kate's breasts hovering just above his face. "Stay right there, Kate," he whispered. "I feel so much better when you're close."

She smiled. "I will. I'll do what I can to take good care of you."

Frank Cobb shook his head. It seemed like the Texas Rangers could turn any situation, no matter how dire, to their advantage. Finally he said, "Kate, I know he's hurt bad, but he's milking it."

"He's what?" she said, startled.

Frank said quickly, "He's pretending to be worse than he is."

"No, he's not. He's a poor thing."

Despite his pain, JC Brewster looked up and grinned.

CHAPTER FORTY-TWO

By dawn the storm had blown itself out. Somewhere under a mound of sand lay Tilly Madison's body. Neither Kate nor Frank had the time or inclination to look for it.

They rode out just after daybreak. Kate was on Brewster's horse and the Ranger, drifting in and out of consciousness, sat behind Frank and somehow hung on until they reached Eagle Pass, a sprawling, lawless settlement of two thousand people on the Rio Grande.

The doctor in town was a young woman, unusual at that time in the West, unusual at that time anywhere. According to a man Frank spoke to in the street, her name was Ada Jordan and her shingle hung outside the end house on Main Street, right after the Last Chance Saloon & Billiard Room.

Frank, conscious of the presence in town of Jesse Dobbs and his cohorts, felt vulnerable with a wounded man clinging to him. A horseback revolver fighter needs freedom to maneuver, but Brewster denied him that. It was therefore with considerable relief that he and Kate reached the doctor's house without incident, though many curious and possibly hostile eyes had stared in their direction. Or so Frank thought until he realized it could have been something far less sinister—merely men struck by Kate's maturing beauty and the fact that she sat her horse like a warrior queen.

Dr. Jordan's nurse was a middle-aged woman with fine hazel eyes and gray hair scraped back in a bun. She took one look at Brewster and led the way past living quarters to a surgery at the rear of the house. Once the Ranger had been laid out on a steel table with a leather top she said, "The doctor will be right with you."

Ada Jordan MD was a tall, beautifully shaped woman with a thick mane of glossy chestnut hair and expressive brown eyes. She was pretty, but lacked Kate's spectacular beauty. Men looked at her, but not in the same tongue-hanging-out way they looked at Kate.

After brief introductions were made, Dr. Jordan examined the patient. Her manner was brusque and businesslike, perhaps to compensate for her gender. She told Brewster that she would operate to remove the bullet and that she'd give him ether so that he felt no pain.

"Doc, so long as you stay close to me and give me a musket ball to bite on, I'll be fine," Brewster said.

The doctor smiled and allowed herself to unbend a little. "Spoken like a true Texas Ranger, Mr. Brewster, but I believe ether will make it easier for all concerned." She turned to Frank. "Mr. Cobb, perhaps you'd care to wait in my study. Nurse Boxford will show you the way."

After Frank was ushered out by the nurse, Dr. Jordan said, "Mrs. Kerrigan, I believe I have the only bathtub in Eagle Pass. At least it seems that way sometimes. You're welcome to use it and I think we can find something in my closet to fit you."

Kate looked down at her torn, trail-stained dress and smiled. "I look a mess, don't I?"

"I don't think you could ever look a mess, Mrs. Kerrigan."

"But still . . ."

"Yes," the doctor said. "But still."

"Yes, I'd appreciate a bath," Kate said.

Nurse Boxford returned and after the doctor told her about the bath she said, "I'll have Marius, our manservant, heat water and then set up the tub in the parlor by the fire. You'll have privacy there. And now if you'll excuse me, Mrs. Kerrigan, I have to prepare for surgery." Dr. Jordan was all business again.

All Frank Cobb sought that noon hour as he stepped into the Last Chance Saloon was a beer and a quiet corner. As fate would have it, he got the former but not the latter.

Gunmen of all stripes were not rare in Eagle Pass. Usually they were in transit across the Rio Grande, either leaving or heading toward Old Mexico, and bothered no one. Unfortunately, one of those gunmen, a bully and braggart by the name of Clip Hornage, was in the saloon talking with Jesse Dobbs.

As Frank ordered his beer at the bar, Hornage was in earnest conversation with Dobbs.

"I feel that I'm destined for great things, Mr. Dobbs. That's why I want to throw in with you."

"As what?"

"Anything you want me to be." Hornage puffed up a little. "I've killed men before."

"You don't say?"

"Sure. You ever hear of Lou Hope up Potter County way? No? Well, he had a rep as a fast gun, told folks he'd killed fifteen men. Then he drew down on me and his career ended right there and then. One shot right through the bowels and he died three days later screaming like a woman."

"You're fast, huh?" Dobbs said, enjoying this.

"Maybe the fastest there is," Hornage said.

"Well, that's fast. How did you know about me, Clip?"

The use of his first name by a known gunman and outlaw flattered Hornage and his face glowed. "Everybody's heard of you, Mr. Dobbs. There's talk that you robbed an army payroll and you're on the scout from the Rangers. You need a man like me at your side."

"A fast gun?"

"That's right, Mr. Dobbs."

"Well, you seem eager enough, young feller." Dobbs moved his whiskey bottle to one side and leaned across the table. "Look around the saloon and tell me what you see."

Hornage's pale blue eyes moved around the room. His smile was disdainful. "Nothing much. Looks like a bunch of sodbusters and drummers in here."

"What about the man in the corner nursing a beer?"

Hornage's contemptuous gaze skimmed over Frank. "Cowboy. I never met a puncher who could shoot worth a damn."

"Brace him," Dobbs said.

"Him? Why?"

"You said you're fast, Clip. Show me how fast you are. Gun the cowboy."

"And when I do?"

Dobbs smiled. "Well then, welcome to my gang."

Hornage rose to his feet. "This is gonna be too easy," he said, grinning. "It ain't much of a test." He adjusted the hang of his flashy Smith & Wesson and stepped toward Frank's table, his spurs ringing.

Frank knew trouble when he saw it . . . and he was seeing it.

The young man striding toward him affected the frockcoat and string-tie garb of a frontier gambler and his blond, shoulder-length hair pegged him as a wannabe Hickok. But unlike, Wild Bill he wore his revolver in a low-slung holster. His beard and mustache—meticulously trimmed in the imperial style of the top-rated shootist—was the finishing touch, and Frank wanted no part of him.

The man stopped at Frank's table and said louder than was necessary, "On your feet!"

"Go away," Frank said. "I'm drinking a beer."

The puncher didn't seemed scared and that rattled Hornage a little. He'd killed a cowboy or two before and they didn't show the relaxed self-confidence of this one.

Again loud, he said, "Mister, you've been pretty free with your talk about me around town, saying that I was too much of a coward to meet you. Well, here I am."

The cowboy's eyes were cold as frosted steel. He didn't scare worth a damn and Hornage didn't like it—but he was in too deep to back out now.

"Go away," Frank said again.

Hornage couldn't see the man's gun hand. A glance in the mirror behind the bar revealed a smiling Dobbs. A few other men were grinning, enjoying the show.

The wannabe gunman tried once more. "I said get on your feet."

"Can I buy you a beer?" Frank said.

"I'm a whiskey man. I don't want your damn beer."

"Too bad. It's even pretty cold."

"I told you to get on your feet," Hornage said. "I don't draw on a sitting man, but for you I'm willing to make an exception."

Frank shook his head. "Feller, I never saw you before in my life, but you're determined to kill a man for breakfast. Isn't that a natural fact?"

Somebody laughed and Hornage knew he was beginning to lose it and look bad. "Stand and front me like a man." To save face, he added, "And admit that you're a damn liar and a yellow belly."

Frank sighed deeply, then rose to his feet. "All right, youngster, let's have it over with. Shuck the iron and get your work in."

Hornage felt that he was back in command of the situation. He had confidence in his draw and put it on display for all to see. His hand flashed for his gun.

A gun roared, but it was a Colt, not a Smith.

It took Hornage a few moments to realize what had happened to him. And then the pain of his shattered right wrist hit him like a pile driver. In that instant, as his revolver dropped from his numb hand, the young man knew he was done, that his gun fighting days were over. His wrist was a bloody mass of torn tissue and splintered bone and would heal twisted, stiff, and deformed. He looked at Frank, standing tall and straight, his smoking Colt in his hand.

Then he heard the man say, "I could have killed you just as easily. But there's good news. Now no one else will kill you. You're not fast, boy, not even close to fast."

By nature Frank loved women, little children, and animals, but he was not noted for his compassion toward a defeated enemy, the result of many harsh lessons. He stepped around the table, grabbed the groaning Hornage by the scruff of his neck, and marched him to Jesse Dobbs's table. The young man left a trail of red splotches on the pine floor behind him.

Frank threw Hornage into a chair and said to Dobbs, "You could have stopped this."

The man shrugged. "Young feller wants to test himself, it's no concern of mine."

"There's a doctor in town. Make that your concern."

"The hell I will." Dobbs reached for the bottle on the table but never made it. Frank grabbed it and threw it against a wall, where it shattered, spraying shards of glass and a shower of amber whiskey.

Dobbs, his face like stone, ignored Frank and called out, "Bartender, another bottle here."

Clip Hornage, sobbing in an agony of shame, chose that moment to make a desperation play. He rose from his chair and staggered across the floor. He bent over and, with a triumphant shriek, grabbed for his dropped gun with his left hand.

In one smooth fast motion, Frank drew and fired. He fired again and sent the big Schofield .45 skittering across the saloon's floor, under a table, and thudded against a wall.

Hornage straightened and saw Frank, Colt in hand, eyeing him. He threw himself out of the saloon door and staggered into the street, holding the forearm of his ruined gun hand. The young man's screams announced to everyone within earshot that his days as a feared draw fighter were gone forever.

Frank punched out the empties from his Colt and reloaded from his cartridge belt. Jesse Dobbs, a sure-thing killer, made no move to challenge him.

Frank holstered his Colt and said, "I'm going to take a guess and say that your name is Jesse Dobbs."

"Is that right?"

"You tell me."

"Maybe it's Dobbs. Maybe it isn't."

"Either way, you're coming with me," Frank said. "There's a lady called Kate Kerrigan wants to talk to you."

"What about?"

"About how your boys kidnapped her and planned to sell her in Mexico. Where we come from, that's a hanging offense."

"I didn't kidnap her," Dobbs said. "I've never even met the lady."

"Explain that to Kate." Frank's hand dropped to his gun, but a voice from his left stopped him.

"I wouldn't, mister." The bartender held a scatter-gun and when he eared back the hammers it sounded like the wrath of God. "You've shot up my saloon and one of my customers pretty good and that's where it ends. I'm a fair hand with this here Greener and it's no friend of draw fighters."

"And neither are we." This came from one of two

men who'd walked into the saloon. The man, big and bearded, said, "We'll back your play, bartender."

"There will be no gunplay if the gentlemen will go to another saloon," the bartender said. "The Oriental serves a real nice free lunch. Tell them Miles Dolan sent you."

Dobbs smiled, staring at Frank. "Mister, I got no quarrel with you. Those two hardcases are my boys, and right now they're a couple fingers looking for triggers. If I was you, I'd ease on out of here."

"I'm up against a stacked deck, Dobbs, and I knew when to fold," Frank said. "But this isn't over."

"As far as I'm concerned it is." Dobbs turned to Corcoran and Lucas. "Come have a drink, boys."

The moment had passed and Frank knew it. And so did the bartender. He lowered the scattergun's hammers, laid the Greener behind the bar, and greeted a customer who'd just entered.

Frank walked across the saloon to the door. Behind him someone laughed but he ignored it. He stepped through the door . . . into a bullet.

The .44-40 slug fired from a Winchester hit Frank Cobb on his left side, an inch above the cartridge belt. Clip Hornage stood in the middle of the street, the rifle cradled in his damaged right arm and he worked the lever with his left . . . slowly . . . awkwardly. Missing his first shot was a death sentence and he knew it.

People stopped in the street to watch as Frank drew and fired. There would be no wounding this time. He shot to kill. His bullet slammed into the Winchester's side plate, caromed upward and hit Hornage under the chin. The man dropped the rifle and staggered back, shocked, wearing his blood like a scarlet bib.

Frank fired again, a hit center chest. Hornage went to his knees and then pitched forward into the dirt.

Years later, when the legends were written, people swore that after Frank Cobb watched Hornage fall, he said, "I've had enough of you for one day."

And that was probably the truth.

CHAPTER FORTY-THREE

"You're very lucky, Mr. Cobb," Dr. Ada Jordan said. "A couple inches to the right and I'm afraid you would not live."

"Well that's cheerful news, Doc," Frank said. "What's the damage? It hurts like hell."

"The bullet passed clean through, and the wounds look worse than they are. I've cleaned them and used alcohol to prevent infection. You're young and strong, and you'll heal quickly."

Frank looked at the bandage tight around his middle. "Clip Hornage is dead, huh?"

The doctor's face was stiff. "There was nothing I could do for him."

"And Ranger Brewster?"

"He'll recover, but I don't think he'll ever gain full mobility of his left shoulder."

"He shoots off his right shoulder, so that's good," Frank said.

"Yes, good news for him, I suppose." Dr. Jordan's pretty face revealed nothing.

The surgery door opened and Kate stepped inside. Her hair hung over her shoulders in damp ringlets and a few tumbled over her forehead. She wore a calico dress that fitted her well and she smelled of lavender water. "How are my patients, Doctor?"

"The Ranger is sleeping off the effects of the ether, and Mr. Cobb will live to fight another day."

Kate ignored the irony in the physician's tone. "How did it happen, Frank?"

Frank's immediate answer was, "Kate, Jesse Dobbs was in the Last Chance Saloon. I'm sure it was him. Two of his boys came in later."

"That would be Ben Lucas and Bob Corcoran," Kate said.

Frank winced as he put on his shirt. "How do we play this? I mean what are your intentions, Kate?"

Dr. Jordan said, "I guess I should leave and let you two talk."

"No, stay," Kate said. "My intentions are no secret. I plan to see Lucas and Corcoran stand trial for kidnapping and conspiracy to commit murder. Then I'll hang them."

"What about Jesse Dobbs?" Frank said.

"He'll hang with them."

Dr. Jordan said, "Mrs. Kerrigan—"

"Please call me Kate." She smiled. "I'm wearing your clothes and that makes us almost kin."

"Kate, there are Pinkertons in town. Why not let them deal with the outlaws?"

"Pinkertons. Are you sure?"

"Three of them. I treated one for a spider bite. I remember he was annoyed because he said his trigger finger was swollen up like a sausage."

Kate, aware that Brewster was out of commission, possibly for weeks, and Frank was wounded, seized on an opportunity to recruit allies. "They'll be at the hotel. Do you know their names?"

"The one I treated was called Bernard Rigby. He mentioned the given names of the two with him as Byron and Arch. They're all young men and seemed very capable."

"Then I'll go talk with them. I can use their help."

Frank said, "Kate, why would there be Pinkertons in Eagle Pass?"

"I'm sure I don't know."

"They're here because Jesse Dobbs is in town. You can bet the farm that the army hired them to recover the stolen payroll."

"Well, that's all to the good, Frank. Isn't it?"

"All the Pinkertons want is the money back. I don't think they'll have any interest in helping you arrest Dobbs or anybody else."

"We'll discuss that when I meet them," Kate said. "I will insist they give me the help I need or their superiors will hear about it. In short, I will not take no for an answer. That is out of the question. Ada . . . may I call you Ada? Can Ranger Brewster remain here until we return?"

The doctor smiled. "Of course. He's a model patient . . . when he's unconscious."

Kate reserved a couple rooms at the hotel, one for herself and the other for her wounded warriors to share. She then asked the desk clerk if Mr. Bernard Rigby was in residence.

"I'm afraid you just missed him, Mrs. Kerrigan." The clerk was young and eager to please the beautiful lady, and the light of adoration radiated from him. Frank, hurting and in a foul mood, disliked him on sight.

"Where has he gone?" Kate said.

"He and the other Pinkertons, Mr. Buchanan and Mr. Poole, rode out an hour ago on urgent business. They carried rifles, so something is afoot."

"How did you know they were Pinkertons?" Frank said, his face sour.

The clerk smiled. "The whole town knows. What we don't know is why they're here." The young man leaned closer and whispered, "There's talk that they're after a fortune in gold bars stolen from a bank in Austin." He straightened and tapped the side of his nose with a forefinger. "But you didn't hear that from me."

"Did the Pinkertons say where they were headed?" Kate said.

"They didn't say, but old Mr. McKinney in room twenty-three said he saw three riders headed north and they looked like the Pinkertons."

"Frank, do you feel like riding?" Kate said.

"No."

"But I need your scouting ability should I lose their tracks."

"Kate, if the Pinkertons are after Jesse Dobbs and the payroll, let them shoot it out. Later, we can pick up the bodies."

"And be cheated of my justice, Frank? No. I want Lucas and Corcoran alive. And Jesse Dobbs." She sighed with considerable drama. "Oh, very well then, I'll go by myself."

"I can ride," Frank said. His shoulders slumped.

Kate smiled. "I knew you would say that, Frank. You're my knight in shining armor."

No, I'm not, Kate. My armor is rusted from my blood. Frank thought that, but he didn't say it.

CHAPTER FORTY-FOUR

Two words recently carved into a scrap of wood taken from the bed of a long-abandoned wagon had attracted the attention of the Pinkertons.

DEAD MAN

Frank read the tracks. Three men wearing shoes, not boots, had stood around the grave and one of them had toed a shallow depression in the sand and rock to see what lay underneath. A scrap of homespun cloth, probably from a shirtsleeve, poked above the surface, and the stench of death hung in the air like a poisonous fog.

"Like it says, there's a dead man here," Frank said. "The Pinkertons stayed for a while and then rode on."

Kate stood in the stirrups and shaded her eyes, studying the sun-blasted rock and cactus wilderness around her. "There's dust to the northwest, Frank."

"Probably Jesse Dobbs and his boys. And the Pinkertons, but for the time being they're holding back."

"Why? What's going on?" she said.

Frank climbed stiffly into the saddle. "My guess is the Pinks hope Dobbs will lead them to the stolen payroll and then they'll force his hand . . . the money in exchange for letting him live."

"But Dobbs won't lead them to the money," Kate said. "He can see the Pinkertons are right behind him."

"Kate, I don't know who those three big-city boys are, but they seem mighty confident. Look at the dust. They're not following Dobbs, they're catching up. They stopped at the dead man's grave and let Dobbs and his men get ahead of them. They'll surprise the hell out of him with a sudden attack, drop a couple men in the first volley, and force the survivors to lead them to the payroll."

"Frank, that's thin. I don't think—" A sudden rattle of gunfire stilled Kate's tongue.

Frank said, "Well, it's started. Now we light a shuck."

"Have they seen us?"

"I don't know. But right now they've got other things on their mind."

The gunfire was constant as mounted men exchanged shots in a cloud of dust.

"Kate, as I told you, we'll pick up the pieces. Right now I'm in no shape for a gunfight."

"I hope Lucas and Corcoran survive," Kate said. "My business with those two is not yet done."

Frank swung his horse around. "Time will tell, Kate. Time will tell."

Even with a gray tinge under his tanned skin and his shoulder under a fat bandage obviously paining him, JC Brewster was still a Texas Ranger. Enduring bullet wounds without complaining came with the job. He sat up in the hotel bed while Kate spooned him beef broth, blithely ignoring Frank's muttered comments about his own wound and how much it hurt.

She dabbed Brewster's mustache with a napkin. "There, that will help you regain your strength."

Frank built a cigarette, lit it, and stepped over to the bed. "I don't know why I'm doing this," he said as he stuck the smoke between Brewster's lips.

"I do," the ranger said. "It's because you're such a fine human being, Frank, a Southern gentleman to your fingertips."

"Don't count on it," Frank said. "You roll the next one yourself."

Kate said, "Frank, be kind. JC is wounded."

An obvious retort was on the tip of Frank's tongue, but he didn't make it. He strolled to the window and stared into a street lit only by the oil lamps that hung outside the stores and other commercial buildings. The result was a strange orange-tinted twilight that never reached the alleys where the black shadows crouched.

Brewster said, "Now, do you want to tell me what the hell is happening and why you took a woman with you to trail some mighty dangerous characters?"

"It was my idea," Kate said. "I thought the Pinkertons would make arrests and I'd force them to surrender Ben Lucas and Bob Corcoran into my custody, but it wasn't that simple."

"Tell me what happened out there," Brewster said.

Kate described the Pinkertons' slow chase in pursuit of Jesse Dobbs and his boys and the subsequent gunfire. "I've no idea what took place next. We thought it prudent to leave."

Brewster absorbed that and then said, "Those

Pinkertons aren't detectives. They're strikebreakers and strong-arm men, sap and billy club bullies paid by rich men to threaten and terrify the starvation-wage slaves that toil for them. I've met those kinds of Pinkertons before. They come down from the big cities up north and reckon they can do in Texas what they've done in Detroit or Chicago and a dozen other towns. But you can bet your bottom dollar they learned a lesson today . . . that Western men like Jesse Dobbs don't terrify worth a damn."

"Rider just came in," Frank said. "He stopped in the middle of the street and he's drawing a crowd."

"Is he a Pinkerton or Jesse Dobbs?" Brewster said.

"Hard to tell, but I think he's wearing a bowler hat."

"Frank, help me up. I got to go down there and find out what happened."

Kate said, "You will stay right where you are, Ranger Brewster. You're too weak to stand. I will not allow you out of bed."

"Frank, give me my hat."

"Don't you dare, Frank Cobb," Kate said.

"Here's your hat, JC," Frank said. "Now you're properly dressed."

"Help me," Brewster said.

Frank steadied the Ranger as he crossed the floor, passed the fuming Kate, and grabbed his boots. He sat on the bed and pulled them. "Get me the slicker over there in the corner with my saddle and bedroll."

"I will not be held responsible for your well-being if you go out into the street in your underwear, Ranger Brewster," Kate said. "I am adamant on that."

Frank helped Brewster into the slicker. "I guess he's going, Kate."

"I guess I am." Brewster buckled his gun belt over his long johns and stepped to the door.

"Then we'll go with you," Kate said. "You're a stubborn, headstrong man, JC. I've never known the like."

The hour was late, the night dark, and Eagle Pass was not Dodge City. Few people were on the street, and the crowd gathered around the man on the horse numbered only a dozen.

"Texas Ranger, make way there," JC Brewster said. "Has this man identified himself?"

"Only in hell, Ranger. He's dead," said a portly man with a red face.

As his eyes grew accustomed to the gloom, Brewster saw that the rider was indeed dead, as dead as a bullet through the center of his forehead could make him. The corpse sat stiff and upright in the saddle, hands on the reins, shadows gathered in the hollows of his eyes and cheeks. He had a placid, almost peaceful expression on his face as though he'd died instantly without ever realizing it had happened.

"You men, get him down from there," Brewster said. "And somebody take the horse away."

The dead man was laid out on the street and his coat fell open, revealing his Pinkerton badge.

"Where are the other two?" Kate said.

"I guess we'll find out come morning," Brewster said. "I'll ride out to where you and Frank heard the gunfight."

A woman who'd arrived on the scene said, "Does that poor man need a doctor?"

"No, he needs an undertaker. Who does such work in Eagle Pass?"

"That would be Charlie Gill," the portly man said. "I'll go get him."

Frank saw Kate suddenly stare into space, her face troubled. He took her arm and said, "Kate, you look like you've seen a ghost."

"Yes . . . maybe I have. Frank, I think I know where the army payroll is buried."

CHAPTER FORTY-FIVE

"I sure hope the nag can see in the dark," JC Brewster said.

"She's doing all right," Kate said. "The moonlight helps."

The Ranger, in pain and irritated, scowled at the equally pained and irritated Frank. "Do you need all that room for your legs?"

"It's a small wagon," Frank said. "I got to put them someplace."

"Why didn't you bring your hoss?" Brewster said.

"Because he's all used up, like me."

"Damn it all, Frank. You could have taken mine," Brewster said, stretching his legs.

"No I couldn't," Frank said. "I never took to riding twenty-dollar mustangs."

"That's because you ain't a Ranger. A Ranger can ride anything with hair on it."

"Damn it, JC. You kicked me," Frank said.

"It was an accident. There's no room in the back of this wagon."

"It's all I could get at the livery," Kate said. "You

boys stop squabbling like children. We'll soon be there."

"Why does that mare keep stumbling?" Brewster said. "Pains my shoulder every time."

"Because she's old," Kate said. "But she's got eyes like a hawk in the dark."

Moonlight lay on the surrounding terrain like a frosting of snow and the coolness of early fall was in the air. There were no animal or night bird sounds, only the steady *clop-clop* of the horse and the iron-shod rumble of the wagon wheels. The sound of metal on rock made Frank think about the Tin Man back in Dodge, and he wondered idly if he'd ever completely recovered from the bullet Kate had put into his vitals. Probably not. His boiler must have burst.

"Frank, I think we're getting close," Kate said.

"Good. Stop the rig and I'll walk ahead with the lamp." He clambered out of the wagon, ignored Brewster's agonized protests, and retrieved the lamp from Kate, who had stored it under the driver's seat. It was only then that he realized how much the wound in his side had weakened him. His head reeled and pain gnawed at him like a living thing.

"Frank, are you all right?" Kate said, alarm lifting her voice.

"I'm fine. Real good." He held the lantern high in his left hand, pulled his Colt, and stepped in front of the mare. "Never better."

"Can you see anything?" Kate said.

"Not much," Frank said. "I'll walk ahead for a spell and then you come after me."

Brewster said, "Hell, it's getting darker, Frank. You be careful."

"Could be fixing to rain," Frank said. "I'll be fine

with the lamp." The sound of his feet crunching on sand and rock grew dimmer and then was gone, but the bobbing orange orb of the lamp glowed in the distance.

"Follow him, Kate," Brewster said. "I got my Winchester handy."

"You think Jesse Dobbs could still be around?" Kate said.

"I don't know. I don't know what could be around here, and that includes boogermen."

Kate's laugh made music in the quiet. "I didn't know Texas Rangers were scared of boogermen."

"You'd be surprised how many things scare us," Brewster said. "But most times we get un-scared pretty damn fast."

From ahead came a cry from the darkness.

"Kate! Come quick!"

"All right. Now I'm scared again," Brewster said.

The lamp above his head, Frank stood in a shifting cone of amber light, an open grave at his feet and a dead man on the ground behind him.

Kate stopped the wagon, but the mare, disturbed by the smell of the corpse, whinnied and reared in the traces. Arcs of white shone in her eyes. Kate jumped from the seat, grabbed the horse's browband and reins, and spoke soothing words to the scared animal. As soon as the mare settled a little, Kate led her away from the grave and the smell of death.

Brewster limped out the rear and indignantly said, "Did you forget about me?"

"Sorry, I didn't have time to rescue you," Kate said. "Are you all right?"

"Apart from being shot through and through I'm just fine, I guess."

"You were right, Kate. They buried the money under a dead man," Frank saidt. "And now they've reclaimed it."

Brewster peered at the corpse that had been torn from the grave. After a while, he said, "I know him. That's Zeb Magan, ran with Jesse Dobbs and them. Looks like they shot him and then tossed him on top of the money sacks, figuring no one would disturb a grave."

"Except resurrectionists like us," Kate said. "But we were too late."

"Jesse must be in Eagle Pass by now," Brewster said. "Or he's already crossed the Rio Grande into Mexico."

"Maybe not," Kate said. Frank and Brewster stared at her in the hazy orange lamplight.

"When Corcoran and Lucas helped Dobbs recover the money, they didn't know I'd escaped from Tilly Madison. As far as they're concerned, I'm still at the cabin. Those animals wouldn't pass up the chance to sell Kate Kerrigan in Mexico, so I'm certain they left here and headed for the Madison place."

"When they saw you were gone, they probably headed south with Dobbs," Brewster said.

"But there's a chance they decided to spend the night at the cabin," Kate said. "I want to go there."

"You sure got it in for those boys, Kate," Brewster said.

"If they were outlaws who happened to steal an army payroll, I could forgive them, but they talked about selling me in Mexico and discussed raping me. That I cannot forgive." Kate stepped to the wagon, removed a shovel, and returned to the grave. "I can't let this man lie unburied. I'll say proper prayers for the dead later." Frank extended his hand for the shovel, but Kate shook her head. "No, you and JC are too stove up. I'll do it."

She dragged Magan's body into the grave and then began to shovel dirt. Her lips moved in a silent prayer.

CHAPTER FORTY-SIX

In the moonlit mist, the Madison cabin looked like an abandoned ark adrift on a gray sea. There were no horses in sight, no smoke from the chimney, and no sound but the gibbering of ghostly night birds and the rustle of crawling things among sand and rock.

The stillness of the night made Frank whisper. "I guess they didn't come this way, Kate. The place is deserted."

Above the wagon, the moon was as white as a skull.

JC Brewster looked around him, his eyes big. "Seems like."

"We'll go on ahead on foot." Kate jumped from the wagon. "Frank, pass me my Winchester."

"Kate, if Jesse Dobbs and his boys survived the fight with the Pinkertons, we might find ourselves over-matched," Frank said. "Me and JC are in no shape for gun fighting."

Kate levered a round into the chamber. "We're not overmatched, Frank. Even stove-up, you and JC are more than able to shade motherless scum like Jesse

Dobbs and his thugs. We faced bigger odds in Dodge, remember?"

Frank smiled. "It would be nice to have Bat Masterson with us, though."

"You don't need Bat Masterson when you've got me." She looked at Frank. "But you're right. I wish Bat was here."

Frank and JC took up positions on either side of Kate as they stepped warily toward the cabin. The windows stared at them blankly, like black, dead eyes.

Kate stopped. "Frank, to the left by the well. What is that? A sleeping hog?"

Frank's eyes searched into the darkness. His hand opened and closed on his Colt. "Can't see from here. It could be a hog."

"Or a dead man," Brewster said.

"Or somebody laying for us." Kate said. "Let's take a look."

"No." Brewster said. "I'm the Texas Ranger here and it's my job. Kate, you and Frank cover me. If I shriek like my maiden aunt when she saw the mouse, come a-shooting."

"Be careful, JC," Kate said.

"That's the only way I know," Brewster said.

Gun in hand, he advanced slowly toward the lump on the ground and the gloom closed around him, falling like a murky curtain. Beside her, Kate heard Frank swallow hard. He was a man who feared nothing, but the strain of his wound and the mysteries of the malevolent night were getting to him. She lightly touched his big hand with the tips of her fingers.

He nodded. "I'm all right, Kate."

"I know you are. Now what's JC doing?"

The Ranger stepped away from the dark bulk on

the ground and walked to the cabin. He raised his boot and kicked the door in, a violent move that pained his shoulder. A few moments later, a lamp was lit within and the cabin's windows glazed with tawny light.

"I suppose that means there's no danger," Kate said.

"And no Jesse Dobbs," Frank said.

"Unless he's dead."

"Then let's go find out."

Bob Corcoran's body lay beside the well. He'd been shot several times in the belly and chest. Judging by the way his convulsing feet had plowed up the ground, he'd lasted a few minutes after he hit the ground.

"Ben Lucas is inside," Brewster said. "Way I piece it together, it looks like he was wounded in the fight with the Pinkertons and laid out in the bed. Dobbs summed things up for him by putting a bullet between his eyes then stepped outside as Corcoran came running and done for him. Dobbs was always quick on the trigger."

"Any sign of the payroll?" Kate said.

"Nah. Dobbs packed it out of here." Brewster looked into Kate's beautiful eyes. "Kate, I guess that does it for you. You'll want to go home now."

"Why?"

"Corcoran and Lucas are dead. Your fight is not with Jesse Dobbs. Leave him to me."

"You're going after him?" Kate said.

Brewster nodded. "It's my job."

"Kate, it's time to head back and find out what's happening with the plague wagons and with Hank

Lowery," Frank said. "Besides all that, what is Barrie Delaney doing with your new house? You can't trust that old pirate."

"And then there are my daughters and my sons," Kate said.

"Yeah, the kids, too," Frank said. "You must be worried about them."

"I'm not. They're Kerrigans and they can fend for themselves. That's how I raised them."

The *segundo* frowned. "Kate, I'm trying hard here, but I'm not catching your drift. Like JC says, what happens or does not happen to Jesse Dobbs is no concern of ours."

Kate looked at Brewster. "When you reach Eagle Pass, will you wire the Rangers for help?"

"No. My superiors expect me to handle whatever comes up," Brewster said. "If I scream for help when the going gets tough, I will never again hold up my head in the company of booted and belted men."

"I thought so." Kate said. "I will never desert a friend in need, and that is why Frank and I are coming with you, Ranger Brewster. To ignore a vicious criminal like Jesse Dobbs is to throw out the rule of law and plunge into anarchy. I will not allow that to happen."

Brewster shook his head. "You're tough, Kate. Tough as any man."

"Perhaps. But I'm also a woman." Kate lifted the hem of her dress and revealed the lacy garter around her shapely thigh. "I wear this always . . . to remind myself of that fact. Do not mistake my determination for my being harsh and inflexibile, Ranger Brewster, because I am neither."

Frank said, "I guess we should grab whatever sleep we can and head for Eagle Pass at first light."

Brewster looked surprised and paid great attention to the other man's face. "You give up easy."

"I don't mistake Kate's determination for anything else. Well, she's determined to bring Jesse Dobbs to justice and when she feels that strongly about a thing, there's no arguing with her."

Brewster stared at the ground and kicked sand with his toe. "Frank, I guess when we meet up with Dobbs, I'd feel better if your gun was backing my play."

"Of course you'll feel better with Frank at your side, JC," Kate said. "Now, I wonder if there's coffee in the cabin. We could all use a cup."

Frank smiled. "I'll back your play, Ranger. Now let's go hunt up that coffee."

CHAPTER FORTY-SEVEN

"Hell, I didn't expect this," Dobbs said. "Now I'm stuck on this side of the border until it blows itself out."

The bartender nodded and looked wise. "June to November is when you can expect storms coming up from the Gulf. If you stand at the door and take a sniff you can smell fish shoaling, or so I'm told. I never could smell them myself but Hug Cluggan the timber merchant says he gets a whiff every time."

"I didn't. This damn town always has the same stink." Dobbs pushed his whiskey glass across the bar. "Fill it."

The bartender, a fat, jolly kind of man with a network of broken red veins on both cheeks, poured his best bourbon from a dusty bottle. "Rain is getting heavier, and listen to the wind. Sounds like the wail of a damned soul."

"Yeah, getting his first glimpse of Eagle Pass."

The bartender grinned. "You're a rum one, mister." He put the bottle under the bar and left to serve another customer, leaving Dobbs to sit in silence, morose, armed, and dangerous.

He picked up his glass and stepped to the door that rattled in its frame, making a racket like chattering castanets. He peered out of the rain-lashed glass panel into the empty street. Muddy puddles rippled in the wind, and a couple of tarpaper shacks to the rear of the stores had already lost their roofs. Across the street, a brave matron battled the weather to do some emergency shopping, but when her umbrella turned inside out into a V she gave up the struggle and turned into an alley out of the wind.

"Mister, you look like a feller who's bored."

Dobbs turned and studied the man standing next to him. "You could say that."

The man was a city slicker by the look of his fancy duds. Slender and of medium height, he had the sly eyes of an outhouse rat. "I got a remedy for boredom. She goes by the name of High Timber Hattie Dickson, six foot tall and all woman." The man smiled. "She'll give you such a time, you won't be bored for a week, just thinking back on it."

"Where is this woman?" Dobbs said.

"Just down the street a ways. You won't even get wet."

"How much?"

The man smiled. He had a gold tooth. "Well, that's between you and Hattie, but five dollars will guarantee you a good time and ten a real good time."

Dobbs thought about that. "Sure. It beats staying here waiting for the wrath of God to strike."

"Finish your drink and follow me." The man pushed out his hand. "Name is Mordecai Benger."

"I don't care what your name is," Dobbs said, ignoring the proffered handshake. He pulled out a thick wad of notes that made the man's eyes pop out of his head. "First I got to pay my score."

"Oh yes, certainly," Benger said. "A man should always pay what he owes."

Dobbs saw greed in the pimp's eyes, but he ignored it. A man who's good with a gun could ignore much.

High Timber Hattie was tall and shapely but not real pretty. Her front teeth protruded and horses had slept on better straw than the bleached blond hair that grew on her head. "What do you want me to be?"

"A whore," Dobbs said.

Hattie smiled and drew back the curtain of a recessed closet. She waved to the packed clothes hanging on a rail. "I can be a schoolmarm, a nun, a little girl with a little curl, an equestrienne with a whip, a Chinese, a—"

"Just take your clothes off, lie on your back, and be what you are," Dobbs said. "That's all I want. I'm here to pass time."

"Whatever you say. You are my master."

"Yeah, for as long as I pay you."

"Business is business, so let's get to it."

As the storm raged outside and a relentless rain rattled on the bedroom window of Hattie's shack, she got out of bed and tossed on a silk robe. "I'll get us something to drink, lover." She smiled. "By the way, you were great. A real lively gent. My favorite kind of guest."

When he'd climbed into bed, Dobbs had dropped his holstered Colt on the floor next to the bed, well away from his scattered clothes. He drew the revolver and placed it between the sheets out of sight. Hattie and her pimp had no way of knowing it, but Dobbs figured he was about to get rolled. He'd been there before and he read the signs. He'd seen it happen many times, but this con was cruder and more obvious than most.

As he'd suspected, Hattie stepped into the bedroom, a Smith & Wesson .38 in her hand. Behind her, announced by a thunder roll, was the dressed-up dude with the gold tooth. He carried a nickel-plated Colt with a bone handle.

The man smiled. "You know the drill, mister. We want your wallet, watch, gun, and horses."

"And then you'll kill me." Dobbs put a quaver in his voice, acting scared.

"I'm afraid so," said the man who'd introduced himself as Mordecai Benger. "Three in the belly and you'll be dead so quick it won't even hurt."

"Get up," Hattie said. "You're not going to bleed all over my bed. Go into the kitchen where I can mop up afterward."

"You heard the lady. Get the hell out of there. Make a fancy move and I'll gun you right where you stand."

Dobbs decided to have some fun. "Carry me."

Benger was stunned. "What the hell are you talking about?"

"I don't want to get up. You'll have to carry me."

"Damn you. I'll gun you right now." Benger raised his Colt.

"No!" Hattie yelled. "I just got a new feather mattress."

"I saw the rube flash his wad, Hattie. Hell, he's got

enough money to buy you another one and a new bed to go with it."

"Then we'll give it to him in the head, Mordecai. He won't bleed as much." She raised her .38. "Like this."

Playtime was over.

Dobbs pulled his gun and fired at Hattie. His bullet hit between her breasts and she went down hard, her convulsing finger triggering a wild shot.

Benger was appalled by the suddenness of Dobbs's attack. He hesitated for a second, maybe two, but realized instantly that he'd made a fatal mistake. You can't give a gun-talented man that much time. Dobbs thumbed off three shots, all of them hits to the belly. Benger screamed as he saw death rush to meet him, the dreaded sickle slashing. The man sank slowly to the floor and lay groaning in agony. A gut shooting was one of the worst of all deaths and its torment lasted for a long . . . long time.

Dobbs dressed hurriedly then checked on Hattie. She was dead. He pried the Smith & Wesson from her fingers and stuck it in his waistband. Benger still lived, dying hard, cursing the mother that bore him.

"Do you recollect what you told me, old fellow? Three to the belly and I'd die quick." Dobbs grinned. "Well, how does it feel? You dying quick?"

Engulfed in a sea of pain, Benger was no longer capable of speech. Dobbs shrugged, kicked the man hard in the face, and made his way outside into the tempest.

"The sacks are still there, Mr. Dobbs, just as you left them," the liveryman said. "I don't let anybody get near."

Dobbs stepped to the rear of the stable where the rats and spiders lived. He lifted the tarp that covered the money sacks and nodded. "You done good, Matt."

"Your horses are all in good shape, too. Been feeding them a scoop of oats with their hay just like you said."

Dobbs walked to the door of the barn and the old man followed. "You seen the likes of this before?" Dobbs said.

Matt nodded. "Maybe five, six times in my score of years here in Eagle Pass. This one is stronger than most I've seen."

"How long will I be stuck here?"

"You can travel tomorrow, Mr. Dobbs, maybe so. These here storms don't last very long. They blow into town, do their damage, and move on. Kinda like folks."

Dobbs stared at the old man, but Matt's face was empty. "I thought I heard gunshots earlier."

Matt shook his head. "Hard to tell. Heard plenty of thunder, though."

"I was probably mistaken then."

"Easy mistake to make. Ha! There goes another bang. Just like a pistol shot, huh?"

Dobbs glanced at the sky heavy with banded ramparts of black and purple clouds. Lightning scrawled like the signature of God. Torrential rain danced all over the surface of a large muddy puddle in front of the stable, kicking up exclamation points of water.

"Sure wouldn't want to be traveling on a day like this, Mr. Dobbs," Matt said. "It ain't fit for man nor beast."

CHAPTER FORTY-EIGHT

"I swear, in this kind of weather the ducks drown as soon as they get airborne," JC Brewster said.

"It's coming down all right," Kate said. "And I don't see any chance of it letting up."

She, Brewster, and Frank huddled in the back of the wagon, sharing the shelter of the single slicker they'd brought from the Madison cabin. The slicker was old and full of holes but was better than nothing. The mare had been freed from the traces, but she stood close, her head down, as wet and miserable as the three humans.

"You ever experience anything like this before?" Frank asked Brewster.

The Ranger shook his head. "No, but I've heard about it. Big storms come up from the Gulf and play hob."

"The weather will keep Dobbs in Eagle Pass," Kate said.

"Unless he's already in Old Mexico," Brewster said.

Kate pushed a damp strand of hair off her forehead.

"Does anybody think we could be any more miserable, wet, and hungry than we already are?"

"Not me," Brewster said.

"Frank?" Kate said.

"Not me, either" Frank said.

Kate said, "Good. Then we might as well continue our journey to Eagle Pass. It's better than sitting here."

"It will be slow going and the lightning is dangerous," Frank said.

"It's dangerous right here as well," she said. "I've said a prayer to Our Lady of the Storm for her protection and she will not fail us."

Blown by a gust of wind, rain hammered on the ragged slicker, soaking everybody. Thunder crashed and the air sizzled from a nearby lightning strike.

"Kate, I sure hope you're right," Frank said.

"Have faith, Frank. Our Lady may not shelter us from dangers, but she will give us the courage to face them."

"Amen." Brewster looked at Frank and winked.

As Kate and the others drove into Eagle Pass with the mare faltering in the traces, the wild oaks no longer sang their wind song and the dark sky manifested stars and was calm. The storm had passed and the town would have seemed at peace if not for the score of armed men that patrolled its debris-strewn streets.

Frank planned to drive Kate to the hotel, where she could get out of her damp clothes, but he pulled up the mare when a man wearing a battered top hat and long black coat beckoned to him.

"You folks just get in?" the man said, looking over the wagon and its drenched occupants.

"Yeah," Frank said. "What's happened here?"

"Somebody took advantage of the storm to murder High Timber Hattie Dickson and her paramour Mordecai Benger. Seems like a crime of passion to me, two men after the same whore. Well, we're looking for the murderer whoever he is. You folks be careful." He saw Kate and touched his hat brim. "Ma'am. Myself and the armed men you see are members of the Eagle Pass Peace Command, so you have nothing to fear, young lady."

Kate fluttered her eyelashes. "Why, thank you, sir. You are very gallant. I shall sleep better tonight knowing that you and the other stalwarts are on duty."

The man gave a little bow. "Your obedient servant, ma'am. My name is Marcellus Twining and I own the general store. For this week only, I'm selling ladies' shoes at cost and ditto for the finest French bloomers. Do stop by."

"I most assuredly will, Mr. Twining," Kate said. "You are very kind."

Frank clucked the mare into motion. "Got yourself another admirer, Kate."

"He's trying to sell shoes is all."

"And bloomers," JC Brewster said.

"Ranger Brewster, a gentleman must refrain from using that word or any other word pertaining to underclothing in the presence of a lady," Kate said, frowning.

"But the storekeeper said it," Brewster said.

"I'm aware of that, but he is of the merchant class and doesn't know any better."

"Real nice night," Frank said, a smile tugging at the corners of his mouth.

The desk clerk assured Kate that he would send a copper bathtub and a plentiful supply of towels to her room and that her clothes would soon dry in front of the furnace that heated the hotel's hot water. He made no such assurances to Frank and Brewster, who were assigned a room and left to their own devices. Since he was the only one with money to pay the bill, the Ranger thought himself ill done by.

Kate consoled him when she told him he could also dry his clothing at the furnace. "So long as our intimate garments don't touch. That would be most improper."

CHAPTER FORTY-NINE

Frank left the wagon outside the livery and led the exhausted mare inside.

The man in charge was a gouty oldster with no teeth but a ready, gummy smile. "What can I do fer you, mister?"

"It's what you can do for the horse," Frank said. "I'll rub her down, but she needs a dry stall and oats along with her hay."

"I can do that. Put her back there beside your other hosses. Cost you an extry two bits for tonight, though."

His last dollar light as a feather in his pocket, Frank nodded. "Sounds like a deal." He handed over the dollar.

The man said, "I'll get your change. Name's Matt Lister, but most folks call me Gimp."

"I'll call you Matt," Frank said.

"Much appreciated. There's a piece of sacking over there and a brush."

Frank spent considerable time on the old horse, getting her grooming right, and then led her to a stall at the rear of the barn.

"Not that stall, mister, the one next to it," Lister said. "I'm storing stuff in there for a gent."

A pile of something covered by a tarp lay against the stall's far wall and Frank idly toed it, expecting the feel of leather or canvas. Instead, he heard the clink of coin.

"Your man doesn't believe in banks, huh?" Frank gave that some thought for a few moments. "Can you describe the man who left this here?"

"Sure. Big man, bearded, a gruff way about him. Wears a gun like he was born to it."

"By any chance is his name Jesse Dobbs?"

Lister shook his head. "I don't know his name. He never put it out and I didn't ask. Like I didn't ask your'n"

"Frank Cobb." He led the horse to its stall and forked hay while Lister supplied a scoop of oats.

Frank returned to the mysterious pile, opened his Barlow, and took a knee beside the tarp. He threw it aside and cut into one of the sacks. It was filled with gold and silver coin. He grabbed a handful and held it up. The coins gleamed in the light of the oil lamp the old man held high.

"Did you know it was money?"

"Surely didn't. I suspicioned it might be treasure of some kind, but I wasn't sure. The gent said he'd pay me fifty dollars to keep a close eye on it."

"If it's Jesse Dobbs's money, he would have paid you in lead," Frank said. "I believe this is a stolen army payroll and a lot of men have died because of it."

The old man's face took on a stricken look. "Mister, you're funnin' me about paying me in lead, right? Fifty dollars buys a heap of cartridges."

"When he leaves with the money, Dobbs will not let you live. That's a natural fact."

"Well, what the hell do I do? I ain't a gunman."

"You do what I tell you, Matt."

"And what's that?"

Frank told him.

The tap on Kate's door was soft, almost apologetic. She wrapped a towel around herself and picked up the derringer. "Who is it?"

"It's old Matt Lister from the livery stable as ever was, with an urgent message from Frank Cobb."

"Hold on." She turned the key in the door lock and then stepped behind the dressing screen. "Come in."

Dressed in an old Confederate greatcoat and a battered bowler hat, the small man stepped into the room. He looked at Kate, her naked shoulders visible above the screen, and if he was flustered he didn't let it show. Lister was silent for a few moments, recalling what Frank had told him, then said, "You want to hear the message, ma'am, or should I come back when you're decent?"

"I'm always decent. State your business."

"Beggin' your pardon, ma'am, but my business is to tell you that Frank says he's found the missing army payroll."

"Found it? Where?"

"In the livery stable. See, I was keeping an eye on it fer a feller Frank says is Jesse Boggs."

"Dobbs?"

"Yeah, right. That was the name."

"Is there anything else?" Kate said.

"Sure is, ma'am. Frank says you and the Ranger are

to stay away from the livery, that he'll handle things his own self. And he says not to mention the money to the vigilantes that are prowling all over town doin' nothing but getting drunk and drunker. Frank didn't say the drunk part. I said that."

Lister doffed his hat. "Frank said one more thing, ma'am. He said I was to steer clear of the livery because Dobbs would shoot me for sure. He said I was to throw myself on your mercy, like, and that you'd protect me."

"A difficult thing to do when I don't have any clothes," Kate said. Then her face brightened. "Matt. It is Matt, isn't it?"

"As ever was, ma'am."

"Matt, go down to the boiler room and bring me the clothes that are drying on a rack before the furnace. There are both male and female garments, but bring them all to me."

"Who put them there, if you don't mind me asking?"

"The desk clerk. But I want you to go get them. The less he knows the better. Are you a married man, Matt?"

"I got hitched one time, lasted three years afore she ran off with a banjo player."

"Good. You had a wife. Handling female undergarments will not get you overly stimulated."

"Are you certain Frank said he'd go it alone?" Brewster asked. "He's shot through and through, you know." He'd pulled his pants over his long-handled underwear after Kate had passed his clothes through the door. His suspenders hung loose at his sides. The bandage on his wounded shoulder was fat as a boardinghouse cat.

Lister shrugged. "If he is, he didn't let it show."

"I should be there. A Texas Ranger can't stand idly by while others are performing stirring deeds."

Kate, wearing clothes that were still damp in places, said, "JC, there is no doubt in my mind that you are bold and courageous, but wounded as you are, Frank knows that if it comes to a gunfight you're no match for Jesse Dobbs."

"But Frank's wounded," Brewster said. "He's shot all to pieces."

"I know, but Frank is a different breed. He's strong and enduring as though forged from steel. He's ridden outlaw trails and learned how to survive in a hard, unforgiving land among men equally hard and unforgiving. He's been wounded before, many times, and by sheer strength of will lived on to fight another day. Strange as it may seem, and though Frank would deny it, he and Dobbs are two of a kind, opposite sides of the same coin. The West is changing and there are folks who think that men like Dobbs and Frank don't stack up to much and maybe they're right . . . but in my lifetime, they'll all be gone and I'll never see their like again."

"Dobbs is a murderer and a thief," Brewster said.

"He is indeed," Kate said. "But Dobbs is a hard man to kill, and Frank knows it."

Brewster seemed offended. "I'm a Texas Ranger and I can handle anything that comes my way."

"Of course you can. It's men like you who are bringing law to the West and making it a fine place to live for decent folks. But at this moment in time, we must still depend on men like Frank. Today, the only thing that matters is how fast a man can draw a gun. I've seen Frank do that very thing, JC, and he's faster than you will ever be. Stand aside this once, Ranger Brewster, and let Frank do what he was bred to do."

"I could round up the vigilantes and arrest Dobbs as soon as he steps into the barn," Brewster said.

"And how many widows would there be in Eagle Pass by this time tomorrow?" Kate asked.

"And dead Rangers?" Matt Lister spoke for the first time since he and Kate stepped into Brewster's room. "I've been measuring men all my life and if the feller I spoke with is Jesse Dobbs then he's a handful." His faded, tired eyes turned to the Ranger. "After the war I was a lawman for a spell my own self, but I never amounted to much. The day I watched John Wesley Hardin practice with his guns was the day I turned in my badge. Hell, I knew if I ever had to go up against a fast draw fighter, I was a dead man. Sometimes a man has to face reality and leave the serious shooting to somebody who's more experienced and a sight faster than he is."

Brewster rose from his chair, stepped to the window, and looked into the dark street, where the members of the Eagle Pass Peace Command huddled together and passed bottles around. None of them was sober. "Then I guess we wait."

"'They also serve who only stand and wait,'" Kate said. "The poet John Milton wrote that."

"Was he ever in Eagle Pass?" Brewster said.

"No. No he wasn't," Kate said.

"I didn't think so."

CHAPTER FIFTY

Restless rats rustled near Frank as he sat in a dark corner of the livery stable and awaited the dawn. The bell in the Methodist church tower dinged softly to the errant rhythm of a gusting south wind. He built himself a cigarette, glad that his tobacco sack was almost full. It was going to be a long night.

Around two in the morning, three men stepped out of the gloom and into the barn. Frank tensed, his fingers closing on his gun.

After a few moments came the sound of gushing water hitting the floor and a man said, "Hell, I needed that. I've been holding it for an hour."

"Me, too, Tom," another man said. "Seems that Old Crow goes right through me."

The men left and again the livery was silent but for the rats.

Frank leaned the back of his head against the wall and dozed, treading the narrow ledge between wakefulness and sleep. He woke several times, once from a dream that he walked among blossoming trees showering him with gold and silver coins that chimed on hard ground. It was the knell of the church bell in a rising wind that had trespassed on his sleep, that and nothing more.

Cramped, he rose to his feet and stretched the kinks out of his back. He stepped to the door and looked outside. Eagle Pass was lost in darkness and its buildings looked like shadowy ghost ships anchored for the night. A single oil lamp burned somewhere in the murk and cast no light. He turned and walked back to his uncomfortable corner. Would the night never end?

The dawn arrived as it must.

It is a strange, opalescent time between darkness and light that wakes a man so that he sits up in his blankets expecting to see . . . something different. But always, it's the same . . . the same things he saw the day before. Only the sky changes.

Frank woke from sleep with a start. His hand on his Colt, he quickly looked around. The horses were quiet in their stalls, the barn door was a rectangle of gray, and beyond, the wakening town laid in a drift of rain, the child of the Gulf storm clutching at its coattails.

Rising to his feet, he stood in shadow. Jesse Dobbs would come. He must come. Getting the money out of the country into Mexico was a top priority after the storm delay. The rain wouldn't stop him. He would come . . .

* * *

Frank's prediction came to pass thirty minutes later.

He watched Dobbs come through the rain. The man wore an ankle-length slicker and carried a rifle at his side. Above him, the sky was ashen and gloomy, making the morning damp and depressing.

Dobbs stepped into the barn. "Gimpy!" After a few moments of silence, he called, "Where the hell are you?"

Frank walked out of shadow. "He's not here, Jesse. Even think about raising the Winchester and I'll kill you."

"Who are you?" Dobbs said.

"Name's Frank Cobb. I'm here to arrest you and take the payroll you stole back to the army."

Dobbs smiled. "Hell, I've heard of you. As I recollect, back in the day you ran with some wild ones."

"I still do," Frank said.

Dobbs propped the rifle against the wall of the barn. "We don't need to quarrel, you and me. Come with me to Mexico and we'll split the money. Hell, there's enough for both of us and we can have us a time."

"Until I turn my back and your bullet puts an end to the good times. You're scum, Jesse."

Dobbs had been smiling, but his face hardened. "And what does that make you, outlaw?"

"I could have ended up like you, Jesse, but I went straight, saved myself. You never will."

Dobbs made a visible effort to remain calm. When he succeeded in pulling himself together he said, "Last chance, Cobb, and then my talking is done. Throw in with me and we'll blow this burg as rich men."

"Not a chance in hell, Jesse. We have it out here and now."

"You can't shade me, Cobb."

"Try me."

Dobbs's hand streaked for his gun. He was sudden. Lightning-bolt sudden. Frank, weakened by his wound and far from being at his best, was way slower. But it didn't matter. The rifle bullet that crashed onto Dobbs's back as his Colt cleared leather dropped him like a puppet that just had its strings cut. He was alive when he hit the dung on the floor, but he was beyond movement. With his spine between his shoulder blades shattered and splintered like a dry stick, he died within moments.

Frank looked at the figure in the doorway. "You didn't give him much of a chance to make his play."

"You gave him his chance. He didn't take it." Kate lowered her rifle. "You're family, Frank. I fight like a tigress for my family and win any way I can."

"And now you'll have to live with it, Kate."

"I shot a mad dog, Frank. I can live with that just fine."

Under the fussy supervision of Texas Ranger JC Brewster, Eagle Pass vigilantes moved the payroll money to the town hall and placed it under guard. The army was informed by wire and it promised that a wagon detail would arrive to pick up the money "sooner or later depending on the exigencies of the service."

"The brass don't seem to be in too much of a hurry to get their money back," Frank said.

Brewster said, "Probably the job will end up being done by the Rangers. The army will hold a court of inquiry into the robbery before it does anything else and that could take months."

"You'll stay here with the money, JC?" Kate said.

"I reckon so, unless I'm ordered otherwise. You're heading back to the ranch?"

"Yes," Kate said. "We've been gone too long."

"Going to be quiet around here without you two," Brewster said.

"If you're ever up in the Pecos River country—"

"I'll be sure to stop by."

"We'll have tea and sponge cake," she said.

"I look forward to it." Brewster had been smiling, but his face became serious. "Kate, about Jesse Dobbs—"

"I'd do the same thing again."

"You saved Frank's life. That's what he told me."

"Do you think I did wrong, JC? Kate said.

"Nope. The only part of Dobbs that was facing you was his back."

Kate smiled. "That's one way of looking at it."

"That's the only way to look at it." Ranger Brewster held out his hand. "Good luck, Kate. You, too, Frank."

She took his hand. "And you, JC. Good luck."

BOOK THREE
Sacrifice

CHAPTER FIFTY-ONE

"Did I not say I'd build a house fit for an Irish queen?" Barrie Delaney bowed.

"You did and you have." Kate looked into the old pirate's crafty eyes. "There's glass in the windows, Captain."

"Ah, the eyes of a beautiful woman miss nothing, to be sure. The glass was founded, Kate. Founded by my associate and fellow gentleman of fortune, Coot Lawson, Esquire."

"Found where?"

"A-laying on the prairie where somebody had thrown them away, pane by pane. 'Ah-ha,' says Coot, 'here's a fine kettle o' fish. A dangerous pile of glass lying in the path of any innocent rider.' Now Coot, being such a caring cove, got his men to remove the glass and then he thought to himself, 'I know. I'll take it to Captain Delaney, who is building a fine house for Mrs. Kate Kerrigan. Surely every window needs glass and these panes will not go to waste.'"

Then, triumphantly, Delaney said, "And that's how

come there is glass in every window of the Kerrigan mansion."

"Coot found it, huh? How much did you, or rather me, pay him?"

"A small reward, Kate my darlin'," the captain said. "It was such a mere trifle that I've forgotten the amount, but I'll remember when I put it on my bill."

"And maybe I'll remember to hang you and Coot Lawson from the same tree," Kate said. "Mr. Webbe, you did a fine job with the columns. I declare, it makes the house look like a Southern mansion indeed."

"They need some finishing touches. I won't leave a job half done," Hargate Webbe said.

"I will pay you for your work, Mr. Webbe," Kate said. "You can be assured of that."

Delaney laid his hand on the hilt of his cutlass and eyed the little stonemason. "And there will be no padding of the bill, or you'll answer to me."

"I'm an honest man, Mrs. Kerrigan." He returned the captain's baleful stare. "Unlike some I could mention."

He was spared further abuse when Kate's youngest daughter said, "Ma, can I see my room now? When you were gone, Trace and Quinn wouldn't let me."

"Yes, Shannon, but the house isn't finished yet and you must step carefully. Captain Delaney will take you upstairs and show it to you. Where is your sister?"

"Ivy is already in the house, Kate, pestering my men about making her furniture." Delaney stretched out a hand to Shannon. "Come, lass, I'll show you your room. I built it meself by hand, knowing it was for a right pretty girl."

After Delaney and Shannon left, Webbe said, "You'll

use that fine door from the cabin for your new house, Mrs. Kerrigan?"

"Yes. The people who lived in the cabin before us brought it with them by wagon from up north somewhere. The entire family was killed by Indians."

"A tragedy indeed."

"We gave their remains a decent, Christian burial," Kate said, "so there is always that."

"Amen." He turned and left her standing in front of the almost finished house.

Kate stood for a while listening to the tuneless cacophony of hammering as Delaney's men worked on the interior of the house. She had to concede that for a crew of pirate rogues they were doing a fine job and there had not been a single shooting or cutting since the work started.

She turned to the sound of hooves behind her. Quinn was out on the range with the hands and she'd sent Frank and Trace to check on the cholera wagons. She thought it was possible that the disease had run its course and the survivors had moved on.

Frank's face was grim, and Trace was gray around the gills, his blue eyes haunted as though he'd been given a glimpse of hell.

Speaking from the saddle, Frank said, "They haven't moved, Kate. The horses are grazing all over the place, but the wagons are still where we last saw them."

"The people? What about the people?"

"Ma," Trace said, his voice small, "the people are all dead. They all died inside the wagon circle, every last one of them. There are no living people left."

"But . . . but why, Frank? Oh my God, don't tell me they starved to death?"

"No, the cholera took them all," Frank said. "As to

why . . . I think they sacrificed themselves, Kate. They knew if they traveled on, they'd spread the plague far and wide so they stayed, knowing it would be their deaths."

"Frank, are you sure—"

"They're all dead, Kate. I used Delaney's telescope to make sure."

Tears sprang into her eyes. She opened her mouth to say something but couldn't speak. Then she realized that she'd nothing to say that hadn't already been said.

"There will have to be a burying," Frank said, "but I don't know how we can do that without risking other lives."

Kate said, "Trace, I need your horse. Frank, let's ride out there. I want to see the wagons for myself."

"I told you all there is to see, Kate," Frank said. "And you can smell the place from a mile away. Maybe you should sit this one out."

"Frank, the situation concerns the KK Ranch," she said. "I want to go there. Trace, help me mount up."

CHAPTER FIFTY-TWO

Kate sat her horse, the ship's telescope unused in her hands. Her eyes were on the buzzards circling above the wagons with the silent patience of the caretakers of the dead. The smell of death tainted the morning air, that and the rotten-fish reek of cholera. She steeled herself and then scanned the wagons with the telescope.

It was a fine instrument, English made. Engraved on one side were the words, *Thos. Harris & Son. Opticians to the Royal Family. No. 57 Opposite the British Museum.* It was perfectly suited to a close study of the motionless corpses.

Faces . . . men, women, and children, cheeks and eye sockets shadowed, the eyes open, staring, but seeing nothing. The people had died where they fell . . . a long way from Nirvana.

Kate lowered the telescope, her cheeks pale. "Yes, I can see now that everyone is dead."

"Not an easy thing to look at," Frank said.

"Deaths like that never are. As a child in Ireland, I saw bodies of the people who starved to death during the Potato Famine. They looked like the people in the wagon circle, dead where they fell with the death shadows blue on their thin faces." She looked into distance, her memories as vivid as the paintings in a Book of Hours. Taking her rosary from the pocket of her cotton day dress, she clutched it to her breast, its silver cross falling over the back of her hand. "Frank, we'll burn them. We'll set the wagons on fire and burn everything into ashes." In a quieter tone, she added, "It's a terrible thing to do and may God forgive me."

Everyone who could ride was given a horse—the hands called in from the range, Barrie Delaney and his pirates, Trace, Quinn, Marco Salas the blacksmith, Frank, and Kate herself. A wagon was loaded with coal oil and whatever else would ignite. Around the wagon circle there was mesquite and sagebrush that would burn hot with thick black smoke and would help purify the air.

Despite his protests Moses Rice was to be left behind to take care of the girls. "But Miz Kerrigan, I seen the cholera before," he said.

"Mose, you're the only one I trust to stay behind with my daughters and keep an eye on things," Kate said. "God willing, Mr. Lowery will be up and about soon but for now, he must remain in bed, and Jazmin has other duties to attend to."

"But Miz Kerrigan—"

"Please don't add to my woes right now, Mose. I need you right here."

Bowing to the inevitable, Moses said, "I'll do as you say . . . but under protest, mind."

She smiled. "Duly noted, Mr. Rice."

* * *

Kate split her forces into good riders and bad.

Led by Frank, the best riders—KK hands, Trace, and Quinn—were given the job of trotting around the wagon circle throwing coal oil onto the canvas covers. Frank also included Barrie Delaney, who had begun his piratical career in Ireland as a highwayman on the old coast road between Lame and Ballycastle and rode like a Comanche. The other pirates, men who could sit a horse but were not horsemen, were tasked with building a mesquite fire to light the torches.

Kate sat her horse and said to her assembled riders, "Don't stop for anything. I don't know how many ways cholera can spread, so throw the coal oil on the canvases as you pass and then get out of there. Trace, Quinn, the rest of you, do you understand?"

"Sure do, Mrs. Kerrigan," one of the hands said. "I got no intention of stopping to take in the scenery."

"I hope the rest of you feel the same way," Kate said.

Frank grinned. "I guess you can depend on that, Kate."

"The fire is lit, so let's get it done," she said. "I'll ride down with you."

"Kate, you can see just fine from where you're at," Frank hefted his jug of coal oil. "The rest of us will get it done."

"Truer words were never spoke, Kate me darlin'," Delaney said. "When there's dirty work afoot, leave it to the menfolk, I always say."

With considerable trepidation Kate watched the men ride away. Surely if they kept their distance and didn't stop, they'd be safe. She found her rosary again and held it tight.

* * *

The riders did stop. After a few tries, they discovered that they couldn't efficiently toss the coal oil from jugs without drawing rein and standing in the stirrups. Kate was on edge, her nerves frayed. In how much danger were her men? She had no way of knowing and that made her unease grow.

Soon the tinder-dry wagons were fired and the circle blazed like a gigantic Catherine wheel. Thick columns of black smoke rose into the air from the mesquite and sage that had been added to the blaze.

Kate sat her horse with the others and for a while they watched the conflagration. Finally she said to Frank, "We'll let the fire burn itself out and then come back to bury the ashes of the dead."

Frank nodded. "Not even cholera could survive that blaze."

"I certainly hope not. We're fighting an enemy we can't see and it frightens me."

Frank smiled. "You frightened, Kate? I find that hard to believe."

"Believe it, Frank. Confront me with an enemy I can see and identify and I'll fight tooth and nail, but disease . . . well, I'm at a loss."

"I bet a lot of doctors have said that very thing."

After one lingering look at the circle of fire Kate said to the men around her, "We'll head back to the ranch. I'm sure Jazmin has coffee in the pot and there's whiskey for them that want it."

That drew a cheer from all hands.

Kate smiled and added, "And that includes myself."

"Hey, look at that, me hearties."

All eyes turned to the pirate who'd spoken, a

gray-haired, taciturn man known only to Kate as Jolly Jakes. She doubted that was his real name.

"Where away?" Delaney said.

Jakes pointed. "Over there, Cap'n, among the mesquite by the dead tree. See it? It looks like a younker."

Kate put the telescope to her eye. "I don't see anything. Maybe it was an animal."

"Damn your eyes, Jolly," Delaney said. "Have you been at the rum again and seeing things?"

Jakes shook his hoary head. "It's there, Cap'n, among the mesquite. I swear to God I saw a white child moving around."

"There's one way to find out." Trace kicked his horse into a gallop and headed for the dead wild oak.

Through the telescope Kate watched her son dismount and walk into the mesquite thicket. He emerged a few moments later carrying a struggling, kicking child by the armpits. Grinning, Trace lifted the kid into the saddle and got up behind him. When he returned to the others, he lowered the squalling child to the ground and said above the din, "He's a boy and this was pinned to his . . . whatever the hell it is he's wearing."

Kate was too taken aback to chide Trace for swearing. She took the paper and studied it. "The writing is very small." She reached into the pocket of her riding skirt, opened a small tortoiseshell case, and removed a pair of pince-nez spectacles. She settled the glasses on her nose and read aloud, *"My name is Peter Letting and I'm three years old. My ma took me from the wagons because I don't have the cholera. Everyone else is dead and she died holding hands with my pa. If I am found alive please take care of me. If I am dead bury me as a Christian."*

Kate removed her steamed up glasses. "It's not signed."

Frank said, "Give me the paper," Kate."

Kate handed it over. Frank thumbed a match into flame and when the paper was burning well he dropped it to the ground. "Let me have your hands, Kate." He removed his canteen from the saddle horn and poured water over Kate's hands and then his own. "I don't know if that was needed, but we can't take chances." Nodding in the direction of the boy, he said, "What about him?"

"He's got a locket around his neck." She stepped out of the saddle and kneeled beside the boy. He stopped crying as soon as she put her arms around him and hugged him close.

"Kate, should you be doing that?" Frank said.

She looked at him. "He's a frightened child who may have been wandering around for days. He's hungry, thirsty, and dirty, and he needs affection. Let me have your canteen, Frank."

He hesitated. "He may have gone back to the wagons. Have you thought about that?"

"Yes, I have, and that's a chance I'll have to take." Kate said. "Would you have me abandon him out here? I'm surprised he's still alive. This boy is a survivor. I can see it in his eyes. He's brave, Frank, very brave."

"By the way he caterwauls, you could have fooled me." Frank dismounted and passed Kate his canteen. The child drank deeply and she took the opportunity to open the locket on the silver chain around the boy's neck. She answered the question on Frank's face. "A young man and woman. They must have been his parents."

Frank glanced at the open locket. A bearded man and a dark-haired woman, the man unhandsome, the woman plain. Two ordinary people who died in terrible circumstances. "Well, get that dirty shift off him and we'll take him back to the ranch and feed him."

"His name is Peter," Kate said.

Frank nodded. "Then Pete it is."

CHAPTER FIFTY-THREE

Hank Lowery's throat had been cut and a folded piece of paper had been forced between the dead man's teeth . . . his murderer revealing a grotesque sense of humor.

Carrying Peter into the cabin from outside, Frank heard Kate's frantic calls for Moses Rice and her girls, but he heard no answering cry, nor would there be one, as the bloodstained note explained.

THANKEE FER THE MONEY AND GRUB.
WE'LL LEAVE YOOR BRATS AND THE NIGER AT
THE ROONED MISION AT JAKE PIKE DRAW.
DON'T FOLLER OR THE BRATS DIE.
PS. WERE KEEPING THE MEX WOMAN.

Frank walked through the ransacked cabin. The tin box where Kate kept money for day-to-day ranch expenses had been forced open, emptied, and thrown on the floor. Supplies—flour, coffee, bacon, and canned goods—had been stripped from the kitchen shelves and even the peppers had been taken from the rafters.

Kate stepped around the corner of her new house, a worried-looking Barrie Delaney at her side, when she caught sight of Frank. "How is Hank?" she called when she was still a distance away.

Frank stepped closer to her and said, "Kate, Hank is dead."

Disbelief and then horror crossed her face. She brushed past Frank, hiked up her dress, and ran for the cabin. Frank gave her a few moments and then followed her inside.

She stood at Lowery's bedside, pale like a woman formed from alabaster. She stretched out a hand and pushed an errant strand of hair off the dead man's forehead. Blood had stained his pillow scarlet and his hands were cut, slashed to ribbons as he'd tried to defend himself.

"This was on the table," Frank said, a lie to save Kate from further horror. He handed her the note.

She read it slowly, and then it read again. When she looked up again her beautiful green eyes were as cold as winter. "Who—did—this—Frank?" she said with a pause between each word, her voice sounding like a death knell.

"I don't know," Frank said.

"We'll find whoever did it and kill him," Kate said.

A yell of protest from outside was followed by Delaney's harsh order to "Shut the hell up!" Then Hargate Webbe was hurled headlong through the open bedroom door.

Delaney was right behind him. "Caught this scurvy swab skulking among the trees." His eyes moved to the dead man. "Lord have mercy on us. Kate, what happened?"

"Hank Lowery was murdered," she said.

Delaney removed his hat. "Poor gentleman. May the Good Lord rest his soul." He drew his cutlass and brandished it murderously in Webbe's face. "By God, if you had anything to do with this, I'll cut you into collops."

"I wasn't skulking. I was hiding," Webbe said.

"Same thing. Damn my eyes, there's treachery afoot, Kate. I have a nose that can sniff it out." Delaney glared at Webbe. "I have a mind to ram three feet of Sheffield steel through your belly, stonemason."

Kate said, "Let us respect the dead by stepping outside. Mr. Webbe, you will explain yourself to my satisfaction or I'll hang you."

Webbe was a thoroughly frightened man when Delaney dragged him away from the cabin and threw him on the ground.

"Who took the two young girls and the black man? And where is Jazmin, as fair a filly as ever trod the earth and a fine cook to boot? Where are they, Webbe? Tell me or I'll cut your heart out."

"I told you, I don't know," Webbe said, looking miserable. "All I can say is that afterward they headed south."

Frank said, "Webbe, get a grip of yourself and then tell us what happened."

Webbe took a deep breath and steadied himself. "In my spare time I'm something of an entomologist—"

"I knew it," Delaney bellowed. "There's treachery for you. He's an ento . . . enta . . . whatever the hell he says he is. It sounds like he's aboard with some heathen, murdering crew o' scallywags to me."

"It means I collect butterflies and moths," Webbe said.

Kate said, "Quickly, Mr. Webbe. There's no time to be lost. What happened here?"

"I saw a fine specimen of *Vanessa cardui*—Painted Lady—among the oaks and went after it, hoping to add it to my collection. No sooner had I begun my hunt when I heard rough men yelling and then gunshots."

Kate said, "My daughters!"

"They were not harmed, dear lady," Webbe said. "The miscreants shot into the air. Unfortunately, Moses did not have his pistol with him and could not make a fight of it."

"How many were there?" Frank said.

"Four, four of them."

"Then I'm glad Mose didn't have his pistol," Frank said. "Describe these men."

"Big men, dressed in buckskins," Webbe said. "They had red hair to their shoulders and beards down their chests. That's all I saw or cared to see. I hid in the brush until you and Mrs. Kerrigan arrived."

"Sounds like the Garvan boys," Frank said.

"Who are they?" Kate said.

"Four outlaw brothers spawned in hell, Kate. As I recall, their names are Merrill, Jud, Andy, and the oldest brother is Josiah, the worst of them. Merrill is the fastest with a gun, but Josiah does deadly work with the knife. A couple years ago up in the Indian Territory, he fought a duel with a cavalry sergeant over the affections of a fallen woman. They met on the pine trunk that had dropped across a creek. The sergeant was armed with a saber, but Josiah Garvan cut his heart out."

"Oh my God," Kate said, horrified.

"Kate, I didn't mean to scare you," Frank said.

"Well, you did. We'll change horses and sack up whatever supplies the Garvan brothers left us. Captain Delaney, I want you to mount every one of your rogues who can ride a horse. We'll meet force with force and if my daughters are harmed, I'll hang them all from the same tree."

One of the hands, a round-shouldered man named Dusty Bates, said to Kate, "Where are we headed, boss?"

"Frank, what's the name of that place?" Kate said.

"The ruined mission at Jake Pike Draw. According to Webbe they headed south."

"I know that place, camped there one time when me and another feller was hunting antelope," Bates said. "The mission was burned by the Comanche close to a hundred years ago. All that's left standing are parts of its mud brick walls."

"Can you lead us there, Dusty?" Frank said.

"Sure I can."

"Then get ready to ride," Frank said. Then to Kate, "What about Pete?"

"Jolly Jakes had sons of his own," Delaney said. "He'll stay behind and take care of the tyke."

"Make sure he feeds him," Kate said.

"Feed and wash him and find him something to wear," Delaney said. "Jolly has done all that before."

"I hate to leave him," Kate said.

"Kate, me darlin', if you plan to raise him your own self as a Western man, then he'll need to get used to life's little inconveniences. You can lay to that."

CHAPTER FIFTY-FOUR

Kate Kerrigan's home had been invaded, her children taken, and that was an outrage she'd avenge with equal savagery. As she rode out of the KK Ranch her men behind her, Kate was determined on a war to the finish. There would be no negotiation, no mercy shown . . . only the reckoning.

Barrie Delaney had brought along six of his scoundrels who could be counted on to stay on a horse during a running fight and were not averse to throat cutting if the need arose. Kate had her three toughest hands along with Frank, Trace, and Quinn, giving her a strength of thirteen fighting men. She made fourteen and thus an unlucky number of riders was avoided.

The evening was starting to crowd out the day when Dusty Bates told Kate that the ruined mission was close.

Frank scouted ahead and returned through the darkening twilight. "I saw the girls, but there's no sign of Mose or Jazmin."

"Could it be a trap?" Kate said.

"I don't know. That's why I came back. If the Garvan boys have laid an ambush, I wouldn't last long going it alone."

"Quite right. We'll do this in force." She slid her Winchester from the boot, took a green ribbon from the pocket of her coat, and tied back her hair. She wore a split canvas riding skirt, a Colt belted around her waist. There was no softness in her. She levered a round into the rifle and said, "Spread out, boys. We go in at the gallop." Then Kate yelled her war cry—an ancient Kerrigan battle shriek from the mists of her clan's history—and kneed her horse into motion. The others followed, galloping headlong toward the dark ruin.

Ivy and Shannon were unharmed but scared. They kneeled beside Moses Rice, who'd been badly beaten. Kate joined them there.

Moses's face was bruised and cut, and the shirt had been torn off his back. His ribs on the left side showed signs of having been repeatedly kicked.

"Mose, can you hear me?" Kate said.

The old man nodded his gray head. "I can hear you Miz Kerrigan, but I think they done for me."

Kate looked at Shannon. "What happened?"

"Mose tried to stop them from taking Jazmin and they beat him. Ivy and me tried to stop them, but the man with the knife told us to get away or he'd cut our hearts out." She pulled up the sleeve of her dress and showed purple bruises. "The man with the knife grabbed me and threw me to the ground."

Kate's chin jutted and her eyes blazed with emerald fire, a mother wolf seeing one of her cubs mistreated.

Later, Shannon would say that she'd never seen her ma look like that before and hoped she'd never see her look that way ever again.

"Miz Kerrigan, I couldn't stop them," Moses said. "They took Jazmin."

"You were very brave, Mose," Kate said. "I'm proud of you." Frank passed her a canteen that she held to the old man's lips.

He drank a little and then coughed. "It's all up with me."

"Indeed it is not. Once we get you home to the ranch, plenty of bed rest and Jazmin's good cooking will soon get you back on your feet. How can I run the KK without you?"

"You're very good to me, Miz Kerrigan."

"No I'm not, Mose," Kate said. "I take you for granted and sometimes I don't even notice that you're there. I won't make those mistakes again."

Kate unbuckled her suede coat and made a pillow for Moses's head. Then she said to Quinn, "Stay with them until we get back . . . and keep your rifle handy."

Quinn's face showed his disappointment. "I'd rather ride with you and Trace, Ma."

"I know you would, Quinn, but I want you here. If, God forbid, something happened to Trace and me, you'd be the owner of the KK. I don't want to put all my eggs in one basket. Do you understand?"

Frank said, "Quinn, if you see us galloping back here hell for leather with our tails between our legs, you'll be able to put your rifle to good use. Trust me on that."

Frank's words helped, but as Quinn watched Kate and the others ride away from the mission into the ominous dark, he looked devastated.

* * *

The Garvan brothers made no effort to cover their tracks across the grassland that lay south of the mission. For a time, they'd taken the old *Camino al Cielo* wagon road that had been laid by the Conquistadors, but left it when it petered out into an overgrown barrier of prickly pear cactus and thornbush.

Frank had good tracking skills and even in the dark, he didn't lose the hoofprints left by four horses, one of them carrying double. Around midnight, a small herd of pronghorn emerged from the gloom and crossed directly in front of Kate, startling her as she rode through the cool night with a blanket across her shoulders. The coyotes were up on the ridges talking to the rising moon and once they heard the mournful howls of a hunting pack of gray wolves in the distance. No one talked much, but Barrie Delaney hummed "Brennan on the Moor" to himself, a ballad dear to his heart since it was about an Irish highwayman caught and hanged in County Cork in 1804.

Trace's young eyes were the first to see the red glow of a campfire staining the dark sky ahead of them and he told Frank.

Frank's eyes squinted into the distance. "Are you sure?"

"I see it plain, Frank," Trace said.

"I see it, too. Directly ahead of us, Frank." Kate threw up her arm and drew rein. "Anybody else see it?"

One of the hands said, "Yeah, boss. It's there all right. Big blaze, a white man's fire."

Frank caught the distant glow and estimated the distance, no easy task in the dark. A mile away. Maybe a little farther.

As always in life-and-death situations, Kate deferred to her *segundo*. "How do we play it, Frank?"

"Kate, you and the others stay here. I'm going to scout ahead and take a look-see."

"Be careful, Frank," Kate said.

"I always am, Kate." His lopsided grin made his fine-cut features look ten years younger.

CHAPTER FIFTY-FIVE

On silent feet, Frank ground tied his horse and advanced on the camp. He had no doubt it was the Garvan boys, but there was always the possibility that the fire had been lit by other travelers.

A projecting wedge of limestone rock gave him cover while he viewed the camp from a distance. The moonlight helped visibility, as did the fire, its smoke heavy with the smell of mesquite and greasewood. Four men squatted by the fire, all of them big, red haired, bearded and dressed in greasy buckskins. Each held a rifle across his legs and wore a holstered Colt. Josiah, recognizable by the huge bowie knife stuck into his belt, sat in shadow beside Jazmin. He was trying to make the Mexican woman drink from a bottle and roared with laughter as she choked, the whiskey running down her chin.

In the space of a moment, Josiah Garvan changed from man to raging animal. He tore the front of Jazmin's dress apart, exposing her breasts. Snarling, he drew his knife. His brothers cheered him on, cursing and laughing, urging him to unspeakable violence.

Frank liked Jazmin Salas. She was pretty and a real nice lady. On top of that, she was a wonderful cook. Even more, she was part of the KK Ranch. To Frank that made her within hollerin' distance of kin.

A lesser man would have figured the odds were too steep, turned away, and run for help. Frank Cobb was not such a man. In the West, a man measured his manhood by his readiness to do what needed to be done and by doing it well, without a backward step. If he turned away and left Jazmin to her terrible fate, he would be much less than a man. He would be a craven creature unfit to ever again enter male company.

Driven by a hard, inflexible code, Frank did what he had to do. He drew his Colt and walked into the Garvan camp.

Josiah saw him first. He jumped up, yelled something that Frank didn't understand, and threw his knife, a backward hurling motion calculated to surprise. The Bowie had to cover about ten feet, a split second in time.

A draw fighter's hair-trigger reactions were strong in Frank and he flung himself to the side even as the knife left Josiah's hand. Frank thumbed off a shot while he was in the air. Later, he would say that his bullet and the outlaw's knife crossed each other in flight. Josiah's Bowie missed by a foot. Frank's bullet did not. Only when Josiah slammed onto the ground did Frank know he'd made a solid hit. For the moment, he ignored the big man on the ground and shot at one of his brothers, who stood in the flickering firelight, a rifle to his shoulder. The scarlet-slashed darkness was not good for aimed fire and the man hesitated. He screamed when Frank scored, his bullet hitting Jud Garvan in the belly. He jerked back, his Winchester spiraling away from him.

Josiah Garvan had been hit hard, a sucking chest wound he knew would be the death of him. He pushed to his feet and stumbled toward Frank. With his Colt at eye level, he shot wildly as he went. Frank did not return fire, knowing the man would be dead shortly. That was proven a moment later when Josiah staggered and fell flat on his face, entering hell with a curse on his lips.

From the shadows, the surviving Garvans were firing rifles.

Jazmin, sobbing and bleeding from a thin cut across the top of her breasts, ran to Frank. He had time to yell only one word, "Run!" His breath hissing through his clenched teeth from the pain of his wounded side, he grabbed Jazmin's wrist and dragged her after him. One of the Garvan brothers had found the range and bullets split the air close to Frank's head as he and Jazmin escaped into the darkness.

But not for long.

Frank had seen saddled horses backed up to a stand of stunted live oak and skeletal cottonwood and he knew the remaining two brothers would mount up and come after them.

His horse stood silvered in a shaft of moonlight, as though made of polished iron, and around it the night was vast. The animal raised its head when Frank got near but stood as he mounted, pulled Jazmin behind him, and kicked the bay into a gallop, striving to get a head start.

Frank heard the Garvan boys a distance away, but they were riding hard to catch up. Far off, thunder rolled above the Gulf and with it came a strong wind. Jazmin grabbed on to Frank's waist and buried her face in his back.

He turned his head and yelled above the noise of the wind and his galloping horse. "Not far. Kate is close with a dozen riders."

Frank didn't know if the woman heard him, but she clutched his waist tighter, communicating her fear. His gaze reached out to the darkness ahead of him, probing its limitless depths.

Behind him, Frank heard the flat statement of rifles. He turned and looked. Crimson muzzle flares blinked like the eyes of a dragon. He thought about snapping off a couple shots in return, but Jazmin was already scared and the bang and flash of his Colt would only terrify her further and accomplish nothing.

The Garvans were gaining, firing from the saddle, and with its double load Frank's horse was tiring.

My God, where was Kate?

Kate waited until she saw the flame of firing rifles and the fluttering white skirts of Jazmin became visible in the gloom. She shrugged the blanket off her shoulders and drew her Colt. "Forward!" she yelled, putting heels to her horse.

Her line of riders charged, Barrie Delaney and his pirate brigands yelling war cries in some heathen tongue far from English. She was aware of Frank galloping through her ranks with Jazmin clinging to him for dear life. The way ahead was open but for two buckskinned riders who rapidly drew rein, shocked by the new development.

Then disaster struck under the bright, uncaring moon.

One of the Garvan brothers threw his rifle to his shoulder and snapped off a quick shot. Kate heard the bullet thud into Barrie Delaney, who was riding beside her. The old pirate grunted and swayed in the saddle, but he remained on his horse.

The reaction from Kate's men was immediate and deadly.

Everyone, Kate included, cut loose a barrage of fire that sheeted lead into the Garvans. Both men went down with their horses and for a moment the ground ahead was covered with screaming, kicking horses and cursing men. She drew rein to avoid a collision and yanked her mount to the right of the tangle. One of the fallen riders jumped to his feet. He'd lost his Winchester but grabbed for the Remington on his hip. Several of Kate's men fired at the same time. Hit again and again, the Garvan brother fell. A dying horse's steel-shod hoof crashed into the man's head and if there had been any life left in him, a shattered skull ended his career of rape and murder.

One of the hands dismounted and shot the injured horses. He then checked on the brothers and looked up at Kate. "Dead as they're ever gonna be, boss."

"Where are the others?" Kate said.

Frank rode into the circle of riders. "They're dead, Kate. I killed them both." Jazmin still clung behind him. "She's in a bad way." He helped her down.

Kate stepped out of the saddle and took her in her arms. "Jazmin, are you all right? Did they—"

Jazmin lifted her head, her pained eyes free of tears. "Yes. All four of them."

"Jesus, Mary, and Joseph and all the saints in heaven

help us." Kate hugged Jazmin close, her own eyes filling with tears. "Oh, my poor darling." She looked down at the woman's bloody chest. "My precious girl, what did they do to you?"

It was a time for the women to be together.

Frank called the men away and pointed to the dead Garvans. "One of you men throw a loop on that carrion and drag it somewhere where the coyotes eat. We'll do the same with the other two."

Kate overheard. "Not all of them, Frank. I want the oldest to hang."

"His name was Josiah, but he's dead, Kate. I shot him."

"I know," Kate said, her arm around Jazmin's shoulder. "Carry out my order, Frank. And Trace, see to Captain Delaney. He was hit."

"I'm here." Delaney rode out of the gloom holding an old-fashioned iron breastplate in his hands. He put his forefinger though a hole in the armor and waggled it at Kate. "A rifle bullet did that. Dead center in the dark. Now that's good shooting."

"Are you wounded?" Kate said.

"No. The bullet bruised my chest is all. But for a moment there I thought I was a dead man."

"Captain, where did you get that contraption?" Trace said.

"Well, sonny, I'd like to say I took it from a Portugee sea captain on the Spanish Main or I'd like to say it I inherited it from my old grandpappy, a seafaring gentleman of fortune like meself. But truth to tell, I bought it in a general store in Boston town for three dollars and ten cents." Delaney tossed the punctured breastplate into the darkness. "I was told it would turn any bullet and maybe a cannonball and that was a damn lie. I was robbed, and there's the truth of it."

"You were lucky, Captain," Trace said.

"Aye, lad, I was." Delaney looked around him, his eyes lingering on Jazmin. "But there are some who were not as lucky as me this night, lay to that."

Kate Kerrigan hanged a dead man from a branch of the skeletal cottonwood close to where he died. Jazmin insisted on being there and watched the body strung up. Kate's riders gathered around and watched Josiah Garvan rotate slowly in the breeze. His eyes were wide open, staring into eternity.

There was a profound hush about the place, making Kate's voice clearly heard. "This man was a rapist, a murderer, and a thief. He invaded my home, and I can neither forgive nor forget any of those things. That is why his body will hang here until it rots." She looked around at her men. "Is there anyone who wishes to say something in this man's favor or say a prayer for his soul? In my heart I cannot bring myself to do either of those things."

Her question was met with silence.

"Frank?"

"I have nothing to say," Frank Cobb said.

Barrie Delaney, not the most sensitive of men, spoke. "I have something to say . . . may the souls of him and his brothers burn in hell and be damned."

Frank's smile was faint. "Captain, you have a way with words."

"Aye, the only words the scoundrels deserve." Then Delaney did something that surprised everybody. He reached into a capacious pocket of his blue coat and produced a little medal on a silver chain. He leaned from the saddle and handed it to Jazmin. "It's a Miraculous Medal, me darlin', blessed by a priest back in the old country. Wear it around your neck and it will help bring you peace."

Without a word or a change of expression, she did as he suggested.

Kate fought back a tear. "Now we'll leave this terrible place and return home to the KK." She smiled at Delaney. "God bless you, Captain."

The old pirate nodded. "He's always done that, Kate me darlin'. By His holy grace I became the most feared buccaneer on the Seven Seas and He helped me send many a lively lad to a watery grave with a musket ball in his bowels." Delaney crossed himself. "And there's the honest truth of how the Good Lord has oft times favored me."

"When I say my prayers tonight I will have words with Him about that." She urged her horse into motion. "Now to get Mose and the children. Tonight we'll all pray that they make a speedy recovery from a terrible ordeal that was thrust upon them." She smiled. "And Frank, the good words include you."

CHAPTER FIFTY-SIX

Winter was cracking down hard when Kate and her family moved into their fine new house. Taken from the cabin, the front door with its polished brass fittings was flanked by two Corinthian columns. The front of the house had four windows on the first floor and two bay windows at ground floor level, all glazed thanks to the depredations of Coot Lawson and his gang of rogues. It was a clapboard, white-painted dwelling built in high Victorian style and she considered it a good beginning, replaced only when she built her future mansion in the Greek style with eight columns out front . . . and the same door.

Hank Lowery was buried in the ranch cemetery on the ridge, and Kate placed a gravestone above his grave. Frank wanted the words of "The Longdale Massacre" under Lowery's name, but she would not hear of it, chiding him for wishing to speak ill of the honorable dead.

The ashes of the wagon train dead were placed in timber boxes each marked with a brass plate on the lid that that read NIRVANA. The plates, decorated with angels, were fashioned by Marco Salas, and all agreed that he'd done a magnificent job. Kate had a rock cairn built above the grave.

Marco, Jazmin, and their children moved into Kate's vacated cabin and seemed happy enough, but Jazmin was not well mentally. She still cooked, and did it well, but needed all the care, attention, and understanding that Marco and Kate could give her. The men of the KK Ranch tiptoed around her as though they believed that all the male species shared the blame for what had happened to her.

Captain Barrie Delaney and his rogues decided that life ashore was not for them and they left to return to the *Octopus*. As he explained, "Texas is just a tad too lively for poor sailormen, Kate me darlin'. We long for the quiet solitude of the sea and the cry of gulls instead of the roar of six-shooters."

She hugged the old captain and then said with a tear in her eye, "You're a pirate rascal, Barrie Delaney, but I'll miss you. Please don't return to your old ways. I don't want to hear that you died at the end of a rope."

He grinned. "Well, Kate, here's the good news. I believe that old Queen Vic bears me no personal animosity and I am free to set a course for West Africa, where her majesty's Royal Navy is paying a gold sovereign for every blackamoor freed from a slave ship. The *Octopus* is a fine, fast craft, and her cannon can make short work of any slaver we encounter. Why, a man can become rich, his pockets full of British gold, in no time."

"Then good luck to you, Captain Delaney. I'll say a prayer for you every night of my life."

The old pirate said, "Of course, my offer of marriage still goes, sweet Kate. We can sail the main together."

She smiled and let him down gently. "I'm wed to the KK, Barrie, but your offer is indeed gracious. Now be off with you before I change my mind."

A week before Christmas while a frosting of snow lay on the range and breaths smoked in the cold air, a carriage and pair drew up outside the house with a top-hatted, red-nosed driver at the reins. The ends of his woolen muffler almost trailing to the ground, the man climbed down from the seat and opened the door. A portly man in a fur-collared astrakhan coat stepped down, walked to the house, and introduced himself to Moses, who was acting as a butler in a splendid tailcoat with silver buttons. He bowed the gentleman inside.

Kate met the man in the hallway as Moses announced in a deep tone, "Mr. Barnabas Vanstone Lynn of the Atchison, Topeka and Santa Fe Railroad."

The man bowed. "At your service, madam."

"I'm Kate Kerrigan, owner of the KK ranch. What can I do for you, Mr. Lynn?"

"I have made a somewhat arduous journey to speak to you on a matter of the utmost importance, dear lady, to wit: the continuing prosperity of the Kerrigan Ranch."

"Are you selling something, Mr. Lynn?" Kate said, frowning.

"Selling something? Yes, I am. I'm selling the future, Mrs. Kerrigan. Your future."

"Then you'd better come into the parlor. Did you use a crystal ball to peer into my future, Mr. Lynn?"

"No, ma'am. I used only my good business sense."

Moses relieved Lynn of his coat, cane, and hat, and

the man sat by the fire and accepted Kate's offer of brandy.

"I've just moved into my house and I apologize for the sparse furnishings," she said, handing him a glass.

"Your ravishing beauty is furnishing enough for any parlor, dear lady. To say it dazzles the eye is indeed an understatement."

Kate smiled. "Thank you, Mr. Lynn. You are very gallant."

Lynn produced a silver cigar case from the inside pocket of his broadcloth coat. "May I beg your indulgence, ma'am?"

"Please do. I enjoy the fragrance of a good cigar." She waited until the railroad man lit his cigar. "Shall we discuss your business now? Oh dear, I'd quite forgotten your coach driver, Mr. Lynn. I can't leave him waiting outside in the cold."

"Do you have a kitchen, ma'am?"

"Of course."

"Then never fear, Jonathan Thorne will find his way to it. He has a nose for such things," Lynn said. "And now to business, and no, I don't have a crystal ball. You are no doubt aware, Mrs. Kerrigan, that several railroads, including the Atchison, Topeka and Santa Fe, and the Union Pacific have recently laid tracks deep into West Texas."

"Yes, I have heard that." She found his gleaming head more interesting than his talk of railroads. He was completely bald and his scalp looked as though it had been shined with furniture polish.

"Now let me ask you this. Are you wedded to the Chisholm Trail? In other words do your cow"—he put in a verbal space—"boys enjoy a two- to three-month cattle drive through some of the most hostile country in the nation?"

"I've found it both tiring and dangerous." Where was this talk leading?

Lynn was shocked. "You, a lady, went up the trail to Kansas?"

"I surely did, Mr. Lynn. After all, it was my herd, was it not?"

"Mrs. Kerrigan, you are indeed a remarkable woman, brave as well as beautiful. Now I have another question to ask. Is it true you recently acquired the ranch of one"—he took a small notebook out of a pocket, flipped it open, and read briefly—"Ezra Raven?"

Kate was surprised, but she answered evenly, "Yes, I did. Mr. Raven is deceased and I took over his range."

"And that makes the KK Ranch the largest in this part of Texas, does it not?"

"Yes. I now run cattle on one and a quarter million acres. But there are bigger ranches elsewhere in Texas if your railroad is interested in buying. I'm afraid the KK is not for sale."

Lynn smiled. "I'm selling, not buying, Mrs. Kerrigan, remember?"

"Then it is of the greatest moment that you state your business in its entirety." She drew her eyebrows together, a warning sign that she was growing impatient.

Lynn took the hint. "In short, then here is the case. I put it to you that since yours is the largest ranch in this part of Texas, the Atchison, Topeka and Santa Fe is willing to lay a branch line that would terminate at a depot on your northern range. In return, we require that you sell us sufficient land for the right-of-way and for the cattle pens and other service buildings pertaining thereto. Of course, these structures will be located only in and around the rail terminal."

Pouring Lynn another brandy gave Kate time to think. She understood the advantages of the branch line but wanted the railroad man to spell them out. "What do I have to gain, Mr. Lynn?" She fluttered her eyelashes, playing the innocent.

But Barnabas Lynn was not fooled, and he smiled, enjoying the young woman's ruse. The railroad man raised his hand in what was almost a benediction. "Here are the facts, ma'am, succinctly told and with the utmost sincerity. One—you will never need to make a trail drive to Kansas ever again. Your cattle will be loaded into boxcars and carried directly to the Chicago stockyards. Two—other ranchers will drive their herds to the KK for shipment and you can charge a toll for access. Three, and here is more good news—the Atchison, Topeka and Santa Fe will discount the fee it charges for your cattle shipments by twenty percent." Lynn beamed. "There is bounty for you."

Kate nodded. "Since your rails will cross my range and the depot will be on my property, the discount will be thirty-three-and-a-third percent . . . one third of the usual charge."

"You drive a hard bargain, Mrs. Kerrigan." He looked like someone had just hung a black wreath on his door.

"Yes, I do, don't I?"

"And you don't seem at all impressed by the fact

that the railroads will forever end the trail drives to Dodge City and other places," Lynn said.

"I've long anticipated such a development, Mr. Lynn. The times are changing and I will change with them," Kate said. "Running beef off my cattle during their two months on the trail never seemed to me like a winning proposition. Besides, on a personal note, I have no love for Dodge City, nor, I fear, for any other Kansas cow town."

Lynn leaned back in his chair, his brandy glass parked just under his nose. He seemed deep in thought.

"Well? Is it a deal, Mr. Lynn?"

"The railroad will make you a rich woman, Mrs. Kerrigan. You will find that shipping by rail is fairly expensive, but that cost is offset by the fact that it is a considerably more efficient way to move cattle. Your herds will arrive at market heavier and healthier and that means more money per head in the pocket of the rancher. I will provide you with the facts and figures with the contract at a later date." Making a weak attempt at a joke, "You'll soon be able to buy all the furniture you want, Mrs. Kerrigan."

"Do we have an agreement, Mr. Lynn?"

"Yes. The AT&SF will waive one-third of our normal shipping fee in return for rail access as far as the piney woods."

Kate and Lynn talked for a while about cattle pens, train availability, and how much damage there would be to her northern range. Later, satisfied with his answers, she led him into the hallway. Moses rousted the coachman from the warm kitchen, where he'd been sampling Jazmin's bacon and biscuits.

Lynn's parting words before he climbed into his

coach were, "Weather permitting, we will start to lay track right away, Mrs. Kerrigan. I confidently expect that you and the other ranchers will be able to ship cattle after the coming spring roundup."

After Lynn drove away, Frank Cobb stepped beside Kate. "What was that about? He was here for an hour at least."

Kate drew her shawl closer around her shoulders and shivered. "Come inside and I'll tell you all about it."

Kate had poured a brandy for Frank, but he held the drink in his hand without tasting it. Only when she stopped talking did he down the brandy in one gulp.

"If what you're telling me comes true, this is the end of an age, Kate. Soon the cattle drives will pass into history along with Jesse Chisholm and Charlie Goodnight and the rest of them. It was a way of life, a good way, and I'll be sorry to see it go."

"It will come to pass, Frank. It's the beginning of a new era of growth and expansion, and the KK will grow right along with it."

"You're building an empire, Kate. I'm not much of a one for empire building. Sometimes a man grows so big and so rich so fast he loses sight of the things in life that really matter."

Kate shook her head. "I'm not building an empire, Frank. I'm laying the foundation of a dynasty and I want you to be a part of it. In due time, my sons will take over the running of the KK, and I'll need you at their side. You're my rock, Frank, and I want you to be a rock for Trace and Quinn." She smiled. "And for little Peter Letting, Esquire."

"I'll be here as long as you need me, Kate." That was all Frank needed to say.

"Thank you," Kate said.

And to a man like Frank Cobb, that was all she needed to say.

CHAPTER ONE

"Let's take a ride on a riverboat, you said," Ace Jensen muttered to his brother as they backed away from the group of angry men stalking toward them across the deck. "It'll be fun, you said."

"Well, I didn't count on this," Chance Jensen replied. "How was I to know we'd wind up in such a mess of trouble?"

Ace glanced over at Chance as if amazed that his brother could ask such a stupid question. "When do we ever *not* wind up in trouble?"

"Yeah, you've got a point there," Chance agreed. "It seems to have a way of finding us."

Their backs hit the railing along the edge of the deck. Behind them, the giant wooden blades of the side-wheeler's paddles churned the muddy waters of the Missouri River.

They were on the right side of the riverboat—the starboard side, Ace thought, then chided himself for allowing such an irrelevant detail to intrude on his brain at such a moment—and so far out in the middle of the stream that jumping overboard and swimming for shore wasn't practical.

Besides, the brothers weren't in the habit of fleeing from trouble. If they started doing that, most likely they would never stop running.

The man who was slightly in the forefront of the group confronting them pointed a finger at Chance. "All right, kid, I'll have that watch back now."

"I'm not a kid," Chance snapped. "I'm a grown man. And so are you, so you shouldn't have bet the watch if you didn't want to take a chance on losing it."

The Jensen brothers were grown men, all right, but not by much. They were in their early twenties, and although they had knocked around the frontier all their lives, had faced all sorts of danger, and burned plenty of powder, there was still a certain . . . *innocence* . . . about them, for want of a better word. They still made their way through life with enthusiasm and an eagerness to embrace all the joy the world had to offer.

They were twins, although that wasn't instantly apparent. They were fraternal rather than identical. Ace was taller, broader through the shoulders, and had black hair instead of his brother's sandy brown. He preferred range clothes, wearing jeans, a buckskin shirt, and a battered old Stetson, while Chance was much more dapper in a brown tweed suit, vest, white shirt, a fancy cravat with an ivory stickpin, and a straw planter's hat.

Ace was armed with a Colt .45 Peacemaker with well-worn walnut grips that rode easily in a holster on his right hip. Chance didn't carry a visible gun, but he had a Smith & Wesson .38 caliber double-action Second Model revolver in a shoulder holster under his left arm.

However, neither young man wanted to start a gunfight on the deck of the *Missouri Belle*. It was a tranquil summer night, and gunshots and spilled blood would just about ruin it.

The leader of the group confronting them was an expensively dressed, middle-aged man with a beefy, well-fed look about him. Still pointing that accusing finger at Chance, he went on. "Leland Stanford himself gave me that watch in appreciation for my help in getting the transcontinental railroad built. You know who Leland Stanford is, don't you? President of the Central Pacific Railroad?"

"We've heard of him," Ace said. "Rich fella out California way. Used to be governor out there, didn't he?"

"That's right. And he's a good friend of mine. I'm a stockholder in the Central Pacific, in fact."

"Then likely you can afford to buy yourself another watch," Chance said.

The man's already red face flushed even more as it twisted in a snarl. "You mouthy little pup. Hand it over, or we'll throw the two of you right off this boat."

"I won it fair and square, mister. Doc Monday always says the cards know more about our fate than we do."

"I don't know who in blazes Doc Monday is, but your fate is to take a beating and then a swim. Grab 'em, boys, but don't throw 'em overboard until I get my watch back!"

The other four men rushed Ace and Chance. With their backs to the railing, they had nowhere to go.

Doc Monday, the gambler who had raised the Jensen brothers after their mother died in childbirth, had taught them many things, including the fact that it was usually a mistake to wait for trouble to come to you. Better to go out and meet it head-on. In other words, the best defense was the proverbial good offense, so Ace and Chance met the charge with one of their own, going low to tackle the nearest two men around the knees.

The hired ruffians weren't expecting it, and the impact swept their legs out from under them. They fell under the feet of their onrushing companions, who stumbled and lost their balance, toppling onto the first two men, and suddenly there was a knot of flailing, punching, and kicking combatants on the deck.

The florid-faced hombre who had foolishly wagered his watch during a poker game in the riverboat's salon earlier hopped around agitatedly and shouted encouragement to his men.

Facing two-to-one odds, the brothers shouldn't have been able to put up much of a fight, but when it came to brawling, Ace and Chance could more than hold their own. Their fists lashed out and crashed against the jaws and into the bellies of their enemies. Ace got behind one of the men, looped an arm around his neck, and hauled him around just in time to receive a kick in the face that had been aimed at Ace's head, knocking the man senseless.

Ace let go of him and rolled out of the way of a dive from another attacker. He clubbed his hands and brought them down on the back of the man's neck. The man's face bounced off the deck, flattening his nose and stunning him.

Chance had his hands full, too. His left hand was clamped around the neck of an enemy while his right clenched into a fist and pounded the man's face. But he was taking punishment himself. His opponent was

choking him at the same time, and the other man in
the fight hammered punches into Chance's ribs from
the side.

Knowing that he had only seconds before he would
be overwhelmed, Chance twisted his body, drew his
legs up, and rammed both boot heels into the chest of
the man hitting him. It wasn't quite the same as being
kicked by a mule, but not far from it. The man flew
backwards and rolled when he landed on the deck.
He almost went under the railing and off the side into
the river, but he stopped just short of the brink.

With the odds even now, Chance was able to batter
his other foe into submission. The man's hand slipped
off Chance's throat as he moaned and slumped back
onto the smooth planks.

That still left the rich man who didn't like losing.

As Ace and Chance looked up from their van-
quished enemies, they saw him pointing a pistol at
them.

"If you think I'm going to allow a couple gutter rats
like you two to make a fool of me, you're sadly mistaken," the man said as a snarl twisted his beefy face.

"You're not gonna shoot us, mister," Ace said. "That
would be murder."

"No, it wouldn't." An ugly smile appeared on the
man's lips. "Not if I tell the captain the two of you
jumped me and tried to rob me. I had to kill you to
protect myself. That's exactly what's about to happen
here."

"Over a blasted watch?" Chance exclaimed in
surprise.

"I don't like losing . . . especially to my inferiors."

"You'd never get away with it," Ace said.

"Won't I? Why do you think none of the crew has

come to see what all the commotion's about? I told
the chief steward I'd be dealing with some cheap
troublemakers—in my own way—and he promised
he'd make sure I wasn't interrupted. You see"—the
red-faced man chuckled—"I'm not involved with just
the railroad. I own part of this riverboat line as well."

Ace and Chance exchanged a glance. If the man
shot them, his hired ruffians could toss their bodies
into the midnight-dark Missouri River and no one
would know they were gone until morning. It was
entirely possible that a man of such wealth and in-
fluence wouldn't even be questioned about the dis-
appearance of a couple drifting nobodies.

But things weren't going to get that far.

Ace said in a hard voice that belied his youth, "That
only works if you're able to shoot both of us, mister.
Problem is, while you're killing one of us, the other
one is going to kill *you.*"

The man's eyes widened. He blustered, "How dare
you threaten me like that?"

"Didn't you just threaten to kill us?" asked Chance.
"My brother's right. You're not fast enough—and
your nerves aren't steady enough—for you to get both
of us. You'll be dead a heartbeat after you pull the
trigger."

The man's lips drew back from his teeth in a gri-
mace. "Maybe I'm willing to take that risk."

Well, that was a problem, all right, thought Ace.
Stubborn pride had been the death of many a man,
and it looked like that was about to contribute to at
least one more.

Then a new voice said, "Krauss, I guarantee that
even if you're lucky enough to kill these two young

men, you won't be able to stop me from putting a bullet in your head."

The rich man's gaze flicked to a newcomer who'd stepped out of the shadows cloaking the deck in places. Wearing a light-colored suit and hat, he was easy to see. Starlight glinted on the barrel of the revolver he held in a rock-steady fist.

"Drake!" exclaimed Krauss. "Stay out of this. It's none of your business."

"I think it is." Drake's voice was a lazy drawl, but there was no mistaking the steel underneath the casual tone. "Ace and Chance are friends of mine."

Krauss sneered. "You wouldn't dare shoot me."

"Think about some of the things you know about me," said Steve Drake, "then make that statement again."

Krauss licked his lips. He looked around at his men, who were starting to recover from the battle with the Jensen brothers. "Don't just lie there!" he snapped at them. "Get up and deal with this!"

One of the men sat up, shook his head, and winced from the pain the movement caused him. "Mr. Krauss, we don't want to tangle with Drake. Rumor says he's killed seven men."

"Rumor sometimes underestimates," said Steve Drake with an easy smile.

"You're worthless!" Krauss raged. "You're all fired!"

"I'd rather be fired than dead," one of the other men mumbled.

Steve Drake gestured with the gun in his hand and told Ace and Chance, "Stand up, boys."

The brothers got to their feet. Chance reached inside his coat to a pocket and brought out a gold turnip watch with an attached chain and fob. "I don't want to have to be looking over my shoulder for you the rest of my life, mister. This watch isn't worth that."

"You mean you'll give it back to me?" asked Krauss.

Ace could tell from the man's tone that he was eager to resolve the situation without any more violence, now that it appeared he might well be one of the victims.

"I mean I'll sell it back to you," said Chance.

Krauss started to puff up again like an angry frog. "I'm not going to buy back my own watch!"

"I won it from you fair and square," Chance reminded him. "Unless you think I cheated you . . ." His voice trailed off in an implied threat.

Krauss shook his head. "I never said that. I suppose you won fair and square." That admission was clearly difficult for him to make. "What do you want for the watch?"

"Well, since it came from a famous man, I reckon it must have quite a bit of sentimental value to you. I was thinking . . . five hundred dollars."

"Five hun—" Krauss stopped short and controlled an angry response with a visible effort. "I don't have that kind of money on me at the moment. That's why I put up the watch as stakes in the game."

Steve Drake said, "We'll be docking at Kansas City in the morning. I'm sure you can send a wire to your bank in St. Louis and get your hands on the cash. That's the only fair thing to do, don't you think? After all, you set your men like a pack of wild dogs on to these boys, and then you threatened to murder them and have their bodies thrown in the river like so much trash. You owe them at least that much."

"Nobody's going to take their word over mine," said Krauss, trying one last bluff.

"Captain Foley will take *my* word," Drake said. "We've known each other for ten years, and I've done a few favors for him in the past. He knows I wouldn't lie to him. You wouldn't want it getting around that you were ready to resort to murder over something as petty as a poker game, would you? Seems to me that would be bad for business."

"All right, all right." Krauss stuck the pistol back under his coat. "It's a deal. Five hundred dollars for the watch."

"Deal," Chance said.

The rich man laughed. "The watch is worth twice that. You should have held out for more."

"I don't care how much it is. I just want you to pay to get it back."

Krauss snorted in contempt, turned, and stalked off along the deck. His men followed him, even though he had fired them. Evidently that dismissal wouldn't last, and they knew it.

A man with a temper like Krauss's probably fired people right and left and then expected them to come right back to work for him once he cooled off, Ace reflected.

Once Krauss and the others were gone, the Jensen boys joined Steve Drake, who tucked away his gun under his jacket and strolled over to the railing to gaze out at the broad, slow-moving Missouri River.

The gambler put a thin black cheroot in his mouth and snapped a match to life with his thumbnail. As he set fire to the gasper, the glare from the lucifer sent garish red light over the rugged planes of his craggy face under the cream-colored Stetson.

"We're obliged to you, Mr. Drake," Ace said.

"You're making a habit out of pulling our fat out of the fire."

"Yeah," Chance added. "If you hadn't come along when you did, we might've had to kill that obnoxious tub of lard."

"Krauss's gun was already in his hand," Steve Drake pointed out, "and yours were in your holsters. He might have gotten one of you, just like you said."

"Yeah, and he might have missed completely," said Chance. "We wouldn't have had any choice but to drill him, though."

"And then we would have been in all kinds of trouble," put in Ace. "The odds of hanging are a lot higher if you kill a rich man instead of a poor one."

"You sound like you have a low opinion of justice," said Steve Drake with a chuckle.

"No, I just know how things work in this world."

The gambler shrugged and blew out a cloud of smoke. "You may be right. We all remember what happened back in St. Louis, don't we?"

CHAPTER TWO

St. Louis, three days earlier

Neither Ace nor Chance was in awe of St. Louis. They had seen big cities before. Traveling with Doc Monday when they were younger had taken them to Denver, San Francisco, New Orleans, and San Antonio, so the buildings crowded together and the throngs of people in the streets were nothing new to the Jensen brothers.

It had been a while since they'd set foot in such a place. They reacted to it totally differently.

Chance looked around with a smile of anticipation on his face as they rode along the street, moving slowly because of all the people, horses, wagons, and buggies. He was at home in cities, liked the hubbub, enjoyed seeing all the different sorts of people.

Because Doc Monday, their surrogate father, made his living as a gambler, he had spent most of his time in settlements. That was where the saloons were, after all. And although Doc had tried to keep the boys out of such places as much as possible while they were growing up, it was inevitable that they had spent a great deal of time in those establishments.

Chance had taken to that life, but Ace had reacted in just the opposite manner. He didn't like being hemmed in and preferred the outdoors. He would rather be out riding the range any day, instead of being stuck in a saloon breathing smoky air and listening to the slap of cards and the raucous laughter of the customers. If he had to spend time in a settlement, the smaller ones were better than the big cities. To Ace's way of thinking, a slower pace and more peaceful was better.

Ever since Doc had gone off to a sanitarium for a rest cure, the boys had been on their own, and they had packed a lot of adventurous living into a relatively short amount of time. Chance was always happy when they drifted into a town, while Ace was ready to leave again as soon as they replenished their supplies and his brother had an opportunity to win enough money to keep them solvent for a while.

St. Louis was the farthest east they had been in their travels, with the exception of New Orleans. There was no particular reason they were there, other than Chance deciding that he'd wanted to see St. Louis.

Ace figured Chance might have assumed St. Louis was like New Orleans, the city he loved, with its moss-dripping trees, its old, fancy buildings, its music, its food, its saloons and gambling halls, and especially its beautiful women. After all, both cities were on the Mississippi River.

He seemed somewhat disappointed in their present

surroundings, which led him to look around and ask, "Is this it? A bunch of people and businesses?"

"That's generally what a big city is," Ace reminded him.

"Yeah, but it doesn't even smell good! In fact, it smells sort of like . . . dead fish."

"That's the waterfront," Ace said with a smile. "New Orleans smelled like that in a lot of places, too. You just didn't notice it because you liked all the other things that were there."

"Maybe," said Chance, but he didn't sound convinced.

"I guess we'd better find a place to stay. We've still got enough in our poke for that, haven't we?"

Chance grunted. "Yeah."

Something else caught his attention and he pointed to a large saloon with a sign on the awning over the boardwalk out front announcing its name. RED MIKE'S. "I think we should have a look inside that place first."

The place took up most of the block on that side of the street. A balcony ran along the second floor. Ace wouldn't have been surprised to see scantily clad women hanging over the railing of that balcony, enticing customers to come up, but it was empty at the moment.

The hitch rails in front of the saloon were packed. The Jensen brothers found space to squeeze in their horses and dismounted, looping the reins around the rail. Chance bounded eagerly onto the boardwalk with Ace following at a more deliberate pace. He would have preferred finding a place to stay first, maybe even getting something to eat, but once Chance felt the call of potential excitement, it wasn't easy to stop him from answering.

Considering the number of horses tied up outside, Red Mike's was crowded with customers. Men of all shapes, sizes, and types lined up at the bar and filled the tables. Ace saw buckskin-clad old-timers and burly men in canvas trousers, homespun shirts, and thick-soled shoes who probably worked on the docks or the riverboats. Also in attendance were cowboys in boots, spurs, and high-crowned hats, frock-coated gamblers who reminded him of Doc, and meek, suit-wearing townsmen.

Circulating among the men were women in low-cut, spangled dresses that came down only to their knees. Some of them looked fresh and innocent despite the provocative garb, while others were starting to show lines of age and weariness on their painted faces. All of them sported professional smiles as they delivered drinks, bantered with the customers, and occasionally perched on someone's knee to flirt for a minute before moving on.

In each front corner of the big room was a platform with steps leading up to it. A man holding a Winchester across his knees sat on a ladder-back chair on each platform. They were there to stop any trouble before it got started.

The tactic seemed to be working. While Red Mike's place was loud, even boisterous, it was peaceful enough in the saloon. Everyone seemed to be getting along.

Ace leaned closer to his brother and said over the hubbub, "It's too busy in here. We'd better move along and come back later."

"No, there's a place at the bar," Chance replied, pointing. "Come on."

Ace followed, unwilling to let Chance stay by himself. It wasn't that he didn't trust his brother, but sometimes Chance could be impulsive, even reckless . . . especially in such surroundings.

They weaved through the crowd to the bar. By the time they got there, the space Chance had noticed was smaller than it had been. There was still room for one of the brothers, but not both of them.

That didn't stop Chance from wedging his way into the opening and then using a shoulder to make it wider by pushing one of the flanking men aside. Ace winced a little when he saw that, because he knew what was liable to happen next.

Chance turned his head and beckoned to his brother. "Come on, Ace. There's room now."

No sooner were those words out of his mouth than a big hand clamped down on his shoulder and jerked him around. The man Chance had nudged aside glared down into his face and demanded in a loud voice, "Who do you think you are, boy?"

"My name's Chance Jensen," Chance said coolly. "If this is a formal introduction, you can go ahead and tell me your name."

The man ignored that. "You can't just push a man around like that and expect to get away with it, *boy*. You done left school too early. You ain't been taught all the lessons you need."

"From the sound of it, I have considerably more education than you do."

The big man's face darkened with anger. He was several inches taller than Chance, about the same height as Ace, and probably weighed fifty or sixty pounds more than either brother. His rough clothes and a shapeless hat jammed down on a thatch of dark hair indicated that he probably worked on the docks. Not the sort of hombre to mess with unless it was absolutely necessary, that was for sure.

The man leaned closer and growled. "Listen to me, you little son of a—"

Ace managed to get a shoulder between the two of them and said quickly, "My brother and I aren't looking for any trouble, sir. Maybe we can patch this up by buying you a drink."

Chance began, "We don't have enough money to throw it away buying drinks for—"

Whatever Chance was about to say, it wasn't going to help matters any, Ace knew. He pushed in between them harder, which made Chance take a step back and bump into the man behind him.

Being jostled made the man spill his beer down the front of his shirt. With an angry shout, the fellow twisted around, brandishing the now-empty mug like a weapon. "What in blazes?" he roared. "I'm gonna—"

The place went quiet, but not because of the man's shout.

Ace heard the familiar sound of a rifle's lever being worked and glanced around to see that both men on the elevated platforms in the front corners of the room were on their feet. Their Winchesters were socketed firmly against their shoulders, and the barrels were leveled at the group involved in the confrontation at the bar.

The dockworker who'd been glaring at the Jensen boys swallowed hard and unclenched his big fists. "Blast it, Mike. Tell those killers o' yours to hold their fire."

A man wearing a gray tweed suit moved along the bar until he was across the hardwood from Ace, Chance, and the other two men. He was short and broad and the color and coarseness of his hair made it resemble rusty nails. "You know the rules, Dave. No fighting in here. My grandfather didn't allow brawling and neither did my father. Neither do I."

Dave glowered at Chance and accused, "This obnoxious little sprout started it, not me."

"Obnoxious," repeated Chance. "That's a longer word than I thought you'd be able to handle."

From the corner of his mouth, Ace told his brother, "Just be quiet, all right?"

Chance looked offended, but Ace ignored him.

"Sorry for causing trouble," Ace went on to the man on the other side of the bar. Judging by the man's attitude and the fact that the dockworker had called him Mike, Ace figured he was the owner of the place, Red Mike himself. "We just wanted to get a quick drink, and then we'll be moving on."

"Speak for yourself," said Chance. "I might like it here. I don't so far, not particularly, but I might."

Mike nodded to the brothers and asked the two offended parties, "If these youngsters were to apologize, would that take care of the problem?"

"Hell, no," replied the man who had spilled his drink when Chance jostled him.

Mike pointed a blunt thumb toward the batwings. "Then there's the door. Get out."

The man stared at him in disbelief. "You're kickin' *me* out? I wasn't doin' anything but standin' here enjoyin' a beer when this little pissant made me spill it all over myself!"

"Come back tomorrow and your first drink is on

me," Mike said. "That's the best offer you're going to get, Wilson."

The man glared and muttered for a moment, then snapped, "All right, fine." He thumped the empty mug on the bar with more force than necessary, then turned and walked out of the saloon, bulling past anybody who was in his way.

"Now, how about you, Dave?" Mike went on. "Will an apology do for you?"

"No," the dockworker said coldly. "It won't. But I don't want those sharpshooters of yours blowin' my brains out, so I'll leave. I reckon that same free drink offer applies to me, too?"

"It does," Mike allowed.

Dave nodded curtly. "You shouldn't take the side of strangers over your faithful customers, Mike. It's these two as should be leavin'."

"You're probably right. Make it two free drinks."

That seemed to mollify Dave somewhat. He frowned at Ace and Chance one more time and said, "Don't let me catch you on the street, boys. You'd be wise to get outta town while you got the chance." With that, he stomped out of the saloon.

The two guards on the platforms sat down again. The noise level in the place swelled back up.

Mike looked at Ace and Chance and asked harshly, "Do you two cause so much trouble everywhere you go or did one of my competitors pay you to come in here and start a ruckus?"

"We're sorry, mister," Ace said. "Things just sort of got out of hand."

Chance looked slightly repentant as he added, "Sometimes my mouth gets away from me."

Mike grunted. "See that it doesn't again, at least not in here." He shook his head. "I don't care what you do elsewhere or what happens to you, either. You said you wanted a drink?"

"A couple beers would be good," Ace said.

Mike signaled to one of his aproned bartenders. "Don't expect 'em to be on the house, though. Not after the way you acted. In fact, I ought to charge you double . . . but I won't."

Ace dug out a coin and slid it across the hardwood. Mike scooped it up with a hand that had more of the rusty hair sprouting from the back of it.

The bartender set the beers in front of them.

Since Mike didn't seem to be in any hurry to move on, Ace started a conversation after picking up a mug and taking a sip from it. "You mentioned your father and grandfather. Did they own this saloon before you?"

"What's it to you, kid?" asked Mike as his eyes narrowed in suspicion.

"Nothing, really," Ace replied honestly. "I'm just interested in history, that's all."

A short, humorless bark of laughter came from the saloonkeeper. "Red Mike's has got some history, all right. The original tavern, back in the days when all the fur trappers and traders came through St. Louis on their way to the Rockies, was over by the docks, almost right on the river. A hell of a place it was, too. Men were men back in those days, especially those fur trappers. Always ready to fight or drink or bed a wench. My grandpap ruled the place with an iron fist. He had to."

"His name was Mike, too?"

"The name's passed down to me from him," the saloonkeeper confirmed. "My pa, whose name was Mike as well, moved the tavern a couple blocks in this direction. When I took over, I figured it was time to make a regular saloon out of the place and moved it again. I kept the name, though." He laughed again, but he sounded more genuinely amused this time.

"A while back, one of those old mountain men wandered in. Claimed he knew my grandpap and used to drink in his tavern, more than forty years ago. I figured he was probably crazy, but there was just enough of a chance he was telling the truth that I bought him a drink for old time's sake. Can't remember what he said his name was. Deacon or something like that."

Chance inclined his head toward the guards on the platforms. "Would they have really started shooting if somebody threw a punch?"

"Damn right they would have," snapped Mike, losing his slightly more jovial attitude. "Both of those boys can hit a gnat at a hundred yards."

Ace wasn't convinced that the saloon owner would resort to execution to break up a fight, especially with so many innocent bystanders around . . . but as long as people believed it was possible, they would be a lot more likely to behave.

"Now drink up," Mike went on, "and then get out."

"You're giving us the boot, too?" asked Chance, sounding surprised.

"That's right. I don't want you hotheads starting anything else."

Ace was equally determined that wouldn't happen, so he didn't argue with the saloonkeeper's edict. He wanted to leave and find a place to stay for the night. He had already seen enough of St. Louis to satisfy any curiosity he had about the city. He drained the rest of his beer and told Mike, "Again, sorry for the trouble."

"Let's just go," Chance muttered after swallowing the last of his beer.

They headed for the entrance, moving past several tables full of drinkers and a couple poker games. Chance pushed through the batwings first with Ace right behind him. They went to the hitch rail, untied their horses, and started along the street leading the animals.

Ace was looking around for a hotel that might be a place they could afford to stay when hands suddenly grabbed him and jerked him away from his horse, flinging him along a narrow alley between two buildings. The hour was late in the afternoon and shadows already gathered in the alley, but as Ace stumbled and then caught his balance, he could see well enough to make out several figures blocking his way back to the street.

A couple of the men had grabbed Chance, too, and dragged him into the narrow alley space. They gave him a hard shove that made him go to one knee. He cursed bitterly as Ace took hold of his arm and helped him up.

"Look what I landed in!" Chance exclaimed.

Ace was less worried about that than he was about the fact that they were surrounded. He recognized not only the burly dockworker called Dave but also the man who had spilled his drink when Chance bumped into him.

"So the two of you are friends," Ace said.

Dave shook his head and grinned. "Naw, I don't even know this fella. But we both have friends of our own, and we both know you two need a good stompin'. So that's what we're gonna give you."

With fists flying, the ring of attackers closed in around the Jensen boys.

J. A. Johnstone on William W. Johnstone
"Print the Legend"

William W. Johnstone was born in southern Missouri, the youngest of four children. He was raised with strong moral and family values by his minister father, and tutored by his schoolteacher mother. Despite this, he quit school at age fifteen.

"I have the highest respect for education," he says, "but such is the folly of youth, and wanting to see the world beyond the four walls and the blackboard."

True to this vow, Bill attempted to enlist in the French Foreign Legion ("I saw Gary Cooper in *Beau Geste* when I was a kid and I thought the French Foreign Legion would be fun") but was rejected, thankfully, for being underage. Instead, he joined a traveling carnival and did all kinds of odd jobs. It was listening to the veteran carny folk, some of whom had been on the circuit since the late 1800s, telling amazing tales about their experiences, that planted the storytelling seed in Bill's imagination.

"They were mostly honest people, despite the bad reputation traveling carny shows had back then," Bill remembers. "Of course, there were exceptions. There was one guy named Picky, who got that name because he was a master pickpocket. He could steal a man's socks right off his feet without him knowing. Believe me, Picky got us chased out of more than a few towns."

After a few months of this grueling existence, Bill returned home and finished high school. Next came stints as a deputy sheriff in the Tallulah, Louisiana, Sheriff's Department, followed by a hitch in the U.S. Army. Then he began a career in radio broadcasting at KTLD in Tallulah, which would last sixteen years.

It was there that he fine-tuned his storytelling skills. He turned to writing in 1970, but it wouldn't be until 1979 that his first novel, *The Devil's Kiss*, was published. Thus began the full-time writing career of William W. Johnstone. He wrote horror (*The Uninvited*), thrillers (*The Last of the Dog Team*), even a romance novel or two. Then, in February 1983, *Out of the Ashes* was published. Searching for his missing family in a postapocalyptic America, rebel mercenary and patriot Ben Raines is united with the civilians of the Resistance forces and moves to the forefront of a revolution for the nation's future.

Out of the Ashes was a smash. The series would continue for the next twenty years, winning Bill three generations of fans all over the world. The series was often imitated but never duplicated. "We all tried to copy the Ashes series," said one publishing executive, "but Bill's uncanny ability, both then and now, to predict in which direction the political winds were blowing brought a certain immediacy to the table no one else could capture." The Ashes series would end its run with more than thirty-four books and twenty million copies in print, making it one of the most successful men's action series in American book publishing. (The Ashes series also, Bill notes with a touch of pride, got him on the FBI's Watch List for its less than flattering portrayal of spineless politicians and the growing power of big government over our lives, among other things. In that respect, I often find myself saying, "Bill was years ahead of his time.")

Always steps ahead of the political curve, Bill's recent thrillers, written with myself, include *Vengeance Is Mine, Invasion USA, Border War, Jackknife, Remember the Alamo,*

Home Invasion, Phoenix Rising, The Blood of Patriots, The Bleeding Edge, and the upcoming *Suicide Mission.*

It is with the western, though, that Bill found his greatest success. His westerns propelled him onto both the *USA Today* and the *New York Times* bestseller lists.

Bill's western series include *Matt Jensen, the Last Mountain Man, Preacher, the First Mountain Man, The Family Jensen, Luke Jensen, Bounty Hunter, Eagles, MacCallister* (an Eagles spin-off), *Sidewinders, The Brothers O'Brien, Sixkiller, Blood Bond, The Last Gunfighter,* and the new series *Flintlock* and *The Trail West.* May 2013 saw the hardcover western *Butch Cassidy: The Lost Years.*

"The western," Bill says, "is one of the few true art forms that is one hundred percent American. I liken the Western as America's version of England's Arthurian legends, like the Knights of the Round Table, or Robin Hood and his Merry Men. Starting with the 1902 publication of *The Virginian* by Owen Wister, and followed by the greats like Zane Grey, Max Brand, Ernest Haycox, and of course Louis L'Amour, the western has helped to shape the cultural landscape of America.

"I'm no goggle-eyed college academic, so when my fans ask me why the western is as popular now as it was a century ago, I don't offer a 200-page thesis. Instead, I can only offer this: The western is honest. In this great country, which is suffering under the yoke of political correctness, the western harks back to an era when justice was sure and swift. Steal a man's horse, rustle his cattle, rob a bank, a stagecoach, or a train, you were hunted down and fitted with a hangman's noose. One size fit all.

"Sure, we westerners are prone to a little embellishment and exaggeration and, I admit it, occasionally play a little fast and loose with the facts. But we do so for a very good reason—to enhance the enjoyment of readers.

"It was Owen Wister, in *The Virginian*, who first coined the phrase 'When you call me that, smile.' Legend has it that Wister actually heard those words spoken by a deputy sheriff in Medicine Bow, Wyoming, when another poker player called him a son of a bitch.

"Did it really happen, or is it one of those myths that have passed down from one generation to the next? I honestly don't know. But there's a line in one of my favorite westerns of all time, *The Man Who Shot Liberty Valance*, where the newspaper editor tells the young reporter, 'When the truth becomes legend, print the legend.'

"These are the words I live by."